D1250235

# RESCUING KATHERINE (SPECIAL FORCES: OPERATION ALPHA)

## BRAVO SERIES BOOK 2

ANNA BLAKELY

Dear Readers,

*Welcome to the Special Forces: Operation Alpha Fan-Fiction world!*

If you are new to this amazing world, in a nutshell the author wrote a story using one or more of my characters in it. Sometimes that character has a major role in the story, and other times they are only mentioned briefly. This is perfectly legal and allowable because they are going through Aces Press to publish the story.

This book is entirely the work of the author who wrote it. While I might have assisted with brainstorming and other ideas about which of my characters to use, I didn't have any part in the process or writing or editing the story.

I'm proud and excited that so many authors loved my characters enough that they wanted to write them into their own story. Thank you for supporting them, and me!

READ ON!
    Xoxo
    Susan Stoker

*This book is for my parents, who always made sure my brother and I had everything we needed. We may not have been rich with money, but we were—and still are—rich with love. Thank you, Mom and Dad...for always believing in us. I love you very much!*

# PROLOGUE

*Ten years ago...*

Matt's fingertips brushed against the small, delicate ring hidden deep in his pocket. His pulse relaxed, knowing it was still there. Not that he should've been surprised...after all, he'd only checked on the damn thing a million times since that morning.

Still, it calmed his nerves to know it was safe and secure. No way in hell could he risk losing it. It was too important. *She's too important.*

Though he couldn't see it, Matt knew the smile spreading across his face was the same, goofy grin his buddies had been giving him shit about for the past few weeks. The past year, really.

A year ago today, he met the girl who'd changed everything. Kat was beautiful, funny, and smart as hell. Like, genius-level smart. But somehow despite the fact that they came from totally separate worlds, she'd chosen to be with him.

Matt's smile grew, knowing in less than an hour Kat would no longer be his girlfriend. She'd be his fiancée.

*If she says yes.*

He ignored the tiny voice threatening to kill his emotional buzz. Of course, she'd say yes. She loved him every bit as much as he loved her. Even more so, to hear Kat tell it. But she was wrong.

The fact that he'd never been in love before didn't matter. Not to Matt. Neither did his young age. Even at twenty, Matt knew he'd never love anyone more than he loved her.

Kat was his and his alone. He'd known it almost from the moment they met, but as he toyed with the simple diamond ring once more, Matt relished in the fact that soon the whole world would know it, too.

*Her dad's gonna be so pissed.*

That tidbit of knowledge only added to the joy he was feeling. Thomas Marsh was a silver-spooned blowhard who owned half of California. Thankfully not the half Matt lived in.

From day one, the prick had fought Kat's decision to date him. Thankfully Kat didn't share her father's opinion of those who lived in a lower tax bracket.

She judged people by the size of their hearts, not their bank accounts. It was one of about a billion reasons Matt loved her.

*Speaking of Kat...*

Matt checked his watch, his nerves ratcheting up once more when he saw what time it was. If he didn't leave now, he'd be late.

With one final pat of his pocket, he threw on his boots, grabbed his sunglasses and keys, and headed to his truck. The fifteen-minute drive to the pier flew by as Matt used that time to mentally rehearse what he planned to say.

*A year ago today, my buddies and I came to this same pier to go fishing. I thought my life was perfect, and then I saw you.*

*You were standing right over there with a group of girls. You were all talking and laughing, and I remember a small breeze blew by, sending some hair into your face.*

*You turned your head against the wind to brush it away, and when our eyes met, it was as if lightning had struck. I knew, from that moment on, my life would never be the same.*

Matt pictured himself pulling the ring from his denim pocket and dropping to one knee. He imagined Kat's face lighting up with surprise and tears of joy welling up and streaming down her soft, flawless cheeks. Then, he'd say...

*"Katherine Jean Marsh, I have loved you from the second I first saw you. Will you make me the happiest man in the world and be my wife?"*

She'd say yes and jump into his arms. And after he placed the modest ring on her hand, they'd go to their special place. They'd make love, then. Like they almost always did when he took her there.

Kat was a virgin when they'd started dating and had wanted to wait a while before having sex. As hard as it was—literally—Matt had respected the hell out of that.

For the first six months of their relationship, he'd walked around with balls as blue as the open sea. But man, had it been worth it. Knowing he was her first...that he would be her only...filled him with a ridiculous amount of alpha pride.

Thankfully, Kat understood the way male hormones worked and didn't fault him for not being a virgin when they'd met, too. He had, however, kept himself only for her. And he would for the rest of his life.

His friends all thought he was crazy to even consider getting married at such a young age, but Matt knew she was worth the commitment. She was...everything.

He spotted the red mini coupe her dad had bought her for her sixteenth birthday and pulled into the space beside it. Through his windshield he could see her at the end of the pier.

Facing the water, she didn't see him, so he took a few extra minutes to relish in the moment. Even from here he could tell she was wearing one of her strappy sundresses and sandals, and like a year ago, the breeze blew against her long hair.

As Matt made his way across the wooden platform, he was grateful for the fact that they were alone. It was always a crapshoot when coming here.

Normally he didn't care if others were around. But today was different, and he wanted their special moment to be private.

"Hey, sweet girl," he said from behind her.

Matt thought maybe she'd swing her body around, but she just stood there. Staring out at the North Pacific waves.

*Maybe she didn't hear you.*

Using the extra minute to its fullest, Matt took in the view, appreciating the slow curve of her lean figure as he silently closed the distance between them. Without another word, he reached for her hips and spoke softly in her ear.

"Hey, beautiful."

On a start, Kat turned to face him. Instead of the smile that always brightened his day, she stared back at him with an uneasy expression.

"Hi, Matt."

*Hi, Matt?*

It had been nearly a month since they'd last seen each other, and that's all he got? No hug and kiss. Not even a ghost of a smile.

Matt's gut began to churn like it did when he was on an op that was about to go sideways. Something was off. Way off.

"What's wrong?"

"N-nothing," she lied badly.

"Kat." His tone brokered no argument.

"I'm sorry," she whispered. Tears welled in her eyes, but not for the reason he'd imagined while driving here.

"It's okay." Matt placed his hands on her bare shoulders. "Take your time and tell me why you're so upset." Though she didn't feel cold, Kat trembled beneath his touch. "Okay, Katherine, seriously. You're starting to scare me. What's going on?"

Without looking at him, she whispered, "I think..." She swallowed and began again. "I think we should...take a break."

What. The. Fuck?

Matt stared back at her as he thought of the ring burning a hole inside his pocket. Unable to believe what he'd just heard, he did everything he could to control his voice.

"You're breaking up with me?"

Sniffling, Kat wiped her nose with the back of her

hand and shook her head. "I didn't say that. I said I thought we needed to take a break."

Matt's voice raised as he dropped his hands and took a step back. "That's pretty much the same damn thing, Kat."

Okay, so maybe his control was already gone, but fuck. He had no idea why she was doing this.

*You know why.*

"This is because of your father, isn't it?"

Kat's dad had been trying to drive a wedge between them from day one. It was the reason Matt hadn't gone to him, asking for permission for her hand. He already knew what the asshole's answer would've been, so he hadn't bothered wasting his breath.

Still avoiding eye contact, Kat looked everywhere but at him. Swiping the tears from her cheeks, she cleared her throat and said, "This is my decision."

"Then why can't you look me in the eye?"

Naturally, the beautiful, stubborn woman did just that. Normally Matt could read her like a book, but there was a guarded, almost emotionless look in her eyes. One he'd never seen before.

"Why are you doing this?" he asked, the pain in his heart reflected in his voice. "This makes no sense. I thought you loved me."

He sounded like a pussy-whipped adolescent, but Christ. She was tearing his heart into pieces, and he had no fucking clue as to why.

"I do love you," Kat whispered before looking away again. She licked her lips—something she did when she was nervous—and looked around.

A nagging feeling tickled the back of his mind, but Kat's crushing blow overshadowed whatever it was.

"Really?" Matt's anger began to shine through. "Sure seems like you have a funny way of showing it."

Shoulders dropping, Kat sighed. "Matt, please. Don't make this harder than it already is."

"*I'm* the one making things hard?" He took a step forward and pointed at himself. "I'm not doing shit, here, Katherine. *You* are."

More tears filled her eyes before falling over her lower lids. With a quivering chin, she said, "I'm only doing what's best."

"For you, maybe," Matt shot back.

Blinking back his own tears, he did his best not to let his emotions take over. If he did, Matt knew he'd break down and bawl like a fucking baby.

"What happened?" he asked in disbelief.

Her answer was a mumbled, "Nothing."

"Bullshit. Two days ago, you couldn't wait for me to get home. Now this?" Matt took a chance and stepped in closer. With a hand cupping her face, he said, "Please, baby. Talk to me."

Eyes the color of dark chocolate stared up at him. A sliver of the love he'd seen reflecting back at him over this past year burrowed its way through, sending Matt's hopeful heart pounding against his ribs.

For a second, he thought she was going to say she'd changed her mind. That she didn't want to end things between them, after all. But it was gone as quickly as it had appeared.

"I told you." Kat stepped out of his reach. "Nothing happened, Matt. I think it would be better for both of us if we were friends. That's all."

He looked down at her as if she'd grown two heads.

"You've got to be kidding me."

"Come on, Matt. We barely see each other as it is." Kat turned and walked toward the edge of the pier. "This past year has been fun, but…"

*"Fun?"* He chuckled humorlessly.

His breath froze inside his lungs, shock leaving him unable to say anymore. Dizzy, he turned away from her, too. Running a hand over his face, Matt shook his head as he tried to make sense of what was happening.

One minute, he's planning to propose, and the next, she's tossing him into the friend zone? What an idiot he'd been.

Using his silence to try to explain the unexplainable, Kat drew in a deep breath before turning back around. With her chin held high, she stared back at him with the same, icy gaze her father used and said, "To be honest, I'd rather be with someone with more—"

"Money?" he accused, unwilling to let her finish the damning thought.

Her cold eyes flickered. "I was going to say time."

"Time." Matt rubbed the clean-shaven skin covering his tightened jaw. "Right. Except, time was never an issue before."

The same, odd look flashed again, but like before it vanished in an instant. "Well, it is now. I'm sorry, Matt. I never meant to hurt you."

"You never meant…" He laughed, unable to finish the ridiculous words. "I think what you were trying to say was you never meant to fall in love with a guy like me. Isn't that right?"

"No." She shook her head vehemently.

He'd never doubted her. Not once in all their time

together. But now, Matt realized he couldn't believe a fucking word coming out of her pretty, bow-shaped mouth.

"I should've seen this coming," he told her coldly. "After all, you're *The* Thomas Marsh's daughter, and I'm just the guy from the other side of the tracks. Your dad owns nearly everything and everyone around here, and mine...well, we both know what my father's like."

"I told you this was my decision."

"I know." Matt nodded calmly. "You decided Daddy was right. You want some suit-wearing guy who can support the lifestyle you're used to."

"Matt—"

"A guy like that...I'm sure time wouldn't be an issue. They're home every night at five o'clock on the dot."

"Matt, please—"

"I guess your father was right."

"What?"

"The first time I met him, he told me you'd come to your senses one day and realize what a...how did he put it? Oh, yeah. You'd realize what a nobody I was."

With a steady stream of tears running down her face, Kat shook her head. "I've *never* thought that."

More hurt and pissed than ever before, Matt needed to get the hell out of there. Needed to get away from her.

Calling upon every ounce of strength he had, he shrugged casually and spit out, "Like you said. This has been fun."

He turned and started for his truck. God, he felt sick to his soul. He'd been planning today for weeks. Had saved every extra penny he could to buy her the perfect ring.

*The ring.*

9

With a sudden urgency to be rid of the damn thing, Matt shoved his hand in his pocket and pulled it out. Chest heaving, his nose and eyes burned as he stared down at it resting in his open palm.

Bile churned deep inside his belly as all his hopes and dreams of a future—a future with Kat—were shattered in an instant.

"I guess I won't be needing this anymore." He tossed the ring at her.

Not expecting it, Kat fumbled to catch the small piece of jewelry. When she opened her hand and saw what it was, she gasped.

"Matt." His name escaped on a whisper, more tears spilling over as she lifted her eyes back to his. "W-what…"

Her voice cracked again, and it was clear she had no idea what to say. Guilt, shame, and pain intermingled behind the eyes that, less than twenty minutes ago, Matt thought he'd find looking back at him for the rest of his life.

Now as he stood there with his heart lying at his feet, he realized he couldn't stand to stare into those same eyes a second longer.

"Have a nice life, Katherine"

Without another word, he walked away from the girl he'd planned a future with. One who owned him, heart and soul.

Each step brought with it a new sense of pain and anger. Devastation unlike anything he'd ever known damn near broke him, and it was all he could do to not run back to her and beg her for another chance.

Instead he got into his truck and drove. For hours, Matt drove everywhere and nowhere, tears falling as he wracked his tortured brain to come up with the signs he had to have missed. Something that would have warned him this was coming. But there was nothing.

Hours later, with less than a quarter of a tank of gas left, he headed back home. That night, as he lay in bed pushing back more tears threatening to fall, Matt made himself a silent vow.

*Never. Again.*

He'd thought falling in love would bring him happiness and a sense of belonging. In the end, the only thing loving Kat had done was bring him pain. A pain he would never, ever risk feeling again.

# CHAPTER 1

*Present day...*

"Not bad."

Matthew Turner shot his teammate a sideways glance. "Not bad? Dude, that shot was dead on."

"I don't know that I'd say *dead* on." Kole Jameson, Bravo Team's lead sniper, shrugged. "But it was close."

The guy's placating tone dug under his skin, which Matt knew was the whole point. Pulling himself off his belly and to his feet, he stood by as Kole did the same.

Matt took his sunglasses off his head and slid them over his eyes. "Not everyone can be a record-breaking super sniper like you."

"I know." The six-three smartass frowned. He began swiping at the dust on his chest and pants and looked back at Matt with a smirk. "It's a shame, really."

Removing his ballcap, Matt used it to swat his teammate's arm before readjusting it on his head. The two men laughed.

"I'm just sayin'," Kole continued to chuckle. "There's good, like you. And then there's me."

"Listen, asshole. Let's see you sew up a five-inch gash in someone's side. Better yet, reach inside a guy's leg, dig through a glob of bloody, mangled flesh and muscle, find his severed femoral artery, and clamp it off...before the guy bleeds out."

Kole made a face. "That's disgusting."

"Exactly."

"Yes, you two are gods among every black ops man and woman around the globe, and we should all bow down to you. But can we please do it while we eat? I'm starving."

Both men turned to see Zade King, the team's other sniper, making his way to Kole's truck. Lowering the tailgate, the former Marine reached for his rifle case.

"Aw, don't be jealous, King. You're a decent shot, too."

Without looking over at them, King flipped Kole the bird before returning to the task of unloading his weapon before securing it in the case.

As he and Kole made their way to the truck as well, Matt shook his head but smiled. Man, he loved these guys.

"I can go for a quick bite, but then I need to head home right after," he told them as he reached into the truck bed and grabbed his own case.

"Let me guess." Kole opened the driver's side passenger door and got his case from behind the back seat. "Hot date?"

"Turner doesn't date." Zade snapped his case closed and slid it up toward the cab.

"Oh, that's right." Kole nodded, feigning a seriousness Matt knew the fucker didn't feel. "He gets in and out as fast as he can. Kind of like a thief in the night."

"Except you can't steal what's given to you freely. And trust me, boys." Matt set his case next to Zade's. "Every woman I've been with has been more than willing to give me anything I want."

With a roll of his eyes, Kole took his place behind the wheel. Matt climbed into the front passenger while Zade occupied the spot behind Kole.

"And why are you all always razzin' *me* about this shit?" Matt spouted off, unable to let it go. "King's still single. Hell, Nate was a total commitment-phobe until he met Gracie." He clicked his seatbelt in place. "Still can't believe the fucker flew off to Vegas last week and eloped. You know, he's the one who needs his balls busted. That would've been one hell of a good time."

"Yes, because weddings are your thing, Turner." Kole put the truck in gear and began driving away from R.I.S.C.'s private range. "And quit trying to change the subject."

Kole looked over at his friend. "I'm not, and what do you mean? I like weddings." A corner of his mouth curved upward. "Actually, most of the time, I look forward to them."

"*You* like weddings?" Zade snorted. "Okay."

"I do," Matt protested fiercely before adding, "No pun intended."

"Right..." Kole let the word hang in the air. "That must be why you snuck out of mine and Sarah's the first chance you got."

Scowling, Matt could feel himself getting worked up.

"Seriously? You're bringing that shit up again? I told you before I didn't fucking sneak out. I left. Last I checked, I was free to do without asking the groom's permission."

"I think it's the fact you left *alone* that has us so perplexed."

Matt glared at Zade from over his shoulder. "Maybe my dick needed a break." "Of course, you don't get enough to know what that feels like, do ya, King?"

"Dude." Zade's brows turned inward.

"Seriously, Turner." Kole glanced away from the gravel road to give him a disapproving look. "We're just giving you shit."

Damn. They were right. These were his teammates. His friends. And what they were saying wasn't anything he hadn't heard before.

*So, why is it bothering you now?*

Matt honestly didn't know. Maybe it was the fact that he hadn't been laid in a while. Not that he'd ever admit it to these jokers, but he hadn't had sex since before Kole's wedding.

So, there it was. He was horny and needed to release all his pent-up frustration. Except he wasn't.

Aaand…that was the real problem behind Matt's short fuse. He *wasn't* horny. Not like he should be after going this long without female companionship.

It wasn't that he couldn't get any. Hell, the way he looked, Matt knew he could walk into any bar in Dallas and have his pick of the single women in attendance. Probably some of the married ones, too. Not that he'd ever do that. Even a guy like him had lines he never crossed.

The problem was him.

Not physically. His extra time spent in the shower this morning confirmed that, which was a huge relief. But it also confirmed something else...something Matt had been in denial over ever since his dry spell started.

*You've been denying it for a hell of a lot longer than that.*

The annoying fucking voice was right, and he knew it. He knew it because lately, there was only one woman his body craved. One woman haunting his dreams at night.

She was the same woman who'd turned him into the uncaring, no-strings asshole he was today. And damn if that didn't piss Matt off something fierce.

He squeezed his eyes shut, pinching the bridge of his nose between his thumb and forefinger in an attempt to knock the decade-long memory away.

"You okay?"

Matt opened his eyes and ran a hand over his face before looking at Kole. "Yeah, man. I'm good. And, uh... sorry I got so wound up."

"It's all right." With a concerning glance, Kole shrugged a shoulder. "Anything you want to talk about?"

"Nope." If he did, he'd have to explain what happened ten years ago. No way in hell was he doing that. The last thing he wanted was for them to know what a schmuck he'd been.

"Fair enough."

The cab of the truck was quiet for the next mile or two before Zade struck up a conversation about where they wanted to eat. Once that happened, Kole called Gabe, Bravo's team leader, and invited him to join them.

When the discussion turned to something work-related, the three went on as if nothing had ever happened, and Matt knew all was forgiven.

Like most men, he and the other Bravo members would sometimes get hot under the collar. Also like most men, they'd run their mouths, say their piece, and move on. None of that holding a grudge bullshit.

Still, he felt like a prick having gotten pissed at their teasing. He really wasn't an asshole. Not to these guys, anyway. They were more like brothers than teammates, and Matt was grateful as hell to have them by his side.

By the time dinner was over, he'd canceled his non-date, claiming something had come up with work. Since then, he'd been sitting here, at the hole-in-the-wall bar he sometimes went to when he didn't want to be around anyone he knew.

The longer he sat, the more he thought about his job and the guys he worked with now. Bravo Team may be less than two years old, but for Matt, it felt as if he'd been part of the team for much longer.

When he'd first enlisted in the military, he was convinced he'd be in for life. But when Jake McQueen approached him about joining R.I.S.C., the elite, private security company Jake owned, Matt was more than willing to listen.

R.I.S.C., which stands for Rescue, Intel, Security, and Capture, was one of the most sought-after private security firms in the nation. Made up of two teams—Alpha and Bravo—they not only worked for civilians in need of protection, they also took on jobs for Homeland Security.

Those ops were sometimes very dangerous and almost always off the books. Homeland would task the men—and one woman—of R.I.S.C. to do jobs ranging from intel gathering to hostage extractions. Or, like the name said, they'd be hired to locate and capture some of the country's most dangerous enemies.

Joining the Navy had been a dream of his ever since he was a kid. One of his best friends growing up had an older brother who was a pilot in the Navy. Matt and his friend always idolized him.

Unlike his worthless father, Matt was determined to make something of himself. Although, in a strange way he probably owed part of his success—albeit a microscopic part—to his old man.

Like his friend's brother, Matt grew up thinking he wanted to be a pilot. That all changed the night his dad got wasted and fell through their glass patio door.

Matt was home and came running when he heard the loud crash. Glass was everywhere, and his dad's leg was bleeding profusely.

Thankfully, the idiot was too out of it to fight Matt when he told him to stay still. After calling 911, Matt went to the drawer by the sink, grabbed a couple clean dishtowels, and made a homemade tourniquet by tying the ends of the towels together and wrapping it around his dad's leg.

When the medics arrived, they asked who had done it. Only thirteen at the time, Matt was afraid to answer, thinking he'd done something wrong. Instead he was shocked when the guy told him he'd saved his dad's life.

Funny thing was, he hadn't even thought about what he was doing. He'd just acted. Which was what he'd told the paramedic that day. The older man smiled and said something that would change Matt's life forever.

*Son, that was a very smart and brave thing you did. Not*

*many adults would've handled themselves that well. You get older, you should think about a career in emergency medicine.*

Rather than choose, Matt decided to combine the two and become a Navy corpsman. By the time he was twenty-three, he'd gotten a bachelor's degree in nursing on the government's dime, allowing him to become an officer.

After that, Matt continued to work his ass off, pushing himself harder than most, earning several Atta-boy's and even more documented commendations. His performance both in and out of the field caught the attention of several higher-ups...as well as Jake McQueen's.

Working alongside the legendary former Delta Force operator and the other members of R.I.S.C. was like a dream come true. He'd heard enough to know McQueen only hired the best, so when he asked Matt to join the new Bravo Team Jake was putting together, Matt hadn't had to think about it.

Now he got to do pretty much the same thing he did in the military, without all the side-stepping bullshit that came with being under Uncle Sam's thumb. For the first time in a very long time, Matt finally felt as though he'd made it.

A shrink would probably tell him his overzealous need to succeed was a big *fuck you* to his dad. They'd be partially right, but his dad wasn't the only one who thought Matt wasn't good enough.

*Nope. Not going there.*

Shaking those thoughts away, he took a sip of the same whiskey he'd been nursing since he sat down half an hour ago. He was about to say screw it and call it a night when an attractive blonde sauntered her way over to him.

"Hey, handsome." She smiled, her perfect teeth framed by a set of bright red lips.

Normally this would be the part where his dick would stand up and take notice, but once again, the fucker was asleep on the job.

"Hi," Matt muttered back with a forced smile.

The woman got even closer. "I couldn't help but notice you've been sittin' here alone for quite a while. Thought maybe you could use some company. Mind if I sit?"

When the exaggeratedly obvious woman tilted her head to the empty bar seat to his right, Matt felt he had no choice but to say, "Sure."

"Good." The blonde's smile grew wider. She sat down, the action causing her already-short skirt to slide up even more. Licking her lips seductively, she said, "You know, you're awfully cute. Way too cute to be alone. Where's your girlfriend?"

He should've said he was waiting for her to meet him here. Instead he heard himself say, "No girlfriend."

Her blue eyes brightened at that. "Really?" She leaned forward, resting her hand on his denim-covered thigh. Running her palm slowly up his leg, she licked her lips again.

"What do you say we find someplace a little quieter?"

*Jesus.* He hoped like hell he didn't come off this desperate when he hit on women.

With her fingertips precariously close to his still-not-hard dick, Matt scrambled to come up with an excuse to get him the hell out of there when his phone screen lit up and began vibrating across the top of the wooden bar.

Relieved to see the name of the caller, Matt abruptly

stood, the woman's hand falling as he blurted, "It's my boss. Sorry, but I have to go."

Ignoring the pouty look on her face—and the fact that Gabe wasn't technically his boss—he spun on his heels and quickly made his way to the door. The second he stepped onto the sidewalk, Matt answered the call.

"Turner."

"I was about to hang up," his team leader quipped. "Is this a bad time?"

*Not even close.* Matt checked for traffic and started walking across the street to the pothole-infested parking lot. "Nah. I'm heading home. What's up?"

"Jake called. He wants us in the office at oh eight hundred."

Matt didn't think anything of the news. Last-minute jobs were pretty much the norm for R.I.S.C.

"He give you anything?"

"No details. Only that he had a new job and Bravo Team's up."

Shortly after its formation, Matt's team began alternating the bigger jobs with Alpha Team. Since that team got back from an overseas op for Homeland last week, it was their turn.

"Copy that. I'll see you at eight."

Shoving his phone back into his pocket, Matt unlocked his truck and climbed inside. By the time he got home and crawled into bed, his mind had returned to the woman at the bar.

Not because he regretted brushing her off but because he didn't. What the hell was wrong with him? One minute, he's perfectly fine with no-strings, consensual one-night-stands, and the next...

A different woman's face filled his mind's eye. One with long, dark hair and eyes the color of chocolate. *Ah, hell no.*

Matt threw his covers off and practically jumped out of bed. Storming barefoot across his loft-style bedroom, he made his way down the open staircase and across his condo into the kitchen.

Bottles clanged together as he opened the refrigerator door with more force than necessary. Grabbing a Heineken from the top shelf, he used his free hand to slam the door shut.

Pissed, it took a few seconds of digging noisily through his utensil drawer before he spotted the bottle opener. Popping the top off, Matt tossed the opener and cap onto the marble counter and downed half the beer in one, long gulp.

He didn't know what the fuck was going on, but if he had to drink himself to sleep in order to quiet the sudden thoughts and memories of that particular mistake, that's exactly what he would do.

A few hours and several beers later, Matt crawled back into bed. This time when he closed his eyes, the only thing floating through his mind was how quickly eight o'clock was going to be here.

As he lay there, he found himself hoping this new job would be enough to distract him from the painful memories. Memories that—for reasons unbeknownst to him—had suddenly resurfaced.

*Never again.*

The words that had become his personal mantra whispered through him as Matt drifted off into a deep, drunken sleep.

The next morning, fueled with plenty of ibuprofen and coffee, Matt shuffled into R.I.S.C.'s downtown office. Oftentimes, they'd meet at Jake's house, which would seem odd if it wasn't so badass.

Sitting on over a hundred acres of highly-secured land, the place was set up with a fully-functional shooting range—both indoor and outdoor, an outdoor training course, and a private air strip, jet and hangar included. For obvious reasons, Matt and the guys preferred to hold their meetings at the ranch.

Right now, however, wasn't the best time to invade their boss's personal space. Jake's wife, Olivia, was due with their first child in a little under two months. For her sake, Jake wanted to try and keep his house as calm and R.I.S.C.-free as possible until that time comes, which means all scheduled meetings were to be held here, in the public office.

Shoving the door open with his shoulder, Matt balanced the two coffees he'd gotten from across the street before coming over here. After his idiotic decision to drink too damn much last night, he'd woken up knowing it was going to be a two-coffee kind of day.

Entering the conference room at the end of the long hallway, Matt carefully set the two paper cups on the long, oval table before rolling out one of the empty, cushioned chairs. Taking a seat beside Kole, he slid his sunglasses to the top of his head, his eyes instantly squinting against the harsh, neon lights.

"Damn, man. What happened to you?" Zade asked from across the table.

Kole snorted. "Better yet, *who* happened to you?"

With a silent flip of the bird, Matt lifted one of the

cups to his lips. He then proceeded to suck down as much of the hot, bitter liquid as he could without burning his throat.

"You good to go, Turner?" Gabe asked from the seat next to Zade's.

"I'm fine. Just had some trouble sleeping." When Kole opened his mouth to spout off yet another smartass comment, Matt shut him down, fast. "Alone, dickwad. I went home alone."

"Oh. That's…different. I don't quite know how to respond to that."

Not in the mood for this shit, Matt turned his head and glared at his friend. "Contrary to what you assholes think, I don't sleep with a different fucking woman every goddamn night."

A low throat cleared from behind him, and Matt didn't have to turn around to know Jake had stepped into the room.

Great.

"Turner, I need to see you in my office. The rest of you, hang tight. This shouldn't take long, and then we'll go over everything you need to know together."

Feeling as though he was being called into the principal's office, Matt grabbed one of his coffees and stood. Though a lot worse had been said in that room—a *hell* of a lot worse—it was the only reason he could come up with that Jake would summons him to his private office…alone.

"Sorry about that, Boss," he mumbled as he followed Jake down the hall. "The guys were giving me shit, and I wasn't in the mood, and—"

"Relax, Turner." Jake stopped in front of his closed

door to face him. "This has nothing to do with that." The dark-haired man shot him a look while shaking his head. "Jesus. When did I become such a dick to work for that you'd think cursing in the conference room would be grounds for a private ass-chewing?"

"You're not a dick, Boss. What I said wasn't very professional and the door was open, and…you know what? Never mind." Matt decided to stop talking before he dug himself any deeper.

One of Jake's dark brows rose in amusement. "Glad we got that cleared up. Come on." He turned and reached for the knob. "I want you to meet our new client."

As he followed the other man through the doorway, Matt had the fleeting thought that he was going to need something a helluva lot stronger than a cup of coffee to get him through this day. A second later, he realized just how right he was.

Stopping dead in his tracks, he couldn't believe what he was seeing. There, standing in the middle of his boss's office, was the one woman he'd spent a decade trying to forget.

It was the only goal in his life he'd ever failed to achieve. Christ, had he failed miserably.

The pretty teenager she was when he'd last seen her was gone, replaced by an even more beautiful, grown woman. She was still lean, but even beneath her dark jeans and plain, olive sweater, he could tell she'd developed delicious curves in all the right places.

*The kind I'd like to—*

Thankfully Jake's voice broke through his thoughts before they could venture down that senseless path.

"Matt, I'd like you to meet—"

"Katherine Anderson," Matt finished for his boss. It was the first time he'd uttered her married name aloud. He still couldn't believe she'd left him and married some rich prick.

A swirling collage of memories assaulted him, both good and bad. Matt's heart kicked the shit out of his chest as he stared back at the only person to have ever made him truly happy.

She was also the person who'd brought him more pain and misery than anyone or anything he'd ever known.

"Matt?"

Dark, round eyes grew wide, and she looked and sounded every bit as shocked to see him as he was her. Of course, she always was a good little actor, so there was that.

Despite his loathing for this woman, Matt felt his cock twitch inside his jeans. He wanted to punch the damn thing for choosing now...choosing *her* to respond to.

He crushed his molars together to the point of pain. Feeling as though he'd stepped into some sort of alternate universe—one he wanted to get the fuck out of—Matt glared at her from across the room.

"What the hell are you doing here?" he growled, not bothering to hide his disdain for her.

Round, dark eyes blinked at his harsh tone. "I-I...um..."

With his blue eyes bouncing back and forth between them, Jake sounded less surprised than Matt would expect when he said, "I take it you two know each other."

"Used to," Matt answered for them both. With a casual shrug, he added, "It was nothing."

A brief flash of pain crossed behind those damning

eyes, but Katherine collected herself before looking to Jake. "It was a long time ago."

Jake looked over at Matt and back to her. "I see. Well, I should give you two a minute to catch up before we get started."

"Okay," she said with a smile Matt knew was forced.

At the exact same time, he practically blurted out, "No." When Jake gave him an odd look, he did his best to recover. "I mean, we should probably get on with whatever this is. I know you're busy, and I still have to finish up my portion of the paperwork from that last bodyguard gig, and..."

"Gracie already took care of it all before she and Nate left."

Well, didn't that blow a huge fucking hole in his reason why they shouldn't be left alone.

"She did?" Matt was genuinely surprised to find that out but not enough to complain. Right now, he would be happy to talk about anything other than the hundred-thirty-pound beauty in the room. "Why'd she do that?"

"She wanted to. Which, as it turns out, is a good thing, because I need you on this."

Matt slid his cold eyes to Kat before focusing on Jake once more. "Need me on what?"

"Your next assignment."

With his jaw muscles working overtime, Matt begrudgingly asked, "And what is that, exactly?"

*Don't say it. Please, God, don't say it.*

"Dr. Marsh needs protection."

"*Dr.* Marsh?" Matt looked back at her. "Didn't realize you'd become a doctor. Of course, I also thought you were married, so..."

In a moment of weakness about two years after they split, Matt had a buddy search her through his social media account. The fact that she'd married someone else shouldn't have surprised him, but it had. What didn't surprise him was how wealthy the asshole was.

Actually, if Matt were being honest—which, he wasn't —it had completely fucking devastated him. Which is why he never bothered looking her up again.

Genuine sadness filled her pretty eyes. "I got my Ph.D. a few years ago. As for being married, I was. I'm not anymore."

If she'd been any other woman, Matt would've stored that bit of information away for future use. But he didn't want to keep it. Didn't want to know a damn thing about her life, now.

Even so, he couldn't help but go for the dig. "What happened? Hubby run out of money?

"Turner," Jake said his last name as a warning.

Kat drew in a deep breath. "Brian died sixyears ago."

*Eight years, and she hasn't remarried?* Not that he cared.

"Dr. Marsh was sent to us because she needs our protection."

Making a snorting sound he didn't bother trying to cover up, Matt nearly rolled his eyes when he asked, "From what?"

Surprising him—because apparently it was Let's Surprise the Ever-Loving Fuck out of Matt Day— Katherine straightened her shoulders and lifted her chin.

Looking him square in the eye, she said, "From whoever's trying to kill me."

# CHAPTER 2

Matthew. Freaking. Turner.

Of course he'd work here. After all, that was par for the course with how her life was going lately.

*Damn it, Kat. Why didn't you check this place out more thoroughly?*

Oh, that's right. She'd been too busy running for her life.

Wanting to crawl into a hole and disappear, Kat did everything she could not to show the reaction she was having from seeing him again. Not that he'd bothered hiding his feelings about her being here.

One look at his face and she knew Matt would rather be anywhere but in this room with her. It had been in his cold, uncaring eyes.

As soon as he recovered from seeing her again, he'd looked back at her as though she were a stranger. Worse than that. An enemy.

Kat had become dizzy with shock when she'd found

herself staring back at the only man she'd truly loved, and when he spoke? God, just hearing his voice again after all this time had damn near brought her to her knees.

Then it turned cold, like his expression. And he'd spit his next words out as if they were a curse.

*It was nothing.*

Though she deserved it, Katherine had to fight to breathe for the pain still spreading inside her chest. To her, what they'd shared was everything.

It shouldn't still hurt this much. Not after so many years apart. Too bad no one had passed that particular memo to her heart.

Over the years, she'd forced herself to imagine him a hundred pounds overweight and balding to help ease the pain of having lost him. With no social media accounts she could find—and she'd searched them all more times than she could count—Kat had almost convinced herself that's how he looked now.

*Not. Even. Close.*

IN SOME WAYS, HE LOOKED EXACTLY THE SAME. IN OTHERS, he looked even better.

His dark hair was still short, but much longer than the military-buzz he'd had the last time they were together. She could still remember the way it felt beneath her fingertips when she'd run her hands over it.

The scruff covering his strong, chiseled jaw was sexier than it should've been, and his lean, youthful body had filled out in the most delicious way.

Kat's fingers itched to touch him as she continued her

covert assessment. Especially where his white button-up stretched across his large, well-defined chest and biceps.

Her gaze lowered to where the material loosened around his narrow waist, her mouthwatering from the way his thick thighs pressed against the denim covering his lower body. A memory of him pressing his legs against hers as they made love flew through her mind, and she had to clear her throat against the moan threatening to escape.

Both men turned their heads in her direction, and she scrambled for an excuse. "Sorry. Had a tickle in my throat."

*A tickle?* Kat mentally sighed at herself. For a genius, she could be a real idiot sometimes.

As if she needed further proof, the man standing three feet away from her was it. Out of all the private security companies in Texas, she'd chosen this one.

*See? Idiot.*

"Why don't we go into the conference room where the rest of the team is waiting." Mr. McQueen's deep voice interrupted the self-deprecating thoughts. "We'll go over everything in detail and figure out a more precise game plan."

Realizing he was speaking to her, Kat nodded and said, "Okay." Because really...what other choice did she have?

The intense man led the way, immediately followed by Matt. He didn't even look at her when he passed by, which was almost worse than if he'd given her the death stare.

Taking up the rear, Kat kept a safe distance between them, trying hard to not pay attention to the way *his* rear looked in those jeans. Like with everything else, lately, she failed miserably.

Matt had always had a nice ass, but damn. The man was seriously perfect, in every single way. Too bad he hated her.

"We're in here." McQueen stopped at the doorway to let them by.

Kat's eyes shot up with the same speed as her pulse. Though he didn't say anything, she had a sneaking suspicion Matt's boss had caught her checking out his employee's ass.

Pretending as if nothing had happened, she forced a smile as she entered the room. That same smile dropped in an instant when she saw the others staring back at her.

Sitting around the table were three very intimidating men. They were also extremely handsome in their own rights.

The one directly across from where she stood was a little older, probably forties, with a very sexy head full of short, salt and pepper hair. The guy was big and built, and the term *silver fox* immediately came to mind.

Sitting next to him was a younger man with light brown hair and gorgeous brown eyes. Closer to her age, Kat noticed he was built a lot like Matt. They both had that 'runner' look. Muscular, for sure, but in a leaner, more streamlined way than the fox.

Spinning around, the third man looked up at her. He was also younger and lean, his light brown hair cut much shorter than the others.

"Hey." He stood and smiled at her. "I'm Kole."

Shaking his outstretched hand, she smiled. "Katherine Marsh."

"Nice to meet you."

Kole returned to his seat while Matt inadvertently brushed against hers as he slid behind her. Without a word, he made his way to the empty chair at the farthest end of the table. The farthest one away from her.

As she sat in the seat to the right of Kole, Mr. McQueen introduced her to the other two men.

Pointing to the larger of the two, Jake said, "Dr. Marsh, this is Gabe Dawson, Bravo Team's team leader."

With a tip of his head, the formidable man said, "Nice to meet you."

"Next to him is Zade King, one of Bravo's two snipers. He also specializes in hand-to-hand combat."

Like Gabe, Zade offered a tip of his head and a friendly smile. "Dr. Marsh."

"Please." Kat looked at the three Bravo Team members before turning to Jake. "Call me Kat or Katherine. I answer to both."

Nodding, Jake's lips curled into a small smile. "Kat, it is. And you can call me Jake." He glanced to Matt and the man next to her. "Of course, you already know Matt, and you've met Kole."

Not looking in Matt's direction was one of the hardest things she'd ever had to do. For years, she'd dreamed of seeing him again. Now that she had, Kat knew she could stare at him for hours and never get her fill.

"Matt is Bravo's medic and Kole is their lead sniper."

"There's also a fifth member of the team," Zade spoke from across the table. "But Nate's on his honeymoon, so…"

*A honeymoon*. She'd never had one of those. Not that it would've been a real one, anyway.

Shaking those thoughts off, Kat looked to Jake for direction. It didn't take long for him to give it.

Pulling out the chair at the head of the room, he sat down and rested his elbows on the table. With his fingers linked together, he said, "Dr..... uh...Kat was sent to us by way of referral because she needs our protection."

"From who?" Gabe asked.

"I don't know."

The next question came from Kole, and it was obvious he didn't understand. *That makes two of us.*

"Wait. Just so I'm clear, you think you need protection, but you don't know who you need protection from?"

"It's...complicated."

"So, uncomplicate it." Matt's deep voice sounded clipped.

She did look at him then, but the second their eyes met, she wished she hadn't. Thankfully, Jake chimed back in.

"Why don't you start by explaining what it is you do for a living," Jake prompted her. "Then, we'll go from there."

"Okay." Kat looked at him before glancing at the others. "I work for a company called Anderson Biomeds."

"Anderson, huh?" Matt's gaze was knowing.

Confirming his suspicions, she said, "Yes. It's owned by Sloane Anderson, my former father-in-law."

"What do they do?" Gabe asked her, ignoring Matt's smug smirk.

"It's a biologics company specializing in the development and distribution of various types of drugs."

"And what is your role?" Kole turned his gaze to hers.

36

"I'm the lead biomedical engineer for our Specialization Department."

Seeing the blank look on his face reminded Kat most people had absolutely no idea what that meant. She tried again.

"My department is in charge of developing formulas that can be used to help protect or strengthen the inner-workings of the human body at the molecular and cellular levels."

"Oh, okay." Kole nodded as if that made perfect sense.

Zade shot his teammate a look and said, "Dude, you have no idea what she said, do you?"

Kole snickered. "Not a clue."

The room filled with chuckles. Hoping to see a smile on Matt's handsome face, too, Kat glanced his way. Instead, she found him staring directly at her, and he was definitely not smiling.

Looking away quickly, Kat apologized to the group. "Sorry. I spend most of my days in a lab working with a team of scientists. I'm not used to having to explain what we do to other people."

"Why don't you dumb it down for us grunts. We'll try to keep up."

Matt's sarcastic remark got everyone's attention, including Gabe's.

"There a problem, Turner?" Gabe looked directly at him.

Not appearing to be intimidated by his team leader, Matt simply shrugged and said, "Just ready to figure out why we're here, that's all."

"Then let the woman talk," Zade joined in.

Matt gestured for her to continue. "Explain away."

Cheeks red with embarrassment, Kat did her best to ignore the strange looks Matt's teammates were giving them both. Clearing her throat, she gave them what she hoped would be a clearer picture of what she and the others on her team did.

"A biomedical engineer uses biological or chemical processes to research and develop formulas or serums for various purposes. My department is directly involved in working on the company's government contracts."

"So, the government pays you to create stuff," Kole simplified it even more.

"Yes."

"Like what?" Gabe asked.

This is where it got tricky. Every government-sanctioned job the company took on required she and her team to all sign non-disclosure agreements.

As if he could read her mind, Jake said, "It's okay, Kat. We're all former military and do contract work for the government as well. We understand the risks involved in disclosing classified material. And I wouldn't ask you to break any sort of legal agreement you may have signed, but if there's something you believe is directly related to what happened, we need to know. I can assure you, whatever you share with us stays with us and will only be used to protect you."

She knew he was right. They couldn't help her unless they knew everything. Besides, even if they did go back on their word, being sued for breach of contract was still better than being dead.

"Okay." Kat inhaled deeply and began telling them

everything she knew. "The U.S. government has contracted with Anderson Biomeds for years. Specifically my department focuses on projects to help aid our military forces overseas."

That got their attention.

"What sort of projects?" Gabe asked curiously.

"Several types, really. We've developed vaccines to fight off area-specific viruses, immune system boosters, things like that. Oh, and the blood clotting agent the military currently uses was also developed in our lab."

"Really?" Kole gave her an approving nod. "That's cool."

Zade agreed. "Yeah. I'm sure we've all used that stuff at one point or another."

Kat refused to allow herself to look at Matt for fear her eyes would give away too much. He'd always been able to read her well. Better than anyone else she'd ever known.

"If you've ever been deployed overseas, I can pretty much guarantee you have."

"These formulas you develop, do the people in your department work on an individual basis, or as a team?"

"Oh, we're very much a team. One that depends greatly on trust. We've also had to learn and understand each other's nuances and strengths, and we use those to our advantage. Each person has a specific job, but we combine those jobs to obtain the desired result. At least, we try to, anyway."

"Back to the company, itself"—Gabe chimed in—"why did the government choose to partner with Anderson Biomeds?"

"Most companies or agencies use contracted laboratories. That means they work on formulas and outsource the rest of the steps. We do everything in-house, from the developmental stages all the way through completion. Everything we create is done so within our own company's walls."

"Really cuts down on cost," the other man stated. "Also lessens the chance for one of your formulas to get leaked to a competitor."

Kat nodded. "Exactly."

"How competitive is this sort of thing?" Zade asked.

"Biomeds is a highly competitive field, world-wide. If someone discovered one of our formulas, they could take it out from under us. They could then sell it at a lower cost, but still make millions. Possibly more. It would ruin us."

"Which brings us to why Kat needs our help." With a nod, Jake gave her the go-ahead to share the incredible, terrifying story.

"Everything started four days ago when I received a strange text on my work phone."

Kole frowned. "What made it seem strange?"

"For one, it was sent after midnight." Her eyes skittered in Matt's direction and back again. "I pretty much live at work, so I don't have much of a social life. I certainly don't have any friends who would text me that late at night. Plus, it was from a number I didn't recognize, and there was nothing in the text to indicate who the sender was."

"What did it say?" Zade's focused gaze found hers.

"The only things on it were instructions to be sure to 'include all the notes along with the formula' and an email to send the information to. But the thing that really struck me as odd was what was at the end of the text."

Gabe tipped his head a bit. "Which was?"

"An order typed in all caps to delete the texts after the email was sent."

The room was silent for a moment before Zade asked, "Any idea what formula they were talking about?"

Kat shook her head. "Not at the time. We sometimes work on multiple projects simultaneously. Anyway, I wrote back as soon as I read it, asking who it was. I got no response. I tried calling the number, but all I got was a recording saying it was invalid. I finally brushed it off as a wrong number and went on with the rest of my night."

"I'll admit that was a bit strange"—Kole looked at Jake —"but random texts really aren't our thing, Boss." His head swung back around to her. "No offense."

A corner of Kat's mouth turned upward. "None taken. Believe me, I wouldn't waste your time if that was all it was."

"So there's more," Zade commented.

Kat looked over at him. "The day after I got that text, there was an explosion in our lab." She drew in a shaky breath, hating that she had to revisit that nightmarish day. "Three members on my team were killed. Two instantly, and another...Amy suffered severe burns over forty percent of her body. She's been in the ICU, but the hospital called early this morning..." her voice cracked. Clearing her throat she said, "Amy didn't make it."

"Damn." Kole's face filled with sympathy. "I'm sorry."

Forcing a smile, Kat offered a low, "Thanks."

With an expression matching Kole's, Zade asked, "Were you there when it happened?"

She nodded, the memories from that day still raw and painful. "I'd just walked out to use the restroom seconds before it happened. I, um…" Swallowing against the knot in her throat, she forced herself to push on. "The force of the blast threw me to the ground. When I realized what had happened, I rushed back in, trying to help. I knew right away that Evan and Todd were dead. I was able to drag Amy into the hallway, away from the flames and smoke, but that was all I could do for her." Kat cleared her throat. "Other than calling 911."

"That took a lot of guts to go back in like that," Jake said sincerely.

Didn't seem like it to her. All she'd felt was helpless.

"Were you injured?" Gabe asked sounding concerned.

Kat shook her head. "Just some bruises."

She fought the urge to touch the tender spot under her hairline. Thankfully, it was on the same side where her hair naturally lay. Not that she was vain. Kat just didn't want to make a big deal out of a few stitches. Especially when the others had gone through far worse.

"Do you know what caused the explosion?"

"Yes." Though part of her wished she didn't. "Due to the nature of my work, I was able to assist the authorities in testing the residue found at the ignition sight. It was a mixture of various chemicals frequently used by our lab. Individually, each of the substances are relatively harmless, but put them together, and—"

"Boom," Kole finished for her.

Kat nodded. "Exactly. The particular combination created a highly explosive compound."

Jake asked the same question she'd been wondering

ever since it happened. "Are we talking an accident, or do you think the explosion was intentional?"

"That's the thing. I-I can't be certain. I can't imagine they would, nor can I begin to fathom a reason why they would. What I can tell you is, my people would've known the risks of having those chemicals together in one workspace."

"What about someone not on the team?" Jake continued to question her as he took down some notes. "Does anyone else have access to the lab?"

"Only a couple of the higher-ups in the company. But they hardly ever come in, and when they do, it's usually because some important investor is visiting. It's been weeks since our last visitor, and authorities checked the building security footage. The only ones in or out of the lab that day were my three teammates and myself. No one else."

"In whose area did the fire start?"

A pang of sadness and guilt struck inside Kat's chest. "Todd's. His station was behind mine."

"Is it possible he could've grabbed the wrong thing by mistake? Like, maybe he got distracted?"

"Possible, yes. But highly improbable."

"If it wasn't a mistake on his part, how do you think those chemicals ended up there?"

"I wish I knew." She shook her head. "Actually, what I really wish is that I'd never left."

"You needed to use the bathroom, Kat," Zade tried to appease her. "Not like anyone can fault you for that."

Kat appreciated the man's attempt to empathize, but she knew she'd never forgive herself for leaving when she had.

"The explosion originated in Todd's workspace, and you said he was directly behind yours, correct?

She looked over at Jake. "Yes."

"So it's safe to assume that, had you stayed, you most likely would've died alongside your teammates."

"Maybe." She'd thought of that, too. "But had I stayed, maybe I could've noticed the chemicals in time to prevent the explosion in the first place."

Gabe's deep voice rumbled as he advised her, "Kat, if there's one thing we've learned in this business, it's that you can't torture yourself with what-ifs."

She knew he was right. Didn't ease the pain in her heart any, though.

"So you receive the odd text and the next day the lab explodes, killing nearly everyone on your team," Kole spoke evenly, summing everything up so far. "What else?"

Kat hesitated to answer because saying it out loud made it real. She looked at Kole and the others.

"With the lab in shambles and my team…anyway. The project has been put on hold until Sloane can get a new team established and the lab back in working order. I went into work yesterday to see what, if anything had been recovered. After that, I stopped by the hospital to check on Amy before going home. When I walked into my apartment, I found the place trashed."

The engrained image of her shredded couch and broken lamps still caused a shiver to run down her spine.

"Was anything taken?" Zade asked.

"My personal laptop and a stack of old notebooks I'd kept from past research projects. Everything else was just…destroyed."

Kole thought a moment. "Anything of value on the computer?"

"Not to anyone else. Like I said, it was my personal computer. The ones we used at the lab are highly encrypted to protect the research. That one was your average laptop. It was never used for anything work-related. Of course, whoever took it would have no way of knowing that."

"Whoever took it and the notebooks were looking for something specific," Gabe noted. "What were you guys working on at the time?"

"For the past four years, we've been developing and fine-tuning a special project. It was in its final stages, but it wasn't quite perfected to the standards it needed to be. We were coming up on a pretty solid deadline, so the team has been working non-stop with barely enough time to eat or sleep. When it gets like that, I pretty much live on coffee, which is why I was headed to the restroom in the first place, and..." Kat stopped herself and took a deep breath. "Sorry. I have a tendency to ramble when I'm upset or nervous."

When Matt coughed loudly, Kat couldn't help but wonder if her nervous ramblings were the cause. It was a habit she'd had since she was a young girl. One he used to love teasing her about.

"It's okay." Jake offered a kind smile. "Just take your time."

After filling her lungs once more, Kat began again. "This particular formula is for a special serum commissioned by the government. It's been slated for military use only, and in my opinion, is the most important thing we've ever done."

45

"What's so special about it?"

*Everything.* This project was the sole reason she'd continued working for Anderson. Not because she felt any sort of loyalty to him. Not even close.

Kat glanced around the room. "With our serum, thousands of American soldiers' lives will be saved. Maybe more."

# CHAPTER 3

"Spit it out, already, Doc," Matt ordered impatiently. He knew he was being a dick, but *fuck*.

How the hell was he supposed to react to seeing her again? Not only that, but he had to sit here while she talked about her job at the super important lab owned by her rich as fuck former father-in-law. Seriously?

*At least he's a former and not current.*

Matt shot that thought down hard. There was no 'at least' in this situation. He wouldn't have given a flying fuck if she'd still been married. Just like he didn't give a shit about *her* anymore.

*So why did your chest tighten when she talked about the explosion and the break-in?*

That was pure coincidence, he told himself. Probably something he ate.

To make matters even worse—as if that were even possible at this point—he had to continue to stare at her gorgeous face while listening to the sexy, sultry voice that once had the power to bring him to his knees.

*Still does.*

*Shut the fuck up!*

Christ. Now he was arguing with his own subconscious. No wonder he was grumpy as shit.

Maybe, if he was lucky, she'd get mad at him and leave. Jake would be pissed, but it would be worth a slap on the wrist if it meant getting her out of here.

Flickering an annoyed glance his way, Kat revealed the supposedly huge government secret.

"My team and I developed a serum that can slow down the body's response to trauma."

Okay, so that *did* sound sort of cool. He and the others remained silent, so Kat continued to explain further.

"Basically, it works on both the cellular and molecular levels to deter a person's normal physical reactions when they've sustained an injury."

"How?" Zade asked the same question rolling through Matt's mind.

"I'm sure you're all well aware of how adrenaline works in the body, yes?"

She was in a room full of former-military badasses who now worked the private sector. *Brilliant assumption, Kat.*

The other guys all responded with nods, but Matt kept his emotionless expression going strong.

"Okay, good. So, when we're injured, our brain signals the release of adrenaline to help combat the pain, sometimes to the point where we aren't even aware of the injury until a few seconds, or in some cases, minutes later. Not only that, but there have been thousands of reports of people becoming uncharacteristically stronger, more focused, even during high-stress situations such as the ones you've all experienced."

"Are you saying this serum your lab has been creating is some kind of synthetic adrenaline?" Kole asked.

Matt gave his teammate a look. "That's what epinephrine is, dumb ass."

"Sort of," Kat answered Kole. "However, what we've been developing is much more advanced than your average epi pen. This stuff will slow your heart rate, which in turn, slows the bleeding. It makes it so you don't feel pain. Or, if you do, it won't be enough to keep you from being able to defend yourself or your teammates. Your breathing remains more even, as opposed to the heaving breaths we tend to take in when we're hurting."

Kat stopped a few seconds to let what she'd shared sink in. When Zade looked back over at her, Matt couldn't tell if the expression on his face meant he was impressed, or he thought she was nuts.

"You're talking super-soldier shit." He sounded in awe.
*He's impressed.*

With the same half-smile he used to love seeing, Kat said, "Not exactly the term we use in the lab, but yes. That's pretty much it."

"Holy shit." Kole fell back into his chair. Looking at each of them, he sounded even more impressed than Zade. "Can you imagine what something like that could mean for our troops? For any of us? Guy takes a hit that would normally bring them down, but is able to keep going?"

"Remember," Kat intervened quickly "It's temporary. The test subjects we've used it on so far have only seen positive changes for anywhere from a few seconds to a few minutes. We've been tweaking the formula so its effects will last longer, but we were unable to test the new serum before the explosion."

Kole shook his head. "Still. I could name half a dozen soldiers who died when they were mere minutes away from getting the help they needed. Something like this..." He glanced around the room. "This is a game changer."

Jake didn't seem as excited. Wheels turning, he nodded but muttered, "In more ways than one."

"Boss is right," Gabe agreed before turning his focus back onto Kat. "If this stuff truly does what you're saying, I know a hell of a lot of people who'd love to get their hands on it. A lot of very bad, very dangerous people."

"That would explain the text." Zade nodded thoughtfully. "Someone *did* find out about it and was working with a person on the inside. That same person was probably paid a lot of money to access and share the formula."

"When they mistakenly sent you the next instructions in the plan, you became a target," Kole joined in.

Jake nodded, apparently agreeing with their theory. "Even if you didn't suspect anything from the text, you survived the explosion. Whoever's in charge knew there was a possibility you'd put two and two together, so they went looking for you at your place."

"They didn't find you," Kole spoke up again. "But they took what they thought would lead them to the formula."

Gabe's face became dead serious when he stared over at her and said, "Problem is, they're going to figure out pretty damn quick the formula isn't anywhere in what they took."

Now it was Kat's turn to be in awe. Matt watched as

she stared wide-eyed at each of the men. *That's right, sweetheart. Not a bunch of dumb grunts, after all.*

"You said you went back to the lab yesterday to see if there was anything salvageable. You find anything?" Jake asked.

"Not really. A few miscellaneous notes, but mostly everything had burned."

"Where do you keep your records from all the testing you do? Research files, that sort of thing?"

"We have one main computer system in the lab that everyone has access to. Or, had. It got destroyed in the explosion."

"Is that the only place?"

"Yes and no. We store the data in a file in that computer, but I also have an external hard drive I would use to download the findings and notes from each day. That's where the recipe for the formula is kept."

"Did that survive?"

Kat shook her head. "It didn't take a direct hit, but it was burned pretty badly. Our head tech guy has been trying to pull what he can from it, but last I heard, he wasn't having any luck."

"Damn. That sucks," Zade commented. "All that time and money wasted. All that research and data just...poof. Gone."

"Except it's not." Matt couldn't keep quiet. "Not really."

All eyes shifted to his.

"What do you mean?" Gabe's brow furrowed.

"Go ahead, Doc." He lifted his chin to Kat. "Tell 'em."

Matt could tell she hated the mocking nickname, making him want to use it that much more.

*Immature much?* Fuck yeah, he was. Wore the badge with pride.

"Tell us what?" Kole asked.

With a sigh, Kat admitted, "I have a very good memory."

*Good, my ass.*

"Ah, come on. You're being modest." To the others, Matt said, "Kat, here, can pretty much remember everything about, well everything. Isn't that right?"

A look of hurt flashed behind her eyes at his mocking tone, but he refused to let it bother him.

"All right, enough." Gabe spun his gaze to Matt's, his intelligent eyes narrowing. "What the hell is going on between you two?"

Matt gave the man a simple shrug. "Absolutely nothing."

"Don't give us that bullshit," Kole called him out next. "The tension's so thick between you guys I can barely see your ass from here."

Kat's eyes shot to Matt's before they skittered over to Kole's. An instant flush began filling her neck and cheeks, and she looked uncomfortable as hell.

*Welcome to my world, Doc.*

"Matt and I know each other." She decided to answer for them both. "Well, we used to. We grew up in the same town."

"Oh." Kole thought about that a moment before his eyes widened and his brows shot up. "*Oh...*" He let the word trail a bit that time. A smug grin began to form on the asshole's baby face as he looked around Kat and to him. "I bet this is awkward."

"Not if we focus on why we're really here," Jake told

them all pointedly. The guy's rugged face appeared impassive, but the look he was giving Matt said the guy felt anything but.

"Back to the situation at hand." Jake turned to Kat. "Is what Matt said true? Do you really have an eidetic memory?"

Still appearing embarrassed, she said, "The jury's still out on the precise term to use, but yes. I can remember everything I see. Have since I was a kid."

"Do the people you work with know this about you?"

"Yes."

"I don't think what happened at the lab was an accident," he announced. "I think whoever sent that text was planning to steal the formula. When you messaged them back, they knew it had been sent to the wrong person. It's possible they somehow learned of your extraordinary memory, and knew you'd give the information from the text to the authorities if the formula were stolen. I think they decided to silence you, and they used Todd to do it."

"But that doesn't make sense."

"Why not?" Matt had to ask.

Chocolate eyes met his. "For one, Todd died. If he was doing this for money, he wouldn't kill himself in the process. Two, all of the research data was destroyed. So if someone hired Todd to steal it, why would they then hire him to destroy it? Sure, they might get rid of me, but they also lost their chance to sell the formula. Plus, the explosion happened after I walked out of the lab. If I was the original target, why wait for me to leave before mixing the compound?"

"You said the chemical combination was highly explosive, right?" Gabe clarified.

"Yes, but—"

He cut her off. "You also said your people don't normally mix those together. So isn't it possible he either put too much of something in there? He messed up, and the explosion happened sooner than planned?"

Kat opened her mouth to answer but closed it. Matt could tell she didn't want to believe her colleague had tried to kill her.

*Wish the fucker was still alive so I could kill him myself.*

Whoa. Where the hell had that come from? Matt didn't care what happened to her. Not anymore.

"It's possible, I guess," she answered hesitantly. "I can't imagine Todd doing something like that."

"I'll need Todd's last name, as well as Evan's and Amy's. Just in case they were involved." Addressing the team, Jake said, "Since Nate's gone, I'll get West on this ASAP. I'll have him run their financials, check for any large deposits or anything out of the ordinary. We'll start with Todd's and go from there."

Derek West was a former SEAL and member of R.I.S.C.'s Alpha team. Apart from Nate, West was the smartest man Matt knew when it came to computers and all that shit.

If there was something in the lab rat's background, D would find it. Matt just wondered what it would be.

Another question ran through his mind. One he knew was going to royally piss Kat off.

Glancing down the table to where she sat, he asked her, "How closely did the authorities question you after the fire?"

Dark, perfect brows turned inward. "I'm not sure I understand what you're asking."

Bullshit. She knew exactly what he was getting at.

"Oh, come on, Doc." Resting his elbows on the table, Matt linked his fingers together in a loose steeple and said, "I'm sure you can figure it out."

She blinked, clearly taken aback by his not-so-subtle accusation. "You think *I* rigged the chemicals to explode?"

"You tell me." He leaned back in his chair. "You said it yourself, no one other than you and your team went in or out of the lab that day. And the point of origin was right behind your work area. Not to mention, it's a pretty big coincidence the place goes up in flames right after you walked out.

A fierce anger replaced the hurt in her eyes. "I can't believe you'd think I could do something like that."

Truth be told, he couldn't either.

He shrugged. "People do all kinds of shocking, totally unexpected things every day."

"I'm the one who came to you guys, remember?" She slapped a palm to her chest. "*I'm* the one who hired you to find out who's behind all this. Why would I do that if I was the guilty one?"

"Criminals insert themselves into investigations all the time, Kat. Just so they can keep an eye on what's going on. What better way to know whether or not authorities are closing in than to be working by their side?"

Matt could hear himself. Knew he should probably stop, but damn if he could make himself.

"Hell, I wouldn't be surprised if whoever you were planning to sell the formula to encouraged you to come to us. Speaking of which, exactly how did you find us?"

"I can't believe this." Kat looked to Jake and the others

as if she expected them to back her up. Honestly, so did Matt.

Instead, their focused eyes staring back at her, waiting for her to answer his questions.

"This was a mistake." Her dark hair swished across her shoulders when she shook her head. "I never should've come here."

Standing, Kat grabbed her purse from the table. After a couple awkward attempts, she shoved her chair back to its rightful place and turned to leave.

"Katherine, wait." Jake stood. "I apologize for Matt's behavior. However, while he was much more abrupt than necessary—"his boss shot him a look—"these *are* questions we need answers to."

With an almost lost look in her glossy eyes, Kat stared up at Jake. "I came here because I thought..." her voice cracked. A tear fell down her cheek.

Matt refused to let it bother him.

Swiping it angrily away, Kat regained her composure and started again. "How I found out about your firm is of no relevance. I came here because I heard you were the best." Surprising the hell out of Matt, she turned to him. "I know you hate me, and you have every right to. If I'd known you worked here, I would never have come." Glancing at the others, she said, "I'm sorry to have wasted your time." And then she walked out.

*Mission. Accomplished.*

"What the fuck just happened?"

Rather than answer Kole's question, Jake told the man, "Go get her."

"Why me?" Kole pointed his thumb at Matt. "He made this mess. He should be the one to clean it up."

"Fuck you." Matt glared at his teammate before looking back at Jake. "Boss, I'm sorry, but you don't understand."

"No, Matt. *You* don't understand. I get there's some bad shit between you two, but that woman came to us for help. And from the sounds of it, she needs it." Before Matt could say anything else, Jake spoke to Kole again. "Go. Get her back here. Gabe, why don't you and Zade go with him in case he needs help talking her down."

Giving Matt a few awkward glances, the other three men did as they were told and left the room.

"Did you know?" Matt asked Jake.

"Know what?"

Because this man was his boss and he respected the hell out of him, Matt resisted the urge to roll his eyes. "Did you know Kat and I used to date? I'm the only one you took into your office earlier, so I assume you did."

Sighing, Jake sat back down. "Ryker contacted me late last night. Told me he referred a woman named Katherine to us. He didn't give me a ton of specifics, only that she was a scientist working on a top-secret project for the military, and she felt she was in danger because of it. As soon as we got off the phone, I looked her up. Saw she grew up in the same town you did, I figured there was a good chance you knew each other. I took you to my office because I wanted to see if you did, in fact, know her. If you did, I wanted to gauge how well the two of you got along."

"Ryker referred her?" Matt felt his brows raise. "How the hell does she know him?"

Jason Ryker was R.I.S.C.'s Homeland Security Handler. He ran a special division within the agency, and some-

ANNA BLAKELY

times hired both Alpha and Bravo teams to either assist or fully execute sensitive jobs.

The guy was like a fucking ghost. Everywhere and nowhere, all at the same time.

"Jason said Kat's father contacted him because he was concerned for her safety and wanted advice. Ryker suggested she come here."

"Hold up. Kat's *dad* is friends with Jason Ryker?" Falling back in his chair, Matt linked his hands behind his head and laughed. "Oh, man. This shit keeps getting better and better."

"Then you're probably going to love this next part."

"There's more?" Matt wasn't sure he could take it.

Jake nodded. "I'm assigning you to be Kat's protection detail."

He stared at Jake, waiting for the 'gotcha' to come. It never did.

*And the hits just keep on coming.*

Matt didn't know who he'd pissed off, but goddamn. He must've done a bang-up fucking job to deserve this shit.

"Boss, that's a terrible idea."

*And understatement of the fucking year goes to...*

"You might be right. But Ryker thinks this is our best shot, and I happen to agree."

"Best shot at what?" Matt looked back at the other man as if he'd lost his damn mind. "Killing each other?"

"You two have a history. I get it."

"All due respect, Boss. You don't."

Jake studied him a few seconds before nodding. "Fair enough. But this isn't about you. It's about finding out who put the target on Kat's back."

"I get that, but I really think it's in everyone's best interest if someone else took this on."

Jake hesitated a half second before dropping yet another bomb. "You brought up the possibility that Kat was involved."

Shit. "I was just…" Matt tried to figure out the best way to say it.

One of the guy's dark brows rose with a knowing smile. "Trying to piss her off so she'd leave?"

Matt sighed before admitting to his boss, "Yeah. I was."

"Well, Ryker is wondering the same thing. We're certain Kat has a target on her back. Question is, is it because someone knows she's the key to getting the formula, or is it because they've given up on the idea and want to get rid of the final loose end? Personally, I think she's telling the truth."

There was a time Matt would've died to defend her honor. The only thing he said was, "But?"

"Ryker wants to be sure."

*Ah, hell.* "You want me to find out if she's lying."

"I want you to protect her. First and foremost, that's your job. But, yeah. While you're protecting her, Ryker thought you could feel her out." When Matt opened his mouth to comment, Jake quickly shut him down. "Not like that. This case is already complicated enough without it turning even more personal."

"It won't," Matt assured him. "That will definitely not be an issue. Trust me."

"Good." Understanding filtered through Jake's tough exterior. "Look, Matt. I can tell I'm asking a lot of you, here. But Ryker was able to confirm this project Kat's been working on was, in fact, top-secret. Commissioned for and by the United States military, like she said. If someone *is* trying to sell it, you can bet they're doing so to use it against us."

"To make their forces less vulnerable."

"That's right. And we've been tasked with preventing that from happening, which is what I need you to stay focused on. Not your past with Kat. Although, it would be nice if the two of you could work your shit out. She's not going to want to open up about a damn thing if you're a complete dick to her the entire time."

Voices from the hall reached his ears, one in particular standing out amongst the rest. Kat had come back, after all.

Matt couldn't believe this was happening. He wanted to tell his boss no, but Jake was right. This wasn't about him.

"All right. I'll do it." The words had no more left his lips when his teammates walked back into the room, Kat picking up the tail behind them.

"Do what?" Zade asked as he made his way back around to his original seat.

Rather than answer him, Matt looked over at Kat with a fake-as-shit grin and said, "Looks like you and I are going to have that chance to catch up after all."

An hour later, he was driving them both to her apartment to pack a bag with only one thought rolling through his mind...

*I'm so screwed.*

# CHAPTER 4

*I'm so screwed.*

It was the first thought in Kat's head when she found out Matt was going to be her bodyguard, and it had been playing on loop ever since.

There were three other men who, from everything Kat knew about them, were perfectly qualified for the job. Instead, she was stuck with the one person on the team who hated her guts.

From the moment Jake told her of his plan to keep her safe, she'd begun to question his sanity. Of course, she'd been questioning her own since this whole thing started.

During the silent drive here, wherever here was going to be, a few optimistic moments had seeped through her despair. For the most part, however, Kat wasn't convinced this was the best option.

Now that she'd actually seen the place where she and Matt—of all people—were going to be laying low, she had no doubt. This was never going to work.

The cabin belonging to Kole and his wife was so far out in the middle of nowhere, Kat couldn't imagine anyone ever finding them here.

*Kind of the whole point, I suppose.*

Standing just inside the door, Kat took a few seconds to study the quaint space.

To her left was a small niche big enough for the round table and chairs there. Directly in front of her was a small, narrow kitchen.

Cabinets, a sink, and a dishwasher took up the wall to her left and the refrigerator, stove, and another small section of cabinets covered the right.

To her right was a decent sized living room. A dark area rug covered its wooden floor. The brown leather couch and recliner appeared a bit worn, and the rustic coffee table and end table matched the small TV stand positioned on the same wall as the door.

A narrow pathway ran between the back of the couch and the far wall, and there was an open doorway Kat assumed led to the bedrooms. Overall, it was a cozy, warm space perfect for a quiet couple's getaway. Which this most definitely was not.

"Bedroom's yours. I'll take the couch." Matt dropped his bag on the floor next to the coffee table.

Crap. There was only one. "I can take the couch," she offered. "I don't want you to be uncomfortable."

He looked back at her with a hateful sneer. "Little late for that, isn't it?"

"I'm sorry. You have to believe me. I had no idea you worked for R.I.S.C."

"Believe you?" He chuckled, but there was nothing but disdain in his eyes. "That's funny. One of the few things I do remember about you is I can't believe a fucking word that comes out of that pretty little mouth of yours."

Kat winced. His words were like tiny, sharp knives. Each one jabbing new holes in her already damaged heart.

"You've changed," she whispered. "You never used to talk that way before."

"Before what, Kat?" Matt's face twisted with feigned confusion. "Before you fooled yourself into thinking someone like you could fall for a guy like me? Before you realized Daddy Dearest was right all along? Or before you decided to leave me so you could go off and marry someone of your stature?"

She frowned. "I never thought any of that. I know you think that's why I left, but you don't understand what it was like for me."

With his hands on his narrow hips, Matt glared as he came back with, "I understand perfectly. You threw me away like I was yesterday's garbage. It all worked out for you in the end though, didn't it? I mean, you landed the rich guy with a country club membership and Daddy's stamp of approval. Sucks that he's dead, but that means more money for you, right?"

Kat was so shocked by his cruel demeanor, she didn't even know how to respond. *You could tell him the truth.*

She gave a mental shake of her head. Sure, she could tell him the whole sordid story of why she'd broken things off with him all those years ago, but what would be the point? Hadn't he just told her he couldn't believe anything she said?

Taking her silence as an admission, Kat was stunned to see him turning to open the door.

Panic instantly set in. "You're leaving?"

"I'm checking the perimeter and setting up surveillance. Don't worry." His lip curled. "I'll still protect that rich little ass of yours, but don't mistake that to mean I care. The minute you're safe, I'm gone. You can go back to your house in the hills and forget all about me. Lord knows I'll have no trouble forgetting you. Did it once before, won't be any different this time."

Without another word, Matt walked out the door, slamming it behind him as he left.

Kat somehow managed to get to the bedroom and shut the door before the dam broke. Crawling onto the bed, she curled into the fetal position and cried harder than she had in years.

She'd already known Matt despised her for what she'd done, but not like this. What she'd witnessed was pure, to his *soul* hatred. The kind Kat knew she'd never be able to change.

Why had she backed down from her father all those years ago? Why couldn't she have trusted Matt—and herself—to be able to deal with the truth rather than tearing them apart like she had?

But even as she lay there, ugly crying with no signs of stopping, Kat knew the answer. She hadn't told Matt the truth because she loved him. Loved him so much, so completely, she'd chosen to protect him by letting him go.

*So, tell him now!*

The tiny voice in the back of her head continued to poke and prod her, but she ignored it. Too much time had passed, and there was too much anger and hurt consuming the great void that would forever exist between them.

The best thing would be for her to stay out of his way and let him do his job. No matter what he said or did, Kat knew she'd always love him. She just prayed someday he'd find it in his hardened heart to forgive her.

Hours later, Kat woke with swollen eyes and a pounding headache. Disoriented, it took her a moment to remember where she was. And who she was with.

The lack of light shining behind the curtains covering the room's only window told her it was already dark outside. Though she'd slept most of the day away—something she never did—Kat felt as if she could sleep another twelve hours, if not for the incessant headache.

Hating to do it, but knowing she'd end up with one hell of a migraine if she didn't, Kat peeled herself off the bed and went in search for some ibuprofen. She checked the medicine cabinet in the bathroom, but the bottle she found only had one pill remaining.

Needing more than that to knock out the throbbing in her temple, she slowly shuffled across the floor toward the bedroom door. With her hand on the knob, she filled her lungs with a steeling breath, fearful of what she was about to walk into.

With hesitant steps, Kat scanned the tiny living room, but saw no sign of Matt. With the fleeting thought that he'd changed his mind and decided to leave her after all, she walked to the kitchen, praying she'd find some sort of pain reliever.

*Maybe this headache will kill me and put us both out of our misery.*

Hating herself for being so dramatic, Kat ran a hand along the wall, flipping the switch when she found it.

Squinting against the painful light, she began searching through the cabinets.

Coming up empty on the first two, she saw some bottles in the third one that could be what she needed, but they were on the very top shelf, out of her reach.

Not wanting to mess with dragging a chair into the room to stand on, Kat climbed onto the counter. Balancing carefully on her knees, she started to reach for one of the bottles right as she heard Matt's deep voice from behind her.

"Need some help?"

With a high-pitched squeal, she jumped. Knocking the bottle from the shelf and throwing herself off balance in the process. When she started to fall, Matt reflexively reached for her, his strong arms catching her before she could hit the floor.

For two full seconds, they stood like that. With his arms around her, holding her close.

Her heart beat forcefully against her ribs, and even though it wasn't for the reasons she wanted, it felt incredible to be in his arms again.

Staring up into those gorgeous, dark eyes of his, she could've sworn she saw a glimmer of heat. But in the next second, he was pushing himself away and stepping as far back as he could.

*It was nice while it lasted.*

"Sorry. I-I didn't see you and thought maybe you'd...left."

He frowned. "I told you I was going to protect you."

"I know. But when I woke up, everything was dark and quiet. I didn't see you, so I assumed..."

"I was sitting at the table."

"In the dark?"

He gave a single nod, glancing over her head to the open cabinet. "What were you searching for?"

"Ibuprofen."

"Headache?"

She nodded and rubbed her right temple. "Yeah."

"Migraine?"

The bit of joy she felt from knowing he remembered was completely ridiculous. "Not yet, but it will be if I don't take something soon. I forgot to grab some when we were at my place, and the bottle I found in the bathroom only had one pill left."

"Here." He pushed himself off the counter and came over to where she was standing, "Let me see if there's anything up here. If not, I think I have some in my bag."

Sliding out of the way, she watched as he searched the labels on the small bottles she'd been trying to reach. Pulling one from the shelf, he opened it and dumped four brown tablets into his palm.

"Here."

Not only had he remembered she sometimes got migraines, he also remembered it took her body more than the recommended dose to combat the pain.

Wanting to roll her eyes at the lame attempt to make something out of nothing, Kat took the pills from his hand.

Ignoring the way it felt to touch his skin again, and how right it had felt being back in his arms, she went to where she'd seen the glasses and grabbed one to use.

Matt stood silently as she filled it with water from the faucet and quickly swallowed the pills down in one gulp.

Setting it in the sink, she turned to face him, leery of what would come next.

"They still as bad as they used to be?"

"Sometimes."

He nodded. "You should probably eat something. Kole stopped by with some groceries earlier while you were sleeping. There's stuff for sandwiches and chips. He also brought some steaks and chicken breasts. I can cook those up, if you'd rather."

Already feeling a bit nauseated from the headache, Kat said, "Sandwiches are fine." Deciding to throw out an olive branch of sorts, she offered, "I can make you one, too. If you want."

"I already had a couple earlier."

"Oh. Okay."

Turning to the fridge, Kat used the time spent searching to try and compose her jumbled thoughts.

When he'd walked out earlier, Matt hadn't even acted like he could stand to look at her. Now he was offering to cook her a steak?

As if he knew exactly what she was thinking, he spoke while she gathered the items needed for a ham sandwich.

"Listen, Kat. I had a lot of time to think while you were sleeping, and I realized I owe you an apology."

"No. You don't."

Hands full with a package of deli meat, sliced cheese, and a jar of mayonnaise, Kat sat the food down onto the counter. Assuming the bread was in the longer cabinet on the other side of the fridge, she looked there first, pleased to see she was right.

"I do. I shouldn't have yelled at you like that. It was unprofessional, and—"

"Matt, stop. Okay?" Kat set the bread down with the other items and turned to him. "If anything, I'm the one who should be apologizing to you."

"For what?"

"Everything." Her shoulders fell with a huge sigh. "Ten years ago. Today." Kat shook her head, then winced. Damn headache. "After finding my apartment had been broken into, I got really scared. I didn't know what to do, so I went to my dad's. He called a guy he knows at Homeland, and that man sent me to you. Well, not *you*. R.I.S.C. I didn't realize you worked there until I saw you. I know you don't believe that, but—"

"I believe you."

Her eyes met his. "You do?"

Matt nodded. "I shouldn't have said that about not being able to trust you. I also shouldn't have said what I did at the office. I was pissed, and..." He sighed. "I don't know. This just wasn't how I expected my day to go, I guess."

"Me, neither." Out of habit, Kat took the hair tie she kept on her wrist and threw her hair up into a messy bun to keep it from getting into her food. "Of course, this whole week hasn't really gone as planned for me, so—"

"What the hell?" A dark scowl crossed over his face.

Kat froze, her hands holding her hair on the top of her head. "What?"

He started toward her. Her mind raced to figure out what she'd said that could've possibly upset him, and then she realized his eyes were focused on the left side of her forehead.

"You said you weren't hurt in the explosion. That looks like more than a couple bruises to me."

*Oh. That.*

Kat quickly plucked a few strands from the bun to make some long bangs. Running her fingers through the tangled cluster, she worked to smooth them out and cover the stitches she'd forgotten about.

"It's nothing."

"You have stitches in your forehead, Katherine. That's not nothing."

In the past, he only used her full name when he wanted her to know he was being serious. Add to that, the concerned look in his eye and tone of voice, and Kat found herself feeling thoroughly confused.

"I told you, I hit my head on the floor when I landed."

In a surprising move, Matt reached up and brushed the newly arranged strands aside for a better look. "Does it hurt?"

Kat's pulse spiked from his gentle touch. "It's tender, but nothing I can't handle."

His eyes dropped to hers. "I'm sorry you had to go through that. Seeing your colleagues hurt and not being able to help them... shit like that can mess with you."

She had a feeling he was speaking from experience. "I see it every time I close my eyes," she admitted quietly.

With a sympathetic expression, Matt said, "I bet you do."

*Maybe he really does still care.*

Memories of being this close to him for a whole other reason threatened to take over. It was almost enough to make her do something stupid like lean up and kiss him.

As much as she'd dreamed of feeling his lips on hers again—God, did she want to—Kat knew it would undo every ounce of civility they'd managed to obtain during these past few minutes.

She took a step back. Understanding filled his dark eyes and Matt's hand dropped back to his side.

Overwhelmed by the whole situation, Kat decided it would be best if she spent the rest of the evening alone.

"Actually." She started gathering the food back into her hands. "I think I'll wait on the sandwich."

"Thought you were hungry."

"I thought I was, too." Kat went about putting the items back into their rightful place.

Matt filled her in on tomorrow's plans while she did. "Derek called earlier. He's Alpha Team's computer specialist."

"I remember."

"Right." He actually gave her a hint of a smile. "Anyway, he's going to be stopping by tomorrow to bring me a few things. Is there anything you need from town? I can send him a list."

The kind gesture was unexpected and actually pretty thoughtful. So why did she feel like he was hiding something?

*Gee, I don't know. Maybe because he's gone from being Asshole of the Year to something closely resembling the sweet, caring man she used to know, in only a few hours' time.*

Still. This was Matt. He used to be *her* Matt. He may not fully trust her yet, but she trusted him with her life. At least she used to.

"I can't think of anything I need." *Other than you.* "Thanks, though."

He nodded. "I'm going to check the perimeter and

surveillance equipment one last time before hitting the couch."

"Okay." Kat gave him a tiny smile. "Goodnight, Matt."

As she stepped past, she heard a low, "'Night, Doc."

That time when he said it, the nickname made her smile.

# CHAPTER 5

*What the fuck was that?*

Matt shut the door behind him and blew out a heavy breath. The spring, Texas air had cooled since sundown, a welcome relief to his feverish skin.

As he made his way around the cabin's exterior and the immediate area surrounding it, he tried to make sense of the entire, fucked up situation.

After his big blow up, Matt had used his time securing the area to cool off and regroup.

He was supposed to be trying to get a feel for whether or not Kat was involved in the suspected plot to steal the formula. In order to do that, he had to at least make her feel comfortable enough to open up to him.

Something that would never happen if he kept throwing their past in her face and treating her like shit.

Determined to take one for the team, he'd gone back inside to swallow his pride and apologize. When he'd heard Kat crying through the bedroom door, he changed his mind and decided to give her some space.

Needing more time to process, himself, Matt had sat down at the table. His mind filling with memories—both good and bad.

Eventually, her sobs slowly faded away. By the time she'd cried herself to sleep, he felt like the biggest dick on the planet.

Matt didn't know which pissed him off more, the fact that everything he'd said to her before was true, or that he'd actually felt bad for making her cry.

Then almost instantly, he'd given himself a mental slap on the head for feeling even an ounce of guilt.

He hadn't been the one to crush her dreams. Didn't tear *her* heart out piece by fucking piece. So why should he feel bad?

The answer was, he shouldn't. But he did. And that made him furious all over again, which was the one thing he was trying to avoid.

Matt hadn't felt this out of control since that day on the pier. It was like he was the lone rider on a goddamn emotional roller coaster.

A big one, with huge-ass twists and turns and no seatbelt. And he fucking hated it.

Matt had only gone into the kitchen to help her. To use the opportunity to try and rebuild at least some of the trust between them in order to do what his job required.

But when he saw she was physically hurting, a very real and unexpected feeling of sympathy rose to the surface. He remembered how debilitating her headaches could sometimes become, and always hated that he couldn't do more to ease her pain.

Then, when he caught a glimpse of those fucking stitches, his protective instincts came rushing back to life.

Before he'd even realized he was moving, Matt had found himself standing in front of her. The need to make sure she was okay overruling any sense of objectivity.

As he walked across the dewy ground now, he wondered how he'd let himself get that close. One minute, he couldn't wait to get away from her. In the next, he was touching her. Had actually considered *kissing* her.

After everything Kat had put him through, that thought shouldn't have been a blip on his fucking radar. And the way she'd looked up at him…

Matt had been with enough women to recognize attraction and arousal. There was no doubt in his mind if he'd started something, she would have been more than willing to finish it.

*Hell. No.*

There had to be a way to put that particular genie back into its bottle. For several reasons. First and foremost being his personal feelings had no place on a job like this.

*A job you shouldn't be on in the first place.*

That didn't matter. Like it or not, McQueen had chosen him for a reason, so he needed to get his head out of his ass and keep his shit straight.

Feeling more level-headed than he had all day, Matt went back inside, sent an 'all secure' text to Jake and the others, and got as comfortable as he could on the couch.

An hour later, after flipping through the few channels the antenna picked up, he turned the TV off and closed his eyes, determined to make tomorrow a better day.

The next morning, things started off a bit more smoothly. Though still a bit awkward, both he and Kat had begun the day on a cordial, almost polite note.

Matt had woken first, and by the time she'd showered

and dressed, he'd not only made a full pot of coffee, but a decent breakfast of scramble eggs, bacon, and toast.

Kat's surprise was obvious when she came out of the bedroom and saw the spread waiting for her on the table.

"Wow. I wasn't expecting all this."

Brushing it off, Matt shrugged. "No big deal. Just some bacon and eggs."

"Still. I can't remember the last time someone cooked me breakfast." Kat grabbed a piece of buttered toast from the small saucer on the table and took a bite. "Actually..." she started to talk but stopped when she remembered her mouth was full. She swallowed before continuing on. "I don't remember the last time I *ate* breakfast."

"You don't have someone who cooks for you?"

When Kat shot him a look, Matt realized how the question had sounded and quickly tried to recover. "That wasn't a dig," he told her truthfully. "I promise. I genuinely assumed you had someone to do that sort of thing."

Accepting his explanation, Kat pulled out the chair closest to her and sat down. "I did. But when Brian...died, I moved out of that house and got my own place."

Her slight hesitation made him curious, but the last thing Matt wanted to talk about was her deceased husband. One who, for all he knew, she was still mourning.

On the other hand, he'd already opened the can of worms, so he may as well get whatever information he could. Strictly for the job, of course. Not because he gave a damn.

After filling up his second cup of coffee, Matt took the

seat to her right and began filling his plate. "How'd he die?"

"He, uh…" Kat paused before answering, her brows turning inward as she worked her throat. "Brian shot himself six years ago."

"Damn." That wasn't what he expected to hear.

"Yeah," she whispered softly, putting a scoop of eggs onto her plate.

He couldn't help but do the math. Kat had only been married for two years, which meant…

"You've been a widow six years, and you never remarried?"

Kat shook her head, a puff of air escaping on a low chuckle. "I never date."

This surprised him even more than the whole suicide bit. "Ever?"

"Nope." She took a bite and swallowed it. "I'm pretty much married to my job. I've been asked out by a few of the guys at the lab, but they aren't really my type."

"And what is your type, Kat?"

Her eyes met his, but she didn't answer. Not with words, anyway.

*Quit reading into shit that isn't there.*

Breaking away, she looked back down at her plate. "What about you?" She moved the eggs around with her fork. "You ever get married?"

A loud snort escaped before he could stop it. "Hell no."

This seemed to surprise her. She waited a few more seconds before asking, "And what about this? You being here with me, I mean."

"What about it?"

Kat licked her lips nervously and shrugged one of her

delicate shoulders. "I didn't know if there was a girlfriend back in the city. Someone who might be...I don't know. Upset that you're stuck in a tiny cabin with another woman?"

She'd tried to make the question sound benign, but Matt knew she was fishing. From the nervous look in her eyes, he could tell she wanted to know for personal reasons rather than casual conversation.

*I'll be damned.*

He could shut her down right now. Lie and say he did have a girlfriend. A serious one. Instead, he decided to play with her in a different way.

Purposely turning his voice lower, he raised a brow and locked his eyes on hers. "You asking for a friend, or are you interested in a...*ride*...down memory lane?"

Kat's lips parted in silent shock as a red hue began to spread beneath her cheeks. Her eyes widened slightly, the chocolate surrounding them becoming nearly as black as her pupils.

*Gotcha.*

"I-I was curious." She blinked and looked away. "That's all."

*Oh, this is starting to be fun.*

"I bet you're curious about a lot of things. After all, we're not kids anymore." Matt let the heat he was pretending meant nothing seep into his teasing eyes. "A lot can change in ten years."

Kat's eyes shot back up to his. Matt gave her a wink, just to fuck with her, and it was all he could do not to laugh when she became flustered while trying to change the subject.

"You, uh..." Her voice cracked, and she had to clear it.

Finding a sudden interest in the food on her plate, Kat finally managed to speak again. "You mentioned Derek coming by today. Do you know if he's learned anything more about the explosion?"

He considered continuing his enjoyable taunts but decided to let her off the hook. For now.

"Not yet. He's supposed to be bringing me the files on all the people we're looking into. Hopefully we'll get a lead from one of those."

Matt didn't tell her *she* was one of those people.

Taking a sip of her coffee, Kat held the warm mug between her hands as if she were cold. "As much as I hate to think of Todd, or anyone else I know, being involved in something so nefarious, part of me hopes Derek finds something. At least that way we'll know if we're looking in the right direction."

"I agree." Matt swallowed a bite of crispy bacon. "Can you think of anything that seemed suspicious or out of place at work lately? Someone you didn't recognize, a co-worker acting strange…things like that?"

"No." Kat shook her head. "Like I said yesterday, we haven't had any investors stop by for a visit in quite a while."

"What about your team? Any of them seem off at all?"

She thought a moment but shook her head again. "Not really. I mean, everyone's been a little on edge, but that's understandable given the hours we've been putting in and the pressure we've been under."

"Tell me what you mean by 'on edge.'"

Kat shrugged. "I don't know. Impatient, I guess. A little grumpy, maybe."

"Anyone in particular?"

"You mean, besides me?" She chuckled nervously but averted her gaze. "We've all been under a lot of stress."

*She's holding something back.* "What is it you're not telling me, Kat?"

"Nothing." Kat shook her head, but her resolve lessened. "I-I'm sure it's nothing."

That didn't sound even remotely convincing, so Matt pressed on. "It could be something. Sometimes even the smallest details can help."

She bit her bottom lip as her dark eyes rose to his. "I hate saying anything, because I know you already suspect him, and I don't want to persuade your judgment. But I overheard Todd having a heated discussion the morning of the fire."

That definitely piqued Matt's interest. "Who was he arguing with?"

"I don't know. He was in the break room, but I could hear him through the closed door. When I walked in, I saw he was on the phone, but he immediately stopped talking and ended the call."

"What did you hear him say?"

She opened her mouth to answer but closed it again. Her hesitation to reveal a potentially vital piece of the puzzle cut some serious length from his patience.

"Damn it, Kat. If you know something."

"I don't." She shook her head vehemently. "At least, I don't know for sure, anyway."

"Not the time to be vague, Doc."

He didn't know what it was about that nickname, but every time he got pissed at her, it seemed to slip out.

*You weren't pissed when you used it last night.* Ignoring the thought, Matt looked at her and waited.

"I'm not trying to be. I just don't want to blame someone who isn't here to defend himself. Especially when I'm not certain what I heard had anything to do with what happened."

Frustrated now—with both himself and her—Matt emphasized each word when he asked, "What did Todd say to the person on the phone?"

His temper was probably ruining the progress they'd made this morning, but one step forward and two steps back seemed to be their new thing.

"This isn't a fucking game, Katherine. The person Todd was arguing with could very well be the same person behind the explosion and your break-in."

"I know." She stood and walked over to the front door.

At first, Matt thought she was going to storm out. Instead, she kept looking out the decorative window with her arms wrapped around herself. Almost as if she needed the comfort.

Part of him understood where she was coming from. Like him, she was loyal to her team. It was an admirable trait, but one that could end up costing her everything.

Finally, he heard her sigh before turning to face him again. "Todd said, 'Fine. I'll do it tomorrow.'"

Matt's eyes felt like they were going to bug out of his head. "And this was the day before the lab blew up?"

Kat nodded, her painful acknowledgement obvious. "Yes."

"Did you tell the police?"

"No."

"Why not?"

"I didn't think about it at the time. The place was in

complete chaos, and I thought...I thought the explosion was an accident."

He wished that were true. "Where would Todd's phone be now?"

"I'm assuming with the rest of the recovered items. Unless it was completely destroyed."

Matt pulled his own phone from his pocket and began typing out a message.

"Who are you texting?" Kat began walking back to the table.

"Derek. I'm relaying what you said and telling him to stop by the lab on his way and grab Todd's phone before he comes here."

"It's evidence. Will they just hand it over to him?"

"Yep." Matt pressed 'send' and returned his phone to his pocket.

Ryker had already gotten Matt's team full clearance to anything pertaining to the investigation, so gaining access shouldn't be an issue.

Two hours later, Derek's gunmetal gray Hellcat Challenger pulled up to the cabin. After breakfast, Kat had insisted on cleaning up and putting everything away, but then she'd locked herself in the bedroom and hadn't been back out since.

As angry as he still was at the frustrating woman for not telling him about Todd's conversation sooner—not to mention all the other shit he was forcing himself not to think about—he also understood she'd been through a lot and was still trying to process everything.

There were still more questions to be asked, but he decided to let her be. For now.

"Hey, man," Derek greeted Matt as he opened the door.

"Thanks for coming out here. I know it's a hell of a drive."

"Gives me an excuse to open Faith up a bit and let her roar like she was meant to."

Faith was Derek's car. The man was seriously in love with the damn thing. If it weren't for the fact that D was engaged to the woman of his dreams, Matt would probably be a little concerned for the former SEAL.

"Here are the files." Derek handed him the stack. "This is the background I could find on the Anderson employees who worked directly with the formula. I'm still workin' through the financials, but it's gonna take some time. Didn't realize scientists were so into investing and all that shit."

"Really?"

"I'm tellin' ya. They've got like an average of five accounts each to go through, plus a couple off-shore ones my system is fine-combin'."

The man's Texas drawl became more prominent the longer he spoke.

"I figured you could do all that stuff in your sleep." Matt gave him a disappointed look. "I mean, Nate seems to act as though he can."

Derek snickered. "Nate's full of shit. It isn't like the shows on TV where you type in a name and two seconds later, the evidence pops up all nice and neat, the authorities make an arrest, and the credits roll. Forensic accounting takes time, my friend. Which is why I'm leavin' all this other background shit for you to go through."

"Gee, thanks."

"What? It's not like you have anything else to do while

83

you're stuck here." Derek glanced over to the closed bedroom door and lowered his voice. "Or maybe you do." His light brown eyebrows waggled.

Matt's cock twitched at the thought, but he forced the fucker to stand down. "Not a chance."

"Oh." Derek seemed genuinely disappointed.

*That makes two of us.*

What the hell? *No. It. Does. Not.*

Oblivious to the internal what-the-fuck moment Matt was experiencing, Derek kept talking. "How's she doin'? I heard she was at the lab when the whole thing went down."

Matt nodded. "Better than most. Kat's pretty tough though, so…"

"Oh, that's right." One corner of Derek's mouth lifted. "Heard you two used to be a thing back in the day."

Matt closed his eyes for a few seconds and took in a deep breath. He swore some of the R.I.S.C. operatives were worse gossipers than a bunch of bored housewives.

"Used to." He opened his lids and stared back at the intelligent man. "Key words to remember."

"What happened? Your needy dick screw it up?" Derek made a clicking sound with his tongue and shook his head full of shaggy, sandy-blond hair. "Knew you were quick to whip it out now, but damn, Turner. You couldn't keep it in your pants even back then?"

Swinging his head to the door to make sure it was still closed, Matt ground out, "It wasn't my dick that screwed it up, asshole. And *I* wasn't the one who ended things."

*Shit.* He hadn't meant to say that last part out loud. Matt also didn't understand why the thought of Kat hearing about his generous sex life bothered him so much. She'd been married to another man, for fuck's sake.

Sympathy swirled behind Derek's blue eyes. "Oh. Sorry."

"Don't be. That split was the best thing that ever happened to me." *Liar.*

Matt could tell Derek wasn't buying it either, but at least he dropped the subject and moved on.

"So...I'm also runnin' a check on Sloane Anderson's financials since he owns the company and obviously knew about the formula. And Ryker's getting me the names of the military contractors who sought out Anderson in the first place. Just in case this whole thing started on that end. And I'll start workin' on Todd's phone as soon as I get back to the office."

Matt sat the files down onto the table. "You want something to drink?"

"Nah. Charlie's got a pretty big wedding coming up, so I thought I'd give her a break and surprise her by taking her out to lunch."

Charlie, or Charlotte, was Derek's fiancée and quickly becoming one of the most sought-after professional party planners in Dallas.

"You'd better get back on the road, then."

Derek grinned. "I'm thinking I may take the scenic route home. Let Faith stretch her wheels while she can."

Matt smiled and shook his head. "You and that damn car."

"Hey, man. Don't knock her 'til you've tried her."

"I *can't* try her, because you won't let anyone else drive her."

Derek stepped off the porch and headed for the car. "Hell no, I won't."

"Not even Charlie?"

The other man turned and smiled as he opened the driver's door. "She likes ridin' while I do the drivin'." With a wink, Derek got into his car and started the ignition.

With a roll of his eyes, Matt went back into the cabin, stopping short when he saw Kat standing inside the doorway.

"Oh. Hey."

"Was that Derek?"

"Yeah." Matt tipped his head in the direction of the table. "He dropped those off. I was going to start looking through them now, but since you're out here, you mind if I take a shower first?"

Why the fuck was he asking her permission?

"No." She shook her head. "Not at all."

"I won't be long. The space will be all yours again, soon."

As worked up as he was, the more space between them right now the better.

"You hungry?" She asked. "I could make us some lunch."

"Sure."

"What sounds good?"

Matt shrugged. "Whatever. I'm not picky."

Kat smiled. "I know."

For some reason, her remembering anything about him at all added even more heat to his confusing-as-fuck frustrations.

Without another word, Matt grabbed his bag and

headed for the shower. When he first got in, he set the water as hot as he could stand it.

He wasn't sure why, maybe he thought it would burn away some of his pent-up anger and frustration. The problem was, he couldn't pinpoint exactly what had him so riled up.

As he grabbed the soap and began washing himself off, Matt's thoughts raced to figure out what the hell was going on inside his head. Or, more importantly, a particular organ inside his chest.

He was pissed at Kat for not sharing Todd's argument initially, and Derek for egging him on to the point he'd admitted he'd been the dump*ee* and not the dump*er*. Matt was also pissed at himself for letting any of this shit get to him on such a deep level.

The thing that had his nutsack twisted the most was his conflicting emotions when it came to Kat.

He should hate her. *Did* hate her. But the longer they were around each other, the more Matt was also starting to feel something else. He just didn't want to admit it.

*Desire, fuckmunch. What you feel for her is desire.*

That tiny voice—the bastard—was right. When he'd first seen her in Jake's office, Matt's vision had filled with nothing but a raw, angry red. But when he looked at her now…

*I want her.*

No. No, he absolutely did not. Except, he kind of did.

Didn't mean anything, right? She was an attractive woman. Of course, he wanted her. Not because it was Kat, but because she was a smart, beautiful, caring woman.

Except she wasn't caring. At least she hadn't been with him.

Goddamnit! This was fucking ridiculous. He was standing in a steaming shower in the middle of the goddamn woods actually contemplating what he wanted or didn't want to do with Katherine Fucking Marsh.

Matt looked down, shaking his head at the solid shaft protruding from his lower half, and something clicked.

*That's it!*

This had nothing to do with his heart. He was just horny.

It had been too damn long since he'd gotten laid, and his dick was pissed because he wouldn't let it slide into Kat's warm heat.

As a medic, Matt understood there were real, physical and mental side-effects that came with sexual frustration.

He felt like such an idiot.

Lathering his hands up nice and good, Matt set the bar of soap back down onto the shower's built-in shelf. Then, wrapping his sudsy fingers around his swollen cock, he began to slide his hand back and forth, using long, slow strokes.

*Ah, yeah. That's better.*

Shoulders relaxing some, Matt closed his eyes to help focus on the task at hand. Or rather, *in* his hand.

This was all he needed. A simple, old-fashioned, do-it-yourselfer. Of course, it would be even nicer if it were someone else's hand stroking his dick.

An image of Kat's smiling face flashed behind his closed lids. His cock jumped against his palm, and Matt blew out a heavy breath.

He began to stroke a little faster.

Another picture formed, one he'd locked safely away years before. This one was of a younger Kat, and she was smiling up at him from the floor of the abandoned boathouse they used to sneak off to.

Matt's fist continued to pump up and down, his breaths increasing with the speed of his hand.

Lying on a pallet of blankets, a youthful Kat lay naked beneath him. He was nude, too, their bodies skin-to-skin as they prepared to make love for the very first time.

Matt had already had sex before her, but that day with Kat had been different. It had been the first time he'd made love.

Panting now, Matt could feel the moisture seeping from the swollen tip as he continued to jerk himself off to the most precious memory his mind had ever held.

With a smile, Kat asked him to make love to her as she spread her legs wide, allowing him to settle himself between her thighs. The tip of his sheathed cock pressed against her wet entrance, more than ready to take the sweetest gift she'd only ever offered to him.

*No!*

Matt's eyes flew open, his hand releasing his aching shaft. The damn thing was seconds away from exploding, but he couldn't do it. He couldn't get himself off to the memory of Kat's first time, knowing she'd gone off and given what was his to another man later.

Was it a fucked up thought? Sure. Had he slept with other women? Too many to count. Was he holding her to a ridiculous and shameful double-standard? Absolutely. But he didn't care.

Yes, he'd had sex since Kat. Lots and lots of sex. But it hadn't meant shit to him or the women he'd been with.

Kat, on the other hand, had *married* another man. Had

said those precious vows to someone else. Had made a life and a home with someone else.

That should have been *his* life. *His* home. She should have said those vows to *him*.

If she had, if Kat hadn't ended things with him that day, Matt knew with utter certainty they'd still be married and have half a dozen kids running around by now.

*Sonofabitch!*

The infuriating woman had ruined everything. And still, to this day, he didn't know why.

Matt looked down at his softening dick and shook his head.

Fuck that. She may have shattered his soul to the point he was no good for any other woman, but he'd be damned if he let her keep him from jerking off in the goddamn shower.

More determine to come than a teenage virgin, Matt lathered himself up again and went to town. It took a few minutes to get back in the groove, but soon he was more primed than before and almost ready to blow.

Just a few more strokes, and he'd be there.

Feeling ridiculously proud of himself, Matt damn near smiled. His body shook, he was so close. And not one minute of this second round had been spent thinking about Kat.

Until the shower door flew open and he saw her standing in front of him. Holding up a folder with her name on it and looking angrier than he could ever remember her being.

# CHAPTER 6

"What the hell?" Kat held the folder up for Matt to see.

His expression went from a wide-eyed shock to an angry scowl in less than a second. "What the hell, Katherine?"

Taken off guard by the unexpected intrusion, Matt quickly covered himself with his hand. At least he tried to.

"I asked first." She raised a brow.

Having made them both a quick lunch of sandwiches and pasta salad, Kat had gone to set the table so everything would be ready when Matt was finished with his shower. When she picked up the files to move them, she'd noticed one with her name written on it.

During breakfast, Matt had told her Derek was bringing files on the people most likely to be involved in the scheme to steal the formula. He'd failed to mention she'd been included in that list.

An instant and fierce anger had risen at the sight of her name amongst the others. By the time she'd stormed into the bathroom to confront him, she was downright pissed.

So pissed, she hadn't even thought about the fact that Matt would be naked behind that shower door.

Kat made the mistake of glancing down.

Now, as she stared at what the infuriating man's large hand was trying to cover, Kat didn't know which she felt more. Anger, shock, or...arousal.

He'd taunted her this morning, making that comment about how things could change after so many years apart. It was blatantly obvious he was referring to a certain part of his anatomy. A part Kat couldn't seem to tear her eyes away from.

Boy, had he been right.

When they were younger, she remembered thinking he had to be larger than the average size. Though, she didn't have anything else to compare him to, Kat had known from that very first time together this man was well-endowed.

Now, standing outside the shower, she couldn't help but noticed the muscles in his arms and chest weren't the only parts on his body that had filled out.

*Holy. Hell.*

The swollen tip peeked out over the top of his large fist, and she could see its base below. Kat's inner muscles involuntarily clenched at the sight of Matt's very full erection.

Memories of him sliding in and out of her body made her legs weak with desire, nearly clouding what she'd seen when she first opened that shower door.

Her eyes shot up to his. The sudden image of Matt pleasuring himself sent an unexpected rush of arousal straight to her core. Refusing to let him see that the idea of him masturbating turned her on in any way, Kat stared back at him with disbelief.

"Were you just..." She struggled to form the question, but the unapologetic expression on his face held the answer, anyway. "Oh, my god. You were." Kat blinked a few times before drawing back, her face twisting with a feigned look of disgust. "Seriously?"

With a simple shrug, Matt's gaze heated as he smirked. "Either get in here and help me finish the job, Doc, or shut the door. You're letting all the cold air in."

She knew the infuriating man had only thrown out the offer to shut her up. It worked.

Kat opened her mouth to respond, but nothing came out. This happened twice more before she was finally able to form a coherent sentence.

Regaining control over the embarrassing situation, she held the folder up again and asked, "Why do you have this?"

"I told you Derek was bringing over a file on everyone in the lab."

"No." Kat shook her head. "You told me he was bringing by files on the people you considered *suspects*."

"That's not what I said."

She quoted him verbatim. "He's supposed to be bringing me the files on all the people we're looking into. Hopefully we'll get a lead from one of those." Kat raised a brow. "That's what you told me, Matt."

A tiny twitch at the corner of one eye was the only sign of recognition he gave. There was a time in their lives he'd found her eidetic memory charming. Clearly, that time had passed.

"We have to look at everyone."

*He can't read this.* "The information in this file is personal. In no way is it related to what happened." Kat licked her lips. "There's nothing in here you need to know."

"Trust me, sweetheart." His face turned emotionless. "I couldn't care less about what's in that fucking folder. Unfortunately for us both, I still have to look. It's protocol."

*Protocol, my ass.* "Don't spout that crap at me, Matt. You apologized, remember? Told me you only said those things back at the office because you were upset." Kat's heart physically hurt knowing he still suspected her. "You made me believe you didn't really think I was capable of killing my colleagues in order to cover up a plan to sell the formula. A formula I've worked years to develop."

*One I put my heart and soul into in order to keep you safe.*

His dark eyes narrowed. "Yeah? Well, you made me believe a lot of things, so I guess we both got screwed."

The dagger twisting inside her chest pressed a little deeper. Doing her best to keep her chin held high, Kat tossed the folder onto the vanity behind her. "I think you should call your boss. Tell him to send someone else from your team to stay with me."

Surprise flickered behind his angry eyes. "Is that what you want?"

*No.* "It's what *you* want."

He shook his head. "You don't have a fucking clue what I want, Katherine."

"No? Why don't you enlighten me?"

"I might scare you."

Kat scoffed. "You could try."

"Maybe I will."

"Good!"

"Fine!"

Kat wasn't sure who moved first. One second they were yelling at one another, and the next, they were in each other's arms.

With his hands firmly cupping her face, Matt's lips worked hard against hers. His tongue invaded her mouth, the intrusion demanding and forceful, but she didn't even consider denying him.

Kat savored every single drop of that first taste, knowing Matt would come to his senses any second now and break free from their spellbinding connection.

His breath was hot as it mixed with hers, his tongue lashing about as he ravished her mouth. She'd done her best to remember everything about him, but those long-ago memories didn't hold a candle to being here, in the present.

A low, grunting sound escaped from his throat as he pulled her into the shower with him. Hot water splashed loudly as it soaked through her t-shirt and jeans, but Kat ignored it. Her entire focus—her entire *being*—only cared about one thing, and that was taking everything this man was offering while it lasted.

Did this make her pathetic? Probably. Did she care? Not one bit. Because this was Matt.

The man of her dreams. The other half of her soul. A soul that had been crushed all those years ago when she'd had no other choice but to break his heart and set him free.

Sure, he'd been a total ass since they'd reconnected, but Kat understood why. She took full responsibility, knowing her past actions were the driving force behind his gruff demeanor. Others may call her a fool, but Kat wasn't worried about anyone else. For the first time in her life, she'd decided to think only of herself.

Dreams of the life she wanted were ruined before she'd ever really had the chance to live, so yes. She was going to take advantage of this moment, however fleeting it may be.

Not because she was naïve or didn't feel worthy of something more…but because she *wanted* this.

With her fingernails digging into Matt's wet, bare shoulders, Kat released a protesting moan as Matt pulled away. Her breasts brushed against his warm, wet chest as her breaths came in hard, heaving puffs.

Fear and panic set in, followed by an immediate rush of overwhelming relief when she realized he wasn't stopping but rather moving his hungry lips down over her chin and beyond.

"This is stupid," he growled. Matt brushed his rough whiskers against her. "So stupid."

His words would've brought with them complete and total devastation had she not felt his teeth continuing to nibble as he made his way along her neck. The impressive cock she'd studied earlier pushed angrily against her belly as Matt left hot, rough kisses against her sensitive skin.

"I know," she breathed, leaning her head to the side.

This *was* stupid. On both their parts. But damn, if she could bring herself to stop.

Working his way back up to her mouth, Matt's lips, tongue, and teeth ate at her as though he were a starving man. The way he was devouring her made Kat feel like his final feast.

He made his way to the crevice at the bottom of her throat. She tilted her head back, allowing the access she could tell he wanted. A wave of hot breath stole hers as his tongue traced the slight dip there before Matt made his way back up to her mouth.

Their next kiss became so raw, so impassioned, Kat could no longer hold back the pleasurable moan that had been building from somewhere deep within. Swallowing the sound, Matt released a guttural groan of his own before suddenly ripping his lips away from hers.

The unsettled way he was staring down at her left Kat feeling as though she were on the edge of a very large cliff. Where she stood now felt safe. Right. But if she fell—if Matt's next words pushed her over—they'd form a cluster of jagged rocks and deadly waves below that would swallow her up and take what was left of her worn and weary heart.

Chest heaving, he kept a strong grip on the sides of her face as he said, "This doesn't change anything."

One foot began to slide over the metaphorical edge, but Kat kept herself from falling. She wasn't that same young, impressionable teenager anymore. No, she was an intelligent adult who knew making a decision such as this would come at a cost. A very high cost.

Being with Matt again would almost certainly cause her more pain and heartache than ever before. She didn't care. It had been far too long since she'd felt a man's touch. *This* man's touch.

She'd spent countless nights pretending her own hand was his, using the memories of those wonderful, stolen moments with him as a guide. But nothing compared to the real thing.

Blinking against the running water, Kat cupped one side of his face and nodded. "I'm not asking for anything more than this. Just this. Just for tonight."

Matt's indecision warred inside him for only a few seconds longer. After that, he was reaching behind her to shut the door and slamming his mouth against hers. Immediately, his hands began tearing at the hem of her shirt as he worked the soaked material up and over her head.

*Thank you, God!*

A loud slapping sound echoed off the shower's walls as her shirt fell onto the tiles next to her feet. Not wanting to waste a precious second of their time together, Kat quickly reached behind her back, releasing the clasp on her white, lacy bra.

Slipping it over her shoulders, she let it join her shirt below, her heart beating with the force of a kick drum as Matt stood back and took his fill.

"Jesus," he mumbled, using a hand to wipe the water from his face. "Even better than I remember." His mouth was on her in less than a second.

Kat cried out, her head falling back as his hot lips formed a seal around one of her hard, sensitive nipples. Matt licked and laved and sucked while his free hand kneaded and caressed the other breast.

Taking a moment to give it the same attention as the first, Matt continued to work his magic as Kat ran her fingers through his dark, wavy hair. Teeth pulled against her solid nub, the sensation falling on just this side of pain.

"Matt," she crooned, his name a rough and needy plea.

As if her breasts were somehow connected to her sex,

Kat involuntarily thrust her hips forward in an attempt to grind away the powerful aching now present between her thighs.

"Don't worry, baby," he snarled. "I'll give you what you need." Heated, almost angry eyes locked on hers as he reached down and yanked the button at her waistband loose. "What we both need."

Squatting, Matt peeled the wet denim roughly down her legs, taking her white laced panties with them as he went. With her help, they awkwardly freed the garments from both her feet, piling the sopping clothes together.

Rather than stand straight up, Matt wrapped a hand around one of her ankles to guide her legs apart. Once she was positioned to his liking, he dug his fingers into her thighs, holding her in place as he half-bit, half-kissed his way up her legs to the center of her core.

He brought himself eye-level with her sex, the water beating down on them both as she watched him revel in what he was seeing.

Kat should probably be embarrassed by the position, but she wasn't. After all, this wasn't the first time he'd had his head between her legs. Somehow, it still felt that way.

Looking down, Kat watched as he brought a hand to the one place she was ready to beg for him to touch. His eyes rose to meet hers, the emotion there so dark, so intense, she couldn't find a word to describe it.

Never before had she been more nervous—or turned on—than she was in that very moment.

Not wasting any time, Matt traced her bare slit with his middle finger before sliding it deep into her core. Kat gasped as an appreciative moan rumbled through his chest.

"Christ, you're wet." He began pumping in and out. "Soaked for me, aren't you, Doc?" His eyes met hers.

"Y-yes," Kat nodded. She closed her eyes, her hand blindly reaching to the side, slipping against the slick, shower door as she grappled for something to hold on to.

"Hold onto my head."

The order had her peeling her eyes back open. "What?"

Rather than answer, Matt used his free hand to move one of hers to the top of his head. "Hold on."

Next, he reached behind one of her knees and lifted her leg up and over his shoulder. The movement would've thrown her off balance had she not been holding on to his head as instructed. With her legs spread wider, the position left her pussy wide open and on display. From the sounds he was making, it was exactly how Matt wanted it.

"Fuck, yeah." He added a second finger, sliding his digits in and out with more speed and force than before.

The rough, incredible movements brought Kat to a different ledge. One she couldn't wait to fall off of.

"Please, Matt."

He stared up at her. "You begging me, Doc?"

She nodded. Hell yes, she was begging.

"Good." He pumped harder. Faster.

Kat hollered for God as he brought his lips to her clit. Matt flicked the distended nub as he continued moving his hand to the beat of the rough, torturous rhythm he'd created. Soon, her body was shaking with need, his delicious torture bringing her precariously close to the release only he could give.

Kat opened her mouth to announce that she was about to come when suddenly, he tore his mouth away. His movements slowed, the change in pace ebbing the glorious pressure his fingers had been working so hard to build.

*No!*

Her eyes shot open, the smugness staring back up at her telling. He'd done it on purpose. Was punishing her. For which sin, she wasn't sure. Didn't care. Kat only knew what she needed, and in that moment, more than anything, she needed him to finish the job.

*Two can play at this game.*

In a surprise move, she slid her leg from his shoulder and knelt down in front of him. Taking his face between her hands, Kat took control and brought her mouth to his. With his fingers still inside her, Matt began pumping them in and out of her velvet heat once more. She would've smiled in triumph had the sensation not been so overwhelmingly good.

Thrusting his tongue between her lips, he started moving it against hers in the same rhythm as his hand, but before she could find what she so desperately wanted, Kat felt him yank his fingers free and start to stand.

"No!" she protested aloud. "W-what are y-you—"

Not giving her the chance to finish the thought, Matt wrapped his strong hands around her shoulders and pulled her back to her feet. Sliding those same hands around the back of her thighs, he positioned them under the heart-shaped curve of her bare cheeks.

"Wrap your arms around my neck."

Willing to do whatever this man wanted, Kat did just that. A half-second later, she felt herself being lifted into the air, her legs instinctively clutching themselves around his narrow waist to keep from falling.

Spinning them around, Matt practically slammed her

back against the shower wall. The blunt tip of his hot, seeping penis pressed eagerly against her swollen and inviting entrance as Matt began to shove himself inside. He stopped.

"Shit."

Her heart dropped. Fearful of what he was about to say, Kat swallowed her pride and asked, "What?"

"Condom."

Kat shook her head. "I haven't been with anyone since—"

"I don't fuck without a condom."

*Right.*

Of course, he'd been with other women. Probably several. She couldn't fault him for that, but still. Irrationally the thought broke her heart in two.

Doing her best to not picture Matt *fucking* anyone else, Kat lowered her legs and straightened her shoulders. Since she had never even bought a condom before, she began to slide between him and the wall, toward the shower door.

"It's fine. We probably shouldn't—"

A hand snaked out and grabbed her wrist. "Didn't say I don't have one."

"Oh." Kat licked some warm water from her upper lip. "O-okay." Not bothering to ask why he'd brought a condom with him, she stood still, waiting for him to take the lead.

"They're in my bag."

Not bothering to dry off, Matt lifted Kat back into his arms. A tiny squealing sound formed in the back of her throat but was cut off when his tongue filled her mouth once more. Carrying her into the living room, he somehow managed to reach for his bag with one hand while keeping her in place with the other.

The move was far more impressive than it should've been, but damn. The man was seriously built. Carrying both her and the bag over to the couch, he plopped it down onto the coffee table, unzipped it with one hand, and pulled out a brand-new box of condoms.

Glancing back at him questioningly, he quickly blew it off with, "Always keep them in my go-bag. Multiple uses in the field."

"Oh," was all she could come up with.

Using his teeth, he ripped open the box before reaching inside for the string of connected foil packets. Matt then held onto her body with his arms and used both hands behind her back to break apart the top packet. Leaving the extras with the box, Matt took them both to the couch where he turned around and sat down, the position leaving Kat straddling his taut lap.

Apparently done with the foreplay, he ripped open the packet and reached between their bodies to sheath his mouthwatering cock. Damn, she wished she'd been the one to do that.

*Next time.*

No. There wouldn't be a next time. This was it for them. He knew it. She knew it. And it was what she'd agreed to, so there was no point in pretending otherwise.

Take what you can, while you can.

With that thought in mind, Kat waited until he was fully protected before lifting herself up on her knees and lining her drenched opening to his hot, angry tip once more. She started to lower herself onto him, but Matt's hands squeezed her hips to stop her.

"I meant what I said, Katherine. You need to be sure."

*This doesn't change anything.*

His words rang clearly through her mind as she looked him square in the eye and said, "I'm sure."

A single nod was the only response he gave before she impaled herself with his body. Two deep, loud moans filled the cabin's still air as they worked together to become one for the first time in a decade.

Being connected to this man—like this—was a feeling unlike any she'd ever known.

A pleasurable pain burned as his adult body stretched her neglected entrance. After a few tries, Matt finally became fully seated, igniting another unified moan.

It was familiar, yet different. So much better, yet insurmountably worse. Kat chose to focus on the better.

"Holy shit, you're tight." His eyes filled with confusion.

Unwilling to let anything ruin the moment, Kat leaned down and began kissing his unspoken question away. Moving her hips forward and back, it didn't take long for him to forget what she knew he was probably wondering, and soon, they were both able to find a compatible rhythm.

Matt's pelvis lifted upward, pushing his steel shaft as deep and far as it would physically go. Gasping, Kat tore her lips from his. Panting hard, her strong breaths blew forcefully against the dark, damp hair caressing his tanned forehead.

Matt grunted and groaned as he pumped himself in and out of her slick channel, the primal sounds letting her know he felt the same, indescribable pleasure she had. Soon, they both began to move faster. Harder.

With her hands on either side of Matt's head, Kat

gripped the back of the couch for leverage. Moving to the beat of a magnificent drum, she raised up and down at a quickened pace. The course hair on his thighs rubbed against her smooth skin as their bodies slapped loudly together.

Just like in the shower, her body began to quiver with an impending explosion. One she couldn't wait to get lost in.

Sensing her orgasm was near, Matt brought his mouth to her neck, biting down with enough force to bring her even closer to what her body craved. Kat cried out, her head tilting to the side for better access, and the next time his teeth sank against her pulse point, she could feel his hand sliding to the place where their bodies were joined.

Moving his fingers in small, tight circles, Matt pressed against her engorged clit. At the same time, he continued to pump himself harder and harder, his hips thrusting against her with such force his entire lower body lifted from the soft couch cushion as he went.

"Oh God, Matt." Kat breathed hard. "I'm so close."

"Come on, baby." He pushed his cock into her again. "Let...go."

"Oh, God!"

"That's it." Matt moved his fingertips faster. Fucked her even harder. "Do it. Now!"

"Ah!"

Kat threw her head back, a low keening sound filling the entire cabin as her climax hit with a vengeance. Her inner muscles clenched down onto Matt's cock, the force of her orgasm sending him straight into his own.

A rush of burning liquid coated his protected shaft as Matt's entire body tensed beneath her. A loud, primal grunt roared from his chest as he pumped a few more, uneven thrusts. When he'd filled the condom with the last drop of his hot seed, they both remained still a few minutes longer.

Their chests rose and fell in tandem. Breaths escaped in hard, rough pants. And Kat felt more satisfied than she had in years.

Physically and emotionally spent, she let her eyes fall shut. Her heart—or what was left of it—broke with the formation of her last conscious thought.

To Kat, what she and Matt had shared was something she'd cherish for the rest of her days. But to him, it hadn't meant a damn thing.

# CHAPTER 7

Being as quiet as he could, Matt gathered Kat's sopping wet clothes, ringing them out over the shower's drain. Careful not to let them drip on the floor, he took them to the closet located on the wall behind the couch where Kole had installed a small, stackable washer/dryer set.

Grabbing a detergent pod from the half-empty container on the shelf above, he started the load so they'd be clean and dry when she woke up.

Once that was taken care of, he went back into the bathroom for the forgotten folder. Before he left the room again, he couldn't help but to glance at her gorgeous, sleeping form.

When he'd realized Kat had fallen asleep while still on top of him, with him still *inside* her, he'd promptly carried her to bed and gotten dressed.

His dick twitched at the thought, no doubt ready for round two. Unfortunately, that was never going to happen.

Silently shutting the door behind him, Matt tossed the

folder onto the couch as he passed by and went into the kitchen.

Once there, he began searching for something, *anything*, he could use to wash down the massive amount of guilt he was having a damn hard time swallowing. Of course, being on the job, he knew anything stronger than soda was out of the question.

He slammed the refrigerator door closed before wincing from fear he'd woken Kat up. Matt needed her to sleep as long as she possibly could.

If she was sleeping, he wouldn't have to own up to the colossal fuck-up he'd made. He wouldn't have to look into those enchanting eyes and remember the soft warmth with which her body had taken him in.

Instead of acting like the strong, disciplined operative he'd worked so hard to become, he'd been weak. Had let his physical wants override the logical side of his brain.

One minute they were arguing, and the next he was pulling her into the shower with him, rather than slamming the door shut and sending her away.

He wasn't even sure what had happened.

*You took what you wanted. And you loved every second of it.*

Matt wanted to argue with the annoying voice in the back of his head, but he couldn't. Did he regret sleeping with her, knowing he'd be walking away once this was over? Sure. Did he regret not having the strength to fight off the irrational desire for the one woman who'd held the power to break him all those years ago? Absolutely.

But another part—a deeper, hidden part—wanted nothing more than to walk back into that bedroom, crawl under those covers, and make love to her all over again.

No, that wasn't right. They hadn't made love. They'd had sex. The kind he'd dreamed of having with her.

When they were younger, their intimate moments were slow and magical. He'd taken his time. Had been loving and gentle.

The way they'd been with each other just now was far and away from that. It was raw and passionate. All-consuming on a level he'd never reached with anyone else.

Despite the fact that Matt knew it was wrong—for a billion and one reasons—sliding into Kat's wet inferno had felt like coming home.

He couldn't count the number of women he'd bedded, but what he and Kat had just shared was...different.

For the first time in years, he felt at peace. With his mouth on hers, their bodies locked together as tightly as possible and his arms around her slender form, it was almost as if he was right where he belonged.

*I am so fucked.*

Or, maybe he wasn't. Maybe he was making more of this than was needed. He was assuming she'd want to pursue something more with him now that they'd slept together, but maybe she wouldn't.

After all, he'd been brutally honest about where he stood. Had told her point-blank sex between them didn't change anything. And in that moment, he'd believed that with every fiber of his hormonal-driven being.

Standing here now, however, with his body still humming from the most intense orgasm ever, Matt knew precisely how full of shit he'd actually been.

Gulping down the remaining drops of his soda, he threw the can in the trash and started for the couch. Plopping down on one of the dry cushions, he glanced over at that damn folder.

*There's nothing in here you need to know.*

Even if she wasn't involved in whatever was going on inside her lab, Kat had been pretty damn adamant he not find out what Derek had found.

If he was being honest, Matt didn't really want to know.

His phone began to ring, momentarily taking the decision out of his hands. Hurrying over to the table where he'd left it, Matt saw it was Derek and answered as quickly and quietly as he could.

"Hey, D," he spoke with a hushed voice. "What's up?"

"Hey, Matt. I know I haven't given you much time, but did you happen to go through those files yet?"

*Sorry. I was too busy having sex with the bane of my existence.*

Matt cleared his throat. "Not yet. Why, what's up?"

"My computer sent me a notification. Pulled over to the side of the highway to check it. Turns out we got a hit on one of the lab employees."

Holding his breath, Matt asked, "Which one?"

"Todd Kennedy."

Matt's profound relief flipped open a valve, releasing the air from his lungs. "What did you find?"

"A money market account was recently opened in his name. His wife is listed as the beneficiary. Two large, electronic deposits were made into the account within the last few weeks. The most recent was dated the day before the explosion."

"So we were right. Kennedy was in bed with someone

wanting that formula. Why didn't he just give it to whoever was paying him off and be done?"

"That may be a question for your girl."

"She's not my girl," Matt growled.

"Right. My bad." There was a pause before Derek said, "Anyway, I'm runnin' a program to trace the originating account. In the meantime, his basic financials came back with what could have been his motive for getting involved in all this in the first place."

"What's that?"

"Six months ago, Kennedy's wife was diagnosed with stage three breast cancer. From what I've found, it's a very aggressive kind. Treatments have been eating into all of their savings, and they were about two months away from foreclosure when the first large deposit hit."

*Damn.* "The guy was trying to get extra money to help with his wife's medical bills."

"Looks that way."

"What about his investment accounts? Could the money have come from any of those?"

"Nah. They weren't doing very well, and even if they were, none showed any signs of withdrawal activity."

So they had the answer to whether or not Todd was involved, but that was only one piece of the puzzle. They needed to know who'd paid him to steal the formula.

Matt felt bad for Todd's situation with his wife, but it didn't excuse what he'd done. He glanced at the bedroom door and thought of the woman currently sleeping behind it.

*Asshole could've killed her.*

"It was a shitty thing to do, for sure," Derek spoke as if

he could read Matt's thoughts. "I gotta say, though. Part of me gets it."

"The guy killed himself and two of his co-workers," Matt bit out. "Damn near killed Kat."

"I'm not sayin' I condone what Kennedy did."

"Then what are you saying, D?"

"That there's not much I wouldn't do to help Charlie if she needed it. I know that may be hard for a guy like you to understand, but—"

*The fuck?* "What the hell is that supposed to mean?"

"Easy, man. I meant no disrespect. Just that, you're the lone wolf type when it comes to women. You know, no relationships. That sort of thing."

Matt scowled. "Doesn't mean I can't empathize, for fuck's sake."

"Like I said, my bad."

A few seconds of silence passed before Derek spoke again. "Well that's all I wanted. I'll keep workin' on that trace to figure out the source of the payments. In the meantime, let me know if you find anything in those files you want me to dig deeper on."

Something about the way D said that last part made Matt's ears perk up. "You have something particular in mind?"

"Me? Nope. Just meant let me know if *you* come across something that doesn't add up for you."

Derek was acting a bit strange, but that wasn't necessarily unusual for the former SEAL. "Thanks, man. Appreciate it."

"No problem."

Matt ended the call and set the phone back down onto

the table. Shit. He hated the idea of having to tell Kat her friend and colleague was guilty as hell.

*See? Things have changed.*

Before, he'd have looked for any and every way he could find to cause her as much pain as she'd caused him. Dick move, he knew. At least Matt was man enough to admit it.

But now, he suddenly found himself wanting to protect her again. To shield her from the pain and grief he knew she'd experience once he broke the news to her.

He pictured the way she'd looked back at him in the shower. The way her pupils had dilated with an unmistakable heat when she'd realized what he'd been doing before she stormed in.

Matt allowed himself a moment to relish in the emotion he'd seen pouring out from behind those guarded eyes when Kat had been riding him, inches from where he sat now.

Those weren't the looks one got from a cold, uncaring person. It was the way Nate's and Kole's wives looked at them when they thought no one else was paying attention.

*Shit.* Matt blinked, fighting to accept what he realized was happening. Whether he wanted it to or not, the hard, unbreakable wall he'd erected around his broken heart that day on the pier was beginning to crack.

For the first time in years, he began to consider the possibility that he'd been wrong about her all along. After all, they were just kids when she'd broken up with him. Maybe it hadn't been some game to her, after all.

Matt guessed it was possible his lower social status

wasn't the driving force behind her decision to end things. Maybe her feelings for him had simply changed.

If that was the case, could he really fault her for that? People fell in and out of love all the time. It was one of the reasons he avoided it altogether.

Was that it? Was it possible Kat wasn't the vicious, vindictive woman he'd come to believe? He looked down at the file again.

*There's nothing in here you need to know.*

She'd warned him away from seeing what was in there, but hell. That was like telling a little kid not to press the big, red button.

Resting his elbows on his knees, Matt put his head into his hands and sighed. Being indecisive wasn't his thing. He knew what he wanted, when he wanted it, and most of the time, he got it.

The confusion swirling around inside him now was unfamiliar territory. And Matt fucking hated it.

*Screw it.*

He reached for the folder, his fingertips barely brushing against the thick, smooth cover when his phone began to ring again. This time it was Kole.

After a quick conversation about the cabin, supplies, and some razzing about his being locked away with a beautiful woman he used to sleep with, Matt ended the call.

Once again, he reached for the folder. Once again, his phone rang.

"Jesus Christ, what now?"

Matt's harsh greeting took Zade by surprise. "Sorry, man. If this is a bad time, I can call back later."

Closing his eyes, Matt forced the air in his lungs to

move in and out of his nostrils at a slow, calming pace. "Sorry, King. What's up?"

"Your blood pressure, from the sound of things."

Matt smirked. "You have no idea."

"Want to talk about it?"

*Not happening.* "Did you need something?"

"Not really. I knew you were in a less-than-ideal situation, so I thought I'd check in. See how you were holding up."

Damn. The former Marine was as tough as they came, but the guy sure didn't hold back with his emotions. It was no secret King had the softest heart out of all the Bravo guys.

"I'm good, but thanks," Matt lied.

"You don't sound good."

He opened his mouth to tell his teammate to fuck off but stopped. Being a surly son of a bitch hadn't done a whole hell of a lot for him lately. Maybe it wouldn't hurt to confide in someone for a change.

"To be honest, I don't really know what I am."

"I take it things with your girl have been a little rough?"

Matt nearly choked from Zade's words. "Uh...you could say that. And for the last time, she's not my girl."

"Look, man. I know I'm the least experienced out of al of us when it comes to women and relationships, but I can tell when a person cares for someone else. That woman definitely still has feelings for you."

Matt's heart thumped against his ribs.

"Question is..." Zade continued. "How do you feel about her?"

*I don't feel anything for her.*

That's what Matt wanted to say. But he'd be lying through his clenched teeth.

"Things with Kat are...complicated."

"I gathered that." The guy's voice was laced with humor. "You gonna let that stop you?"

"From what?"

"Going after what you really want."

"I don't—"

"Come on, Turner. This is me you're talking to. You know whatever you share with me is safe."

Zade was right. The guy may be the most emotional on the team, but he was also the most tight-lipped.

Matt took a deep breath and sighed. "Fine. A small... microscopic part of me *might* still care a *little* bit about Katherine. Maybe."

The other man made a humored, throaty sound. "That's a start, I suppose. So what's the problem?"

*So many things.* "Too much past standing in our way." He picked up that damn folder, but kept it closed. "Too many unanswered questions."

"Doesn't have to stay that way."

"It's not that simple."

"Sure it is. You got questions, go ask her for the answers."

"She doesn't want me to know."

"Have you actually asked?"

"I have. Ten years ago."

Zade's breathy chuckle made Matt want to reach through the phone and punch the guy in the throat.

"Jesus, Turner. She would've been what, eighteen?"

"Seventeen."

"Dude."

"What?"

"Oh, that's right. I forget you're an only child. Explains so much, but that's a whole different story. Anyway, I've got two sisters, and trust me. Teenage girls are a species all their own. If whatever happened between you two went down when she was that young, you need to let that shit go. Now."

"You don't understand."

"Maybe not. But you may not understand, either. If she kept things from you back then, I'm sure she had her reasons. You ever consider they may not be what you're assuming?"

Matt remained quiet for a beat before telling Zade, "Derek brought over folders on all the Biomeds employees working in Kat's lab. Including her."

"And? What did you find out?"

"I haven't looked through it yet."

"Ah..." Zade's trailing voice had that all-knowing Sensei tone that left Matt half-expecting his teammate to call him Daniel Son.

"What? What is 'Ah'?"

"Let me ask you this. Which scares you more...the idea of finding confirmation of your suspicions, or finding evidence that you've been wrong about her this entire time?" When Matt didn't answer, his friend quietly told him, "Read the file, Matt. At least then you'll know. Either way, you can move on."

Matt ran his fingers over the manila cover. "Thanks for checking on me, Z."

"Anytime, man. Holler if you need anything."

Ending the call, Matt set his phone aside. Setting the folder back down, he stood and went into the kitchen to make some coffee. Something told him he was going to need it.

With the pot fully brewed, he filled his mug to the rim and carried it back to the living room. Settling in on the couch once more, he took a few careful sips of the steaming liquid—and several deep, cleansing breaths—before opening the folder and beginning to read.

The first few pages were nothing more than the basic intel. Birth certificate, driver's license information, current address, and copy of her lease. It was actually pretty scary to think of all the things his team could find out about a person.

Matt skimmed through her high school and college transcripts, impressed as always by her straight A's and perfect GPA. His chest filled with a familiar pride as he read through the academic awards she'd earned while in college. His heart feeling heavy, wishing he'd been there to see her receive them.

He wasn't surprised by her educational success. Not in the least.

Sure, Kat's eidetic memory played a big part in it, but there was more to her than that. Much more.

Skipping past other unrelated intel, Matt came to a picture that sent a dull, rusty knife sliding straight into his heart. It was Katherine's wedding picture.

This was the same picture he'd found back in the day when he'd been drunk and had looked her up.

The first time he'd seen it, Matt had slammed his computer closed and found the nearest trash can just in time for everything he'd drank to come right back up. Then, he'd drank more to replace it...and then some.

Seeing it now wasn't any less painful, which didn't

make sense. It shouldn't still hurt like this. Not after all this time. But it did.

Masochist that he was, Matt actually took the time to study the picture more closely. He hadn't done that before.

Wearing a long, traditional white dress and veil, Kat smiled for the camera as she held a large bouquet of roses in one hand. Her other was wrapped around her new husband's bent arm.

The roses struck him as odd, because she'd always told him they were her least favorite flower. They didn't last very long, she'd say.

*She told you a lot of things back then.*

With another deep breath, Matt continued his assessment, forcing himself to look at the man she'd married. Brian Anderson was handsome in a preppy, I've-got-money sort of way.

His sandy blond hair was perfectly parted, not a single strand out of place. The man's straight, white teeth shone for the camera, and his posture was spot-on as he stood next to the woman Matt was supposed to marry.

To the untrained eye, they seemed like the perfect couple. But as Matt looked more closely, he realized something was off. It was the way Kat was smiling that nagged at him, and the longer he focused on that damn picture, the clearer it became.

The smile spread across young Katherine's face wasn't the one he'd seen looking back at him all those times they'd spoken of building a future together. No, this was the very same smile Kat always used while speaking to her father or his rich, important friends.

Unlike the one he'd dreamed about endlessly, this

smile didn't reach her dark, beautiful eyes. Like a two-by-four, it hit him. Kat's smile that day was fake as fuck.

His gaze slid to the groom's, the breath in his lungs damn near catching when he found the same signs of deceit on the young man's face.

Matt knew what his expression would've looked like had it been *him* standing next to Kat that day in place of this silver-spooned bastard. Anyone looking at him would've seen nothing but pure joy if he'd been the one to marry Kat. But this guy…this guy looked as though he would rather be anywhere else in the world.

*How did I not see this before?*

The answer to that question was simple. He'd been so sick at heart, he hadn't taken the time to see it.

Gut screaming, Matt sat the folder down onto the coffee table and began shuffling through the remaining pictures and documents with more urgency. Derek had printed off several photos from Anderson's social media account, so he started with that.

The first several were of him at social gatherings. Katherine wasn't in any of those, but that wasn't surprising. Derek had been sure to print off any comments people had left below the pictures, as well and after a quick perusal, Matt realized those pics were mostly from company parties.

He learned from the pictures and comments that Brian Anderson was a second-year lawyer on the fast track to making partner. Kat said he shot himself two years after they were married, but Matt hadn't bothered to ask anything more. Frankly, he hadn't wanted to know.

Now, all of a sudden, Matt wanted to know everything

he could about the man she'd vowed to spend the rest of her days with.

As he continued his search, he realized nothing glaring stood out. Nothing except the change in Brian's smile.

In the pictures with his co-workers, he appeared to be genuinely happy. But in almost every single one he'd posted of him and Kat, not so much.

Kat's were a different story, altogether. Her social media posts were few and far between, but even in the ones with her and what appeared to be a few girlfriends, her expression was the same. That dull, forced happiness Matt knew was far from the real thing.

He went back to Brian's posts. With an operative's eye, he examined them more closely. Now that he was in the right mindset, he could see it. Or at least, he had a high suspicion of what he thought the real story was.

There was one common thread in all the pictures where Brian Anderson seemed to be truly happy. Another man.

At first glance, Matt assumed they were nothing more than co-workers. Friends, even. But upon closer inspection, his trained eye picked up on the things most people would miss.

Their close proximity to one another. The way they were looking at each other in some of the pics. Their hands centimeters apart, as if they wanted to link fingers but knew they couldn't.

Matt opened his phone and accessed his Facebook app. As fast as his fingers would work, he did a quick search for the other men tagged in Brian's photos until he found the one he was looking for.

It only took a minute for him to confirm what he'd

been thinking. The other man, Chad Winthrop, was a proud, openly gay lawyer at Brian's firm.

*Brian shot himself six years ago.*

Holy. Shit.

Matt's wheels were spinning so fast he feared the centrifugal force would cause his brain to shoot straight out of his ears. Over the next hour, he went through every single document in that file.

Derek had somehow accessed the police report, autopsy findings, and photos from Brian's suicide scene, including a copy of the note he'd left for Kat.

The guy may have married the woman of Matt's dreams, but it was still heartbreaking to read his final words. Brian didn't give specifics, but he eluded to the fact that their marriage was a sham. Said stuff about not being able to be himself, leading a life that wasn't his...living a lie.

Brian never once blamed Kat, though. In fact, by all accounts, Anderson truly did care about her. Just not the way a husband should care for his wife.

Was it possible? Was Kat's husband...gay?

Grabbing his phone, he called Derek. As he waited for the Alpha Team tech genius to answer, Matt wondered if he was on to something, or simply conjuring up things that weren't really there.

He knew what he'd found was purely circumstantial. People killed themselves every day for all sorts of reasons, but fuck. It all made sense.

The fake smiles, the closeness oozing off Brian and Chad in those photos...the incredible tightness Matt had felt while trying to work himself into Kat's pussy less than an hour ago.

At the time, all he could think about was how incredible her snug body felt. But now? Christ, was it possible she and her husband had never even had sex?

*I never date.*

Oh shit. Matt ran a hand over his jaw. Could it be? Could Kat really have gone without having sex with anyone since...

*Me.*

He shook those thoughts away. Getting ahead of himself wasn't going to help the situation. He needed to concentrate on one insanity at a time.

"Miss me so soon?" Derek answered with a smile Matt couldn't see.

"What do you know about Chad Winthrop?"

There was a pause and then, "I take it you read Katherine's file."

"I did. And unless I'm seeing shit that isn't there..."

"You're not."

Matt swallowed hard. "Brian Anderson was gay, wasn't he? That's why he ate a bullet."

Derek cleared his throat. "Kat's husband and Chad Winthrop were lovers for nearly two years before Anderson and Kat got married."

Derek's answer shouldn't have taken him by surprise, but it did. "So their marriage was, what? A cover?"

"Kat will have to answer that one. All I can tell you is what I found in Chad's deleted social media files."

"Which was?"

"Pictures. Several, in fact. It was clear he and Brian were much more than mere colleagues or friends. And according to the electronic footprint I followed, they were all deleted on the same day...a week before Brian and Kat announced their engagement."

*What the hell?*

Derek gave him a moment to process before asking, "You think Kat knew?"

"Yeah," Matt nodded. "I think she knew. What I don't understand is why she'd marry a guy knowing he was gay."

"Like I said, you'll have to ask her that."

"Don't worry," Matt assured him. "I plan to."

By the time he'd finished combing through the rest of the documents, he was pretty sure he knew the answer. And it pissed him the hell off all over again.

# CHAPTER 8

"Where is Doctor Marsh now?" The man on the other end of the phone growled.

"I don't know."

"What the fuck do you mean you don't know?"

He gritted his teeth together. If this guy thought his gruff tone and words scared him, he was wrong.

"I mean exactly what I said. Thanks to your guys, Katherine got spooked and is now under the protection of some private security firm out of Dallas."

"*My* guys?" The dangerous killer laughed. "Your man was the one who blew up the entire fucking lab."

"Yes, well, since Todd killed himself in the process, I think it's safe to say he learned his lesson."

Pressing his luck with a man like this wasn't smart, but the entire situation was getting out of hand. They needed to figure out what they were going to do about it.

"Kennedy knew the risks going in," the other man stated bluntly.

"I could say the same for you and your boss," he shot

back. "If you want to blame someone, how about the dumbass who texted Katherine instead of Todd in the first place. *That's* the real reason we're dealing with this clusterfuck." He took a breath. "Do you even have any idea how much money I risk losing if we don't find her?"

"Enough!" The guy's loud voice made him jump. "You're not the only one who stands to lose if this thing goes sideways. The situation isn't going to right itself, so how about we quit this back and forth shit and figure out how we're going to fix it. Starting with how to get access to the woman."

He swallowed. "What are you planning to do to her?"

"Me? Nothing, other than delivering her to my boss. What happens to her once she gives him the formula, however, is anyone's guess."

He thought of Katherine. There was a time he'd genuinely liked her. Thought she was a sweet person and a brilliant scientist. Exactly what he needed, both personally and professionally. But that was before she ruined everything.

Now he merely saw her as a means to an end. Two ends, really. He'll profit more than he'd ever dreamed of, and at the same time, she'll finally be forced to pay for what she'd done. Like killing two birds with one stone.

*Or a lying, conniving bitch who deserves whatever hell she has coming to her.*

"We won't gain access to her while she's being protected," he informed the other man. "I've learned a bit about R.I.S.C., the security firm watching over her. Apparently, she's being guarded by one of their Bravo Team members. Guy named Turner. He's former-military and very well trained. They all are. If you or your men try to go after her now, it won't end well for you."

The other man waited a beat before responding in a surprising way. "Turner's guarding Marsh?" He laughed. "This deal just got sweeter."

"What the hell are you talking about? Do you know him, or something?"

"Don't worry about Turner," the man ignored his question. "I'll handle him and the rest of Bravo. We need to find a way to bring them out of hiding."

*This guy's supposed to be smart?* "How the hell do you propose we do that? It's not like you can send an invitation and she'll come running."

"Actually, I think that's exactly how this is going to play out."

"What are you planning?"

The frustrating prick answered the question with another question. "Doctor Marsh's mother died several years ago, and she's an only child, correct?"

He shouldn't have been surprised by the man's knowledge of Katherine's family dynamics, but he was. "Yes. That's correct."

"You know her father. Are they close? How is their relationship?"

"Somewhat strained, but okay, I guess. Why do you ask?"

"I think I may know a way to bring the good doctor out of hiding."

His pulse spiked. "You said no one else was going to get hurt. Only Katherine."

"And you promised you had everything under control,"

the other man bit out. "Clearly, that's not the case, so now we do things my way."

"But—"

"Keep this phone nearby. I'll be in touch."

The call was ended, and he was left wondering how things had come to this. He glanced at the picture on his desk, the force behind all his problems staring back at him.

*You did this. Now you have to deal with the consequences.*

Katherine Marsh started this with her lies and deception. If her father got caught in the crosshairs, so be it.

It was past time the bitch paid for what she'd done.

\* \* \*

KAT GLANCED AT HER REFLECTION IN THE SMALL, bathroom mirror. Subconsciously, she ran a finger over her still-swollen lips. Traced the small patch of stubble-burn on the side of her neck, her sensitive inner muscles clinching from the memory of how it got there.

She'd woken from her climax-induced nap feeling sore, but in the very best way possible. She'd also woken up alone. Not that she was surprised.

It wasn't like Kat actually expected Matt to be sleeping beside her. If they were still younger, sure, but not now. Even so, after what they'd done, it would have been nice.

She was still trying to wrap her mind around the fact that she'd had sex with Matthew Turner.

Hard, rough, *hot* sex.

In those first, foggy seconds when she'd awoken, Kat had nearly convinced herself it had all been a dream. A fantasy. Then she moved, her body assuring her it was very, very real.

After a quick shower and change of clothes, she used the blow dryer she found in one of the drawers and threw on a little mascara to help take away from the sleepy look in her eyes.

Feeling like a nervous teenager, she kept trying to find ways to keep from having to leave the bedroom. She didn't want to face him or the indifferent look he'd most likely give her.

Doing her best to stall, Kat decided to make the bed. A bed Matt had carried her to.

She should probably be embarrassed by the fact that she'd fallen asleep on top of him, but she couldn't find it in herself to be. Knowing he'd carried her in here and tucked her in, versus tossing her off his lap like a used-up toy, filled her chest with more satisfaction than it should have.

*This doesn't change anything.*

Those words had stung, but at least he was being honest. Unlike her. She'd lied through her teeth when she told Matt she didn't want anything more than what he was willing to give.

So many nights she'd laid awake, wishing for five more minutes with him. Imagined what it would be like to be pulled into his arms for one more hug. To feel his lips pressing against hers as he gave her one more kiss.

Today, she'd been given all those things and more.

Since she never thought it possible, Kat wasn't going to dwell on the fact that it had only been a means of physical release for him. Because for her, it had been a miracle.

She made her way to the door. With a final, steely

breath, Kat turned, straightened her shoulders, and turned the knob.

The sight of Matt sitting on the couch stopped her in her tracks. His back was to hers, and he was just sitting there, staring at the powerless T.V.

Swallowing down her desire to go to him, she willed a casual tone into her voice and said, "Hey. Sorry I slept so long. Are you hungry?"

He didn't answer. Didn't even move, actually.

*Okay, so maybe this would be more awkward than you anticipated.*

Ignoring the frustrating voice, Kat put on a smile and started for the kitchen. "Those steaks are still in the refrigerator. I thought I could pan-fry them and bake a couple potatoes. I think I saw a few cans of green beans, too, so if you want, I could—"

"Don't do that."

The order was gruff and non-negotiable.

Kat turned back around. Standing in the framed doorway separating the kitchen from the rest of the cabin, she frowned.

"Don't make the food?"

He didn't answer. Nor, did he look at her. Instead, Matt simply continued to stare out at nothing.

"Okay. If you're not hungry, we could—"

"I said, don't." He finally looked at her.

The daggers shooting back at her left Kat shaken. "Do what?" She took a step closer. "Matt, what's going on?"

He gestured toward the coffee table. "You tell me."

It was only then that Kat saw it. The pictures and bank statements. The business contract between Brian's father and hers lying on top of it all.

Her heart dropped. "I-I...I can explain."

He chuckled humorlessly, his voice dripping with sarcasm. "Can you? Because I would *love* to hear an explanation for this."

She glanced back down at the papers, knowing what he must be thinking.

"Matt..." She had to stop to blink away the tears threatening to form. Swallowing down the large lump in her throat, Kat whispered, "It's not what it looks like."

"Really?" His lip curled. "'Cause from where I'm sitting, it looks like the girl I'd planned to marry...the woman I wanted to spend the rest of my life with...sold herself out like a high-dollar whore."

Kat reared back, bile rising in her throat from the horrible accusation. "What? No!" She shook her head.

"Stop. Lying!" Matt swiped his arm angrily across the table, the pictures and papers flying in the air before landing on the wooden floor below.

Her muscles jumped from the deafening outburst. "It wasn't like that, Matt. I promise."

"Then what was it like, Katherine?" He shot up from the couch and faced her. With his hands on his hips, his face turned red with fury. "According to those"—he pointed at the strewn papers—"your father and your *husband's* father went into business together right after you and Anderson got married. I bet the ink wasn't even dry on the marriage license when they signed that fucking contract."

Kat opened her mouth to respond, but shame and grief prevented any sound from escaping.

"What's the matter? Having trouble coming up with another lie?"

"I'm not lying!"

"You married a *gay* man, Katherine! And don't bother denying that one, because Derek found the proof."

"I'm not denying it."

"Well, there's a first." Matt spun around, his booted feet crumbling some of the pictures as he began pacing the small room. "I want to know why." He faced her again. "Why did you do it? No, wait. Let me guess. You and your father came up with this little plan together. Isn't that right?"

"No," she answered adamantly.

"Bullshit," Matt snapped before continuing on with his misguided assumptions. "Your father made all his money partnering up with companies that were in financial trouble. From what Derek found, Sloane Anderson was damn near to the point of filing for bankruptcy when you and Brian got married. All of a sudden, your dad swoops in, partners with Anderson Biomeds, and saves the day. Am I close so far?"

Kat swiped away the tears she was unable to stave off but remained silent.

Matt's face twisted in a disgusted smirk. "That's what I thought. So with the help of your Dad's business connections, your former father-in-law's company takes off by securing government contracts like the one for the formula your team was working on. Contracts like those go for millions, right?"

Kat nodded. "Yes."

"I also did a bit more digging over the last hour, and it turns out good ole Sloane wasn't too keen on the idea of his son being a homosexual."

"No," Kat admitted. "He hated it. Hated Brian because of it."

"Right. So you and Daddy Dearest decided to help the Andersons out by helping yourselves in the process. You marry Brian, taking the stigma of having a homosexual son away from Sloane, get him off Brian's back, and you and your daddy come out on top."

Matt shook his head as he paused. Even though Kat knew his train of thought was way off base, she stayed quiet and let him get it all out.

"Your father profits out the ass from the success of the business—thanks in large part to you jumping on board and becoming the lab's star scientist—and you secure your financial future by becoming Brian's sole beneficiary. Not to mention securing your professional success." Matt shook his head and scoffed. "Now that I say all that shit out loud, I'm thinking maybe the authorities should open up your hubby's case again. Make sure he didn't have *help* with his suicide."

Kat saw red. She could handle him throwing the other shit in her face, but this? Past or not, she refused to stand by and let Matt accuse her of hurting Brian.

With more tears streaming down her heated cheeks, Kat opened her mouth and spilled it all.

"How dare you?" she yelled loudly. "You have *no* idea what it was like for Brian. Or me, for that matter."

He raised a smug brow and crossed his large arms at his chest. "Why don't you enlighten me?"

The fact that he'd tossed back the same words she'd used before they'd had sex angered her even more.

*Asshole.*

"You're right. Brian was gay. He was gay and in love with a man named—"

"Chad Winthrop. I know."

"Good. Did you also know Brian's dad threatened to disown him if he continued with his 'shameful' lifestyle? Or that Sloane told his only son if he didn't find a woman to marry and carry on the family name, he'd not only remove his name from the will, but also use his contacts to force Brian out of the job he loved. The job he was made to do?"

Matt stared back at her but said nothing.

"Brian and I met through a friend during my second year of college. We became close, as friends only. One night over coffee he confided in me about all the horrible things his father was threatening to do. He was a couple years older than me, but he was still just a kid. A kid wanting nothing more than his father's approval."

Kat slapped her chest and continued on. "I knew what that was like because my own father was constantly browbeating me to find a good, wealthy man to marry. The longer Brian and I talked that night, the more we realized we could help each other out."

She licked away another tear. God, this was embarrassing. And hard. So much harder than she'd ever thought it would be.

"Brian and I decided to get married," she continued. "Not for money or power or any of that. Yes, our fathers went into business together, but that was only because they became friends once Brian and I started our dating charade. Brian was a good man." Kat's voice cracked as she wiped her nose with the back of her hand. "He was a wonderful friend. My only one, really.

134

So yes…I agreed to help him out. In turn, he helped me."

Still looking like he wanted to throttle her, Matt asked, "Why'd he off himself?"

Kat cringed at the crass way he'd described Brian's death. "He tried. He really did, but the longer we went along with the fake marriage, the more unhappy Brian became. I did what I could to help him sneak around to be with Chad, but after a while, it wasn't enough. The idea of not being himself, to not be with the one and only person he truly loved…it tore him up inside."

She wiped at her damp cheeks again before describing the second worst day of her life.

"I came home from the lab early one afternoon. I wasn't feeling well, and nothing seemed to be going right, so I decided to go home and rest. Recharge so I could start fresh the following day."

Kat closed her eyes, sending a new trail of tears down over her skin. She could still see the heart wrenching scene as clearly as if it had just happened.

"I knew something was wrong the minute I stepped inside. The door had been left unlocked, and Brian's keys were on the kitchen counter." She looked back at Matt. "He loved his job almost as much as he loved Chad. He never missed a day."

Kat drew in a deep breath before continuing. "I called out for him, worried that maybe he had the same bug I did, but he didn't answer. I searched the house, my concern growing with each empty room I entered. I found him in the bathroom." "He'd shot himself in the shower." She released a watery laugh. "I know it was to make the…clean-up…easier for me."

The anger behind Matt's eyes began to ease. Still, he remained silent.

"What you said before was true. I was Brian's sole beneficiary. But if you or Derek had bothered to look more closely at my financials, you would've seen I used that money to set up several investment accounts. All in Chad Winthrop's name. That's who Brian loved. That's who deserved to get his money. Not me."

Matt blinked, visibly taken aback by what she'd shared. "I didn't realize."

"No." Kat shook her head. "You didn't. Because you didn't bother to ask. You simply assumed and made accusations."

Defensive, he gave her a look. "Come on, Katherine. How the hell did you expect me to react? The entire time we were together, your father hounded you to find someone better. Someone wealthier. The bastard even tried paying me off once."

Her mouth dropped, but she was too shocked to say anything.

"Didn't know about that, did you?"

She lifted her chin. "Guess I'm not the only one keeping secrets."

"Are you kidding?" His face turned red again. "Not the same thing, Katherine. Not even close. I didn't tell you what your father did because I knew it would hurt you. I refused his fucking offer because the love I felt for you was worth way the hell more than your father or anyone else could ever afford."

"I know my dad has done some terrible things. Trust me."

"That's the thing, Kat. I can't trust you."

Those crushing words penetrated her soul. "Yes, you can."

"No. I can't." He took a step toward her. "You've proved that over and over again. Starting with lying about your feelings for me."

"I never lied about that, Matt. I loved you. I still lo—"

"Don't." He threw a hand up, his teeth grinding together. "Do *not* go there."

"But it's true."

"Goddamnit, Katherine!" he bellowed. "We're not fucking kids anymore! And I'm not that stupid, naïve boy you fooled into thinking we had something special. That we had a future together."

"We did!" She willed him to believe her. "I loved you more than anything in the world. All I ever wanted was a future with you."

Instead of taking her at her word, Matt's expression turned cold. Emotionless.

"If that were true, you wouldn't have broken us apart. You would have stayed with me. Married *me* instead of participating in some twisted façade with your boss's gay son." Matt took a few more steps in her direction. "I may not have had a lot, but everything I had in here"—he pointed to his chest—"was yours. I gave it all to you, and you threw it right back in my face."

"I did it to protect you!"

The words were out before she could stop them.

"Protect me?" Matt snorted. "From what, the embarrassment I'd face from your father and his stuck-up friends?"

"No," she answered quietly. "Not from that."

"Then from what?"

She'd never intended on telling him this part. Never wanted him to know how horrible the genes were that ran through her veins. Now that she'd started, Kat knew she needed to finish. Once and for all.

"From going to jail."

He laughed. Actually laughed. "Jail? Jesus, Katherine." Matt ran a hand over his hair, causing those top strands to become mussed. "Are you even listening to yourself? You can't bear to face the fact that you were a selfish, spoiled teenager who wanted someone better, so you keep making shit up as you go along. Grow the fuck up and admit it already."

More tears fell, but Kat didn't bother to wipe them away. Woodenly, she opened her mouth and shared the entire, sordid story.

"My father had us followed."

"What?"

She licked her dry lips. "He hired someone to follow us back then. The man took...pictures." Kat wrapped her arms around her waist, the feeling of being violated still fresh, even now. "My dad came to me that morning, about an hour before we were supposed to meet at the pier. He showed me the pictures of us making love in the boat house, along with a written statement he'd signed and had notarized. It was addressed to Commander Jennings."

He frowned. "My unit commander? Why would he—"

"My father gave me an ultimatum that morning, Matt," she cut him off. "Either I ended things with you that day, or he was going to send those pictures and that statement to Jennings and demand you be brought up on charges of statutory rape."

"*What?*" Matt took a step back, the shock on his face telling. "That's ridiculous. You were…"

"Seventeen," Kat whispered. "The legal age of consent in California was eighteen. Still is."

He blinked a few times. While he tried to process what she'd just said, she shared even more.

"The pictures were all date and time stamped. Even if we had tried to fight it, my father's lawyers would have been able to prove they were legit. And if he'd sent those to your commander…"

"I would've been court-martialed." Matt's voice turned flat as he finished for her.

Kat nodded sadly. "I couldn't let that happen. I knew how much being in the Navy meant to you. I never would've been able to live with myself if you'd been kicked out…or worse…because of me."

Understanding finally began to filter through his dark eyes. "So you broke up with me."

"Yes."

He walked over to the window facing the front of the cabin and ran a hand over his scruffy jaw. She waited for him to say something more, but he didn't. He simply kept staring out at nothing.

"I couldn't tell you the truth," she said honestly. "My father had a guy watching us on the pier that morning. He said if it even looked as though I was trying to tip you off on what was really going on, the man would call him. If that happened, Dad would have gone straight to the post office and mailed the envelope containing the pictures."

When Matt remained silent, Kat continued talking, desperate to make him understand.

"Don't you see?" She moved in closer. "I didn't end

things with you because I didn't care. I broke up with you because I loved you. I loved you so much." Kat paused a moment to work past the painful pressure in her throat. "Enough to let you go so you could have the life you always wanted."

His head turned toward her, his heart breaking all over again before her very eyes. "The only life I ever wanted was with you."

"I was scared, Matt. I knew my father wasn't bluffing. He would have had you arrested if I hadn't gone along with his plan. I couldn't let that happen to you. I didn't know what else to do."

"You could've told me."

"I already explained that. I couldn't or Dad would've—"

"I mean after, Katherine." He shook his head. "If what you're telling me is true—"

"It is," she cut him off again, her eyes pleading with him to believe her. "I swear with every fiber of my being I'm telling you the truth."

"The statute of limitations on that shit was up a long time ago. You could have come to me then. Told me what your father had forced you to do, rather than continuing to let me believe you were some cold, heartless woman who didn't give a shit about me."

"Oh, sure." She chuckled without a hint of humor. "Because you would've believed me, right? Look around, Matt." Kat gestured to the small space surrounding them. "The only reason you're even listening to me now is because we're stuck in this tiny cabin with nowhere else to go. I saw the look in your eyes on the pier that day. I remember every single word you said to me. You talk about how I threw you away like you were nothing, but what about you?"

"Me?" His face twisted with confusion.

"Yes, you. You claim to have been so madly in love with me you were ready to propose. Yet at the first sign of trouble, you bolted."

"Are you fucking kidding me?" He closed much of the distance separating them. "*You* broke up with *me*," he growled.

"And you *let* me!" Kat yelled back. Her chest heaved as she tried to get her point across without crumbling into a million pieces. "You could've fought harder, but you didn't. You claimed to have loved me, but believed me the second I said I didn't want to be with you anymore." She swiped angrily at a tear. "What my father did to us was unforgivable, but *I* didn't have a choice. You did. And you chose to throw that ring in my face and walk away without even *trying* to fight for us."

"What would have been the point?" He threw his arms to his sides before letting them fall back down, his hands slapping loudly against the tight denim stretched across his toned thighs. "By your account, I would've gone to prison had I stayed. So whether or not I tried to fight for us wouldn't have even mattered."

"It would've mattered to me," her voice cracked. When he threw that ring at her that day, she'd watched him walk away, feeling as though he never really knew her at all.

"I can't..." Matt swallowed hard before shaking his head. "I can't be here right now."

Her stomach tightened. Not because she was afraid of who may come after her, but because deep down, she didn't want him to go.

"You promised to watch over me."

"I promised to keep you safe." He pulled his phone out of his pocket.

"W-who are you calling?"

"Zade. I'll have him come stay with you." Without looking at her, he hit a number on his contacts list. "He was a SEAL. He'll protect you."

Kat stood at the edge of the living room, her dizzying mind trying to make sense of what was happening.

"Please," she heard herself say. "Don't go. Let's talk about this."

"Hey, King," he ignored her. "It's Turner. I need a favor."

She listened as Matt explained to Zade what he needed. After, Kat stood frozen while Matt walked over to his bag, securing the items inside.

Without looking at her, he said, "Zade will be here within the hour. I'm going to go outside and check the perimeter and security equipment while I wait."

"Matt, please," she tried again.

He zipped the bag shut, stood straight, and flung it over his shoulder. Not making eye contact, he spoke low as he passed by in a rush.

"I won't leave until he's here. Lock the door behind me, and don't open it for anyone but him."

"Matt!" she hollered after him, but it was too late. He was already gone.

# CHAPTER 9

Matt sat in the quiet of Gabe's modest home, his head still spinning from the nuclear fucking bomb Kat had dropped on him less than two hours before.

The trip from the cabin back to Dallas had been challenging to say the least, given his state of mind. No way in hell was he in any shape to safely make the twenty-two-hour drive to Long Beach, California...where Kat's father lived. Even though that's exactly where he wanted to go.

*Motherfucking bastard.*

He still couldn't believe what that son of a bitch had done. Although, he shouldn't be surprised.

Thomas Marsh was all about appearances. To him, money equaled power. At the time of his and Kat's breakup, Matt had neither.

*A lot has changed, asshole.*

His heart became heavy as he thought of Kat. Once again, the woman had turned his world on its axis, changing more than he was ready to admit.

On his way to the city, Matt had called Gabe and asked

if he could stop by his place. His team leader was a few years older and seemed to always have a good, solid head on his shoulders.

Hopefully, the former SEAL would have some sort of wisdom to bestow upon him. A piece of advice on how to handle a situation like this.

After laying the whole shit show of a mess out for his friend, Gabe hadn't said a word. He'd simply stood and vanished into his kitchen, leaving Matt alone to wonder what the other man was thinking.

"Here." Gabe walked back into the room carrying two long necks of the man's favorite beer. "Thought maybe you could use one of these."

*Or twenty.* "Thanks," Matt mumbled as he took the offered bottle.

"So." Gabe took a swig. "What are you gonna do?"

His shoulders bounced with a loud scoff. "Fuck if I know." The cold beer soothed his dry throat as he swallowed a large gulp of his own. "All this time, I thought Katherine broke things off because I wasn't good enough for her. Wasn't rich enough." He took another drink before admitting, "I've slept my way through half the women in Texas because the idea of actually caring about someone again…"

"Scared the shit out of you?" the inciteful bastard guessed.

He sighed, "Yeah."

Matt had also thought if he had enough meaningless sex, he'd eventually forget about her.

*How'd that work out for you, dickhead?*

"I get it," Gabe nodded. "You were burned once. Only natural to steer clear of any flames after that."

Something about the way he said it made Matt wonder about the big guy's past. "You ever been in love?"

"Once." Gabe's eyes softened slightly, his deep voice rumbling as he added, "A long time ago."

*Interesting.* "What happened?"

The man shrugged. "Right girl. Wrong time."

Sensing that was all he was going to get out of the man, Matt refocused on his own fucked-up situation. "I don't know what to do now."

Gabe thought a moment. "You could start by getting rid of that giant chip on your shoulder."

Matt scowled. "I don't have a fucking chip."

"No. More like a giant-ass boulder." The man smirked as he drew in another sip.

"Fuck you, Dawson. You have no idea what it's been like for me."

"You're right," Gabe agreed. "I don't. All I know is you've spent the past decade working hard and playing even harder and for what? So you can prove yourself to a woman you claim to hate but are clearly still in love with? To give a big fuck you to that same woman's father who, by all accounts, is a narcissistic asshole you shouldn't give two shits about?"

Goddamnit, the man was right. And it pissed Matt the hell off.

"I'm not still in love with her," he lied.

Gabe's raised brow told Matt the guy knew he was full of shit. "Then why are you so upset?"

"What?"

"If you don't still have feelings for Katherine, why does this bother you so much?"

145

"Because I..." He trailed off, not knowing how to answer that question.

"It's okay to admit you still love her, Matt. Especially now that you know the truth. It's also okay to want to see where you two can go from here. To hope for a future you thought was dead and buried."

Matt tipped the bottle back, swallowing its remaining contents to keep from having to respond.

"Look, man," Gabe went on. "I'm far from being an expert when it comes to relationships. Lord knows, I made more than my share of mistakes with my ex. But it's obvious this thing with Katherine is tearing you up. Did she hurt you? Absolutely. But you've gotta look at *why* she did what she did. If what she told you is true, that woman saved your ass."

"Why the hell do you think I left?" Matt strode angrily across the room. "I couldn't face her, Gabe. I've been such a dick to her. Said horrible, unforgivable things because I thought..." His fucking voice cracked.

"So apologize. If she's the kind of woman who deserves to be with you, she'll listen. And from the way she looked at you in that conference room, I bet she'll be more than willing to hear what you have to say."

"That's just it," Matt shot back. "I don't know *what* to say to her. I don't..." He paused a moment. "I don't know what to do now."

"What's your gut say?"

"My gut's telling me to go to California and beat the shit out of her manipulating jackass of a father."

"Then what?"

Matt frowned. "What do you mean?"

"Say you do go beat the guy's ass. What happens after? Between you and Katherine, I mean."

"I don't..." He shook his head. "I-I don't know."

"Did you sleep with her again?"

Matt shot his friend a look, but before he could deny it, Gabe gave him a knowing grin.

"That's what I thought."

"Didn't mean anything," he lamely shrugged it off.

"Right." Gabe tipped his bottle toward him. "Keep telling yourself that."

*Trust me, I've been trying to.*

"Sex aside, you obviously believe her story about her dad's blackmailing scheme."

"Yeah." Matt nodded. "I do."

He wanted to ignore what Kat had told him. To believe it was nothing more than another lie to go along with the pseudo marriage. But as much as his mind wanted to deny it, his heart knew she was telling the truth.

It was there, in her heartbroken, tortured eyes. Kat had crushed both their dreams that day on the pier, but she'd done so in order to protect him. He didn't even know what to do with that.

For years, he'd hated the woman when he should have been *worshiping* her. Had despised a girl who, even at the young age of seventeen, was mature enough—brave enough—to sacrifice her own happiness in order to keep his ass out of the brig.

All those hateful, hurtful words he'd spewed at her, both in the past and the present, came rushing back to him. God, he felt so sick at heart.

Not only did Matt hate himself for saying those things in the first place, but also because rather than call him out on his shit, Kat had stood tall the entire time, stoically taking everything on her shoulders as if she'd deserved it.

And all the while, she'd been every bit as heartbroken as he was. Probably even more so.

More than that, the incredible, amazing woman had spent all this time knowing he despised her for making the decision that had saved his career. Hell, his *life*.

Matt swallowed down a rush of burning bile as he stared out Gabe's living room window. His breathing shallowed and his mouth filling with saliva from the nausea filling his gut.

Raising a shaking hand to his face, his fingertips bit into the stubble covering his hardened jaw as he stood there, trying like hell not to puke and wondering where he went from here.

*You know exactly where you're going.*

For once, Matt didn't feel like punching out that tiny voice. Mainly because, it was right. If he could convince his boss to let him borrow the company jet, he had only one destination in mind.

Right on cue, a loud knock came from the other side of Gabe's front door.

"Sorry to keep you waiting." Jake stepped past Gabe as he opened the door. "Traffic was a bitch."

"Boss." Matt went to the other man and held out his hand.

"Turner." Jake reciprocated the gesture.

"Hey, Matt." Trevor Matthews, Alpha Team's medic and Jake's second in command—followed Jake into the home's entryway.

After calling Gabe on the way here, Matt had immediately called Jake, too, asking if he could meet him here.

He'd told Jake Zade had taken over his bodyguard duties but wanted to wait to explain the rest until they could talk face to face.

The fact that *both* men had come didn't bode well for Matt.

Trevor, a former Delta operator like Jake, stood nearly eye-level with him. His short, dark hair and perfectly symmetrical features made him what everyone on the team called Hollywood handsome. Matt had to agree.

Like him, the guy could probably have any woman he wanted. Having seen the way Trevor looked when he spoke to or about his wife, however, Matt knew the other man only had eyes for her.

He'd been like that with Katherine, once. *Maybe you can be again, now that you know the truth.* Ignoring his subconscious, Matt shook Trevor's hand, too.

"Sorry this one's been such a headache for you," Trevor offered.

Along with Gabe, the other two men took a seat in the living room. Praying he wasn't about to be fired, Matt chose to stand.

Sitting with a semi-relaxed posture, Jake looked up at him from his place on the couch. "I'm sure you'd like to give me a big 'I told you so' speech right about now."

Matt blinked and shook his head. "No, sir. Actually, I wanted to apologize."

"For what?"

After airing out all his embarrassing dirty laundry, including owning up to having sex with a client, Matt stared back at his boss in earnest.

"I let my personal issues with Katherine affect my

ability to do this job. I called in King to take over without getting prior permission, and I—"

"Is Katherine protected?" Jake interrupted.

"Yes," Matt quickly assured him. "I made sure they were both secure inside the cabin before I left."

Jake nodded before taking a moment to process what Matt had told him. Then, the man shocked the hell out of him.

"While I would've appreciated a heads-up prior to your leaving, I understand why you did."

Matt felt his eyes widen. "You do?"

With a tip of his head, Jake explained his thoughts on the situation.

"You have a history with this woman, and not a good one. You tried to tell me assigning you as her bodyguard was a mistake. I didn't listen." Jake sighed, looking a bit chagrined. "I saw the way you two looked at each other in my office and in the conference room. I could tell you were pissed as hell, but the way Katherine looked at you when you walked in...it's the same way Liv still looks at me."

Okay, now he was thoroughly confused. "I don't understand."

"I messed up with my wife, Turner. Before she was my wife. I lied and kept things from her, important things, and it damn near cost me everything. As pissed as you were when you realized Kat was our new client, I saw something else there, behind those guarded eyes of yours that made me think you cared."

Suddenly it all made sense. In a shocking, knock-him-on-his-ass kind of way. "You trying to play Cupid, Boss?" Matt asked the man in charge.

Jake smirked and sat back against the couch. "I guess I was." He ran a hand over the short, dark beard covering his jaw. "Looks like it backfired, huh?"

"You could say that," Matt snorted.

"Damn, man." Trevor turned to Jake. "And here I thought Derek was the hopeless romantic of Alpha Team."

"Shut the fuck up, both of you," Jake ordered, though his tone held no seriousness whatsoever. "Look. Maybe it's the impending birth of our baby. Sympathy hormones or some shit. All I know is, I get what it's like to waist a chunk of time not being with the woman you love. To risk the one chance at happiness with the person who knows you better than you know yourself. I saw that in you and Kat, and I guess I thought if I forced you two into close quarters, maybe you could work through your shit and…I don't know. Be as happy as Liv and I are."

Something hit Matt. "Wait a minute. I thought you said Ryker wanted me to get close to her to figure out if she was in on the scheme to steal the formula."

Jake simply shrugged. "Two birds and all that shit."

Matt laughed at that, the sound almost foreign. He hadn't done much laughing the past couple of days.

Grabbing the back of his neck, he squeezed his tense muscles. After taking in a long, deep breath, he said, "So, I take it I'm not fired?"

Jake looked at him like he was stupid. "You removed yourself from a situation where you felt your ability to efficiently protect our client had been compromised. Katherine is still being guarded by a member of Bravo, and you've been upfront and honest about everything. More than I needed to know, actually." The man smirked.

"So no. You're not fired. Just…maybe next time call me first. *Before* you leave your post."

Matt released the breath he'd been holding. "Hopefully, there won't be a next time, Boss."

"Good answer, Turner," Trevor smiled back at him.

"Now that we have that out of the way." Jake changed the uncomfortable subject. "D filled us in on what he found out about Todd Kennedy. Obviously, someone was paying him to gain access to the formula. Since you're no longer on protection detail, I thought you and Gabe could work with Derek to figure out who that was."

"Actually, there's one more thing." Now came the tricky part.

"Okay. Let's hear it."

Matt filled his lungs once more before blurting, "I want to borrow the jet."

His boss stared back at him silently, studying him with an assessing glance. "You want to confront Katherine's father about what he did."

"I do," Matt answered honestly. He respected Jake too much to lie to the man.

"Can't say I blame you."

"Do you think that's a wise decision?" Trevor asked from beside him. "You seem pretty keyed up. With good reason," he added quickly. "I'd want to beat the hell out of the man, too, if I were you."

"I don't plan on beating Thomas Marsh up. That would only give him more ammunition to use against me. The last thing I want is for the bastard to have more leverage to hold over my head."

"So what is your plan?" Jake eyed him closely.

Matt shrugged. "Just want to talk. Confirm what Kat said was true."

Trevor shook his head. "You realize he'll probably never own up to it."

"Actually, I think that's exactly what he'll do."

Gabe's brows turned inward. "What makes you say that?"

He pictured Marsh's smug face with his perpetually turned-up nose. "Kat's dad is a textbook narcissist with major control issues. Especially when it comes to his daughter. He's also arrogant as fuck. The bastard got what he wanted, so in his mind, he won." Matt shook his head. "No way he passes up on the chance to rub that shit in my face."

"You think that'll bring you closure?" Jake asked pointedly.

"Partial closure. Yes." Matt nodded. "A five-minute conversation. That's all I need. I know it probably sounds stupid, but I need Marsh to know I know. Once that happens, I think I'll finally be able to move forward."

"With Katherine?" his boss asked, sounding hopeful. Damn, the man really was a romantic at heart.

Matt thought for a second. If he'd been asked that question a day ago—hell, two *hours* ago—his answer would've been an immediate and unquestionable 'fuck no'.

Her earlier words still rang loudly behind his ears.

*I did love you. I still...*

She'd tried to tell him she still loved him, but he wouldn't listen. Suddenly, Matt wished he'd have shut the fuck up and let her finish.

"Maybe." Turning to Gabe, he added, "If she'll still have me."

All three men smiled back at him. Then, after sharing a look with Trevor, Jake stood from the couch and made his way around the coffee table. He extended his hand.

"I'll make sure the jet is fueled and ready to go. I'll stay behind to assist Derek with whatever he needs until you get back. Take Trevor and Gabe with you, in case Marsh decides to grow a wild hair and try something stupid."

"Thanks, Jake."

With a nod, the man walked to the front door and pulled it open. Before he left, he turned back around and told Matt, "Say what needs to be said, and get your ass back here. We've got work to do."

A while later, as Gabe flew them to California, Matt thought about his conversation with Jake once more. Not only had the man not fired him, he was actually letting him use the company jet for personal business…while in the middle of a job.

His personal life may be a jumbled mess of shit, but damn. As far as the professional side of things went, Matt couldn't ask for a better boss—or team—to work with.

After the three-plus hour flight into Long Beach, Matt found himself standing across the street, staring at the ornate, wrought-iron gate. He'd gone through it a handful of times with Kat when they were younger.

Back then, his gut had tightened with anxiety every time they came here. And, if he were being completely honest, a little fear. As he stared at the man's ridiculously large house now, the only thing Matt felt was fury.

He was pissed at what Kat's dad had threatened to do

to him, but he was even more upset by what the man had done to her.

"You ready?" Gabe asked beside him.

Matt nodded. "More than you know."

"Just remember," Trevor said, presenting himself as the voice of reason. "Guy like this probably has security cameras in every room. Let him make the first contact."

With nothing more than a tip of his head, Matt checked for traffic before starting across the paved road. The other two men followed, having his back as all R.I.S.C. operatives did.

Unlike before, his hand was steady as he pushed the state-of-the-art intercom. Though he couldn't see whoever answered from inside the house, the small, round camera facing Matt would show them exactly who had come to visit.

"Can I help you?" A man's voice emulated through the system's speaker.

"I'm here to see Thomas Marsh."

"Do you have an appointment?"

No, he didn't have a fucking appointment. "He's gonna to want to talk to me."

"I'm sorry, sir. But without an appointment—"

"Tell your boss Matthew Turner from the R.I.S.C. Security Firm is here to see him. Tell him it's about his daughter."

There was a stretch of silence before the voice said, "Please give me a moment. I'll get Mr. Marsh."

"You do that."

Standing out of the camera's line of sight, Gabe silently raised a brow.

Confident they weren't currently being watched, Matt shrugged his shoulders. "What?"

"The guy hired us to watch his daughter," Gabe stated the obvious.

"And?"

"What if he thinks we're here because something happened to her?"

Matt gave his team leader a smug smile. "My guess is, he'll open the gate and let us in."

The other man shook his head, laughing silently. "Sly bastard."

A few moments passed by before they heard a loud clicking sound. The three men turned their heads as the large gate began to slowly swing open.

Taking it as their invitation to enter, Matt and the others made their way along the paved drive to the home's elaborate front entrance. Before he could ring the bell, the door was opened. Staring back at him for the first time in years, was the bastard himself, Thomas Marsh.

At five-nine, the sixty-two-year-old man was shorter than Matt. His hair was a silver-gray, and there were several new lines that had formed on his aged face.

Marsh quickly scanned the area behind Matt before his blue eyes met Matt's. "Where's Katherine? Is she all right? Did something happen to her?" His voice was laced with genuine concern.

"Kat's fine." Matt stared down at him. "She's being guarded by one of my teammates."

"Why aren't you with her?"

Though he didn't react, Matt couldn't help but be surprised at the question. If he didn't know any better, he'd think Marsh was upset that he wasn't the one guarding his daughter.

*How about that? Guess there really is a first time for everything.*

"We need to talk." Without waiting for a formal invitation, Matt stepped past Kat's father and entered the home.

"Okay." Thomas swallowed hard, following him inside.

Gabe and Trevor came in, too, but kept their distance. Matt appreciated that they were willing to let him handle this on his own. Speaking of which...

"There someplace private we can talk?"

Marsh's nervous gaze slid to the other two operatives before landing back on Matt. "We can go to my office. It's just down the hall."

With a nod, Matt let his co-workers know he had things under control before following the not-so-scary man down the long hallway and into a room on their right. Marsh waited to close the door before speaking.

"Would you like a drink?"

The man walked over to an expensive-looking cabinet. On top was a silver tray housing a crystal bourbon decanter and two matching glasses. Matt remembered the man offering him one of those same glasses the same day the prick had tried to buy him off.

"I didn't come here for a social call, Marsh. I came here to talk."

"I have a feeling I know what this is about, so I'll save you the trouble."

One large, perfectly square ice cube landed with a dull clink as he dropped it into his glass. Pouring two fingers of what Matt assumed to be high-dollar bourbon over the frozen water, he then returned the delicate stopper and took a sip.

"Yes," Marsh continued. "I hired a man to take pictures of you and Katherine. And yes, I used those pictures and the threat of bringing criminal charges against you to entice her to end things."

The asshole didn't even appear sorry for what he'd done.

Before he realized he'd moved, Matt had crossed the room and was fisting the man's crisp dress shirt between his two fists. Bourbon spilled sloppily over the tilted glass and onto Marsh's shirt before he dropped it on the carpeted floor.

"You son of a bitch!" Matt ground out between clenched teeth. "Why?"

Though he appeared afraid, Kat's dad didn't back down. "You remember what it was like back then. What *you* were like. I did what I did for the good of my daughter."

"Bullshit!" Matt's breath flew in and out of his flared nostrils. "You did what you did for yourself. No one else."

With a harsh shove, Matt released the man and stepped back. If he didn't put some space between them, he had no doubt he'd beat the man to a fucking pulp.

"I know exactly what I was like," he continued talking. "I was the man who loved your daughter more than anything in the entire world. I wanted to marry her. Raise a *family* with her. No, I didn't have a lot to offer in the way of money, but I was working my ass off in the Navy, doing everything I could to better myself so I could provide for her. For us."

He looked around the dark, stuffy office. "Maybe I

couldn't afford to build this sort of house, but did you ever stop to think maybe Kat didn't want that? That she was okay living life on our terms?"

"Katherine was seventeen years old." Marsh picked up the now-empty glass and set it back down. Wiping a hand over his damp shirt, he attempted to regain his composure. "She didn't know what she wanted."

"She wanted *me!*" Matt's loud voice echoed off the wooden paneled walls. "But you took that choice away because you were so stuck on your high-society bullshit, you were too blind to see what she wanted. The life she dreamed of having."

Marsh lifted his chin. "She moved on. Did quite well for herself, too. Even married a wealthy lawyer."

Without missing a beat, Matt came back with, "A *gay* lawyer who put a bullet in his brain because he couldn't bear the thought of living a lie for one more day. A lie that included being married to your daughter rather than the man he truly loved."

"That marriage was her choice. Not mine."

"You're right," Matt nodded sarcastically. "It was her choice. Kat chose to marry a man who had no romantic interest in her whatsoever, because she couldn't stand the thought of you pushing her to anymore rich assholes. *That's* the choice you left her with."

Matt crossed the room getting in the bastard's face. "Brian Anderson killed himself because he would've rather been dead than in a fake fucking marriage. Your daughter found him. She still sees the image of him lying in that goddamn shower, his blood and brains splattered all over the fucking walls. *You* did that to her."

A hint of guilt seeped through the guy's unshakeable

demeanor. It was the first real sign of emotion he'd ever seen on the bastard's face.

*About fucking time.*

"You talk about the kind of man I was back then," Matt continued on. "Let me tell you. I was the man who would have done *anything* in order to be with your daughter. I loved Katherine with everything I had. I would have died to protect her."

"And now?" Marsh stared back at him. "After everything that's happened between you two, would you still give your life to keep Katherine safe?"

Matt didn't hesitate. "You bet your ass, I would."

"Good."

The man's response left him blinking.

"Weren't expecting that, were you?" Marsh gave him a sad smile. "No, I don't supposed you would."

He stepped to the side and made his way back over to the bourbon. "I know you probably won't believe me, but I do regret what I did to you both."

"You're right. I don't."

Kat's father studied him a moment before taking another sip. "I suppose I deserve that. Nevertheless, it's true." He drew in a weary breath before asking, "Do you have any children, Matthew?"

"No." *Hopefully, I will soon, though.*

The thought came out of nowhere, but oddly, it didn't freak Matt out like it probably should have.

"Well, when you do, you might understand a little better why I did what I did."

"What you did was wrong, Marsh. No way around that."

"You're right. But my reasoning behind it wasn't."

Matt rolled his eyes as the asshole kept talking.

"As you know, Katherine's mother died very young. What you don't know is the last promise I ever made to her was while she was on her death bed. She was lying before me, struggling for every breath, and her only concern was that of our daughter's well-being. I promised my wife I would do everything in my power to protect Katherine. To make sure she had the best life had to offer for as long as I lived. Now, at the time I was misguided. I believed money equaled happiness. And more than anything, I wanted my daughter to be happy."

"She was happy," Matt growled. "With me."

"I know that, now. I also know that, while Katherine married Brian to help him save face with his father, she also married him to protect herself, too."

"From being hounded by you. She told me."

"There was more to it than that, Matthew. Katherine married Brian because she knew she'd never truly love anyone else the way she loved you. Had no desire to...give herself...to another man the way she had you."

As twisted as it made him, the primal part of Matt wanted to puff his chest and holler to the rafters. Instead, he made sure Thomas Marsh knew exactly where he stood, as far as Kat was concerned.

"She won't ever have to worry about that again. Not as long as I'm still breathing."

The man smiled, the shocking sight nearly knocking Matt on his ass. "I was hoping you'd say that."

Despite the man's sudden turn of heart, Matt glared back at him. "I want the fucking pictures, Thomas. Now." His gut was screaming the man still had them.

Sure enough, he watched as Marsh walked over to a

picture on the wall. Sliding the heavy frame aside, Marsh entered a digital code into the safe concealed behind it. Pulling a large envelope from between a small stack of other papers, he secured the metal door and righted the frame before walking over and handing Matt the envelope.

"I know you and I will probably never be close."

*You fuckin' think?*

"But I want you to know I truly am sorry for the way I handled things. You have my word, I will never do anything to stand between you and my daughter, ever again."

Still fuming, Matt unwound the twine wrapped around the envelope's enclosure and began to pull its contents out.

As if he'd been transported back in time, Matt stared down at one of several pictures of him and Kat making love in the boathouse. At the time, these images could have easily been seen as nothing more than evidence. Proof that Marsh's allegations would have been accurate.

Looking at them now, however, all Matt saw was proof of their love.

"Those are the only copies," Marsh's voice broke through. "My investigator was too concerned about being charged with child pornography to keep pictures such as those."

"But you weren't?" Matt's brow rose.

"Frankly, no. My lawyer would've argued parental concern, and he would've won." The arrogant son of a bitch went on. "At first, I held onto them as leverage. I kept them after the statute of limitations ran out because I think..."The man cleared his crackling throat. "I think deep down, I was hoping this day would come."

Matt's guarded gaze rose to his, but he remained silent.

"I've wanted to have this moment to talk to you. To explain my reason for forcing you two apart." The man's shoulders fell, and suddenly Marsh looked much older than when he'd first opened that door. "Truth be told, I wanted to look you in the eye, man to man, and tell you I was sorry."

*Too little too late.* "I'm not the one you should apologize to."

"I know. Katherine and I..." Marsh swallowed hard. "She hasn't looked at me the same since that day. I'm hoping, now that you two are back together"—he gave Matt a look—"you are back together, aren't you?"

"Yes." Matt nodded. He didn't consider it a lie, since he planned to make that clear the second he walked back into Kole's cabin.

Kat's father nodded. "Good. I'm hoping that will be the first in a long list of steps I know will be required for my daughter and I to make amends."

"I hope so, too. For Katherine's sake." Matt made himself clear. "But don't think that means I will ever trust you or your motives."

"Understood."

Turning for the door, Matt was about to open it when he thought of one final thing that needed to be said. He faced Marsh again. "You're not the only one with a fierce need to protect Katherine. You hurt her again, in any way, I'll fucking kill you."

Having laid everything out on the table, he opened the

office door and walked out. As soon as he saw them, Matt let Gabe and Trevor know he was ready to go. More than ready, actually.

A sudden urgency raced through him. He needed to get back to the cabin. Needed to look Kat in the eye and tell her he was wrong. About everything.

Matt just prayed she'd find a way to forgive him. Because if she didn't, he didn't know what he was going to do.

# CHAPTER 10

Kat rubbed her throbbing temple as she stared at the moon through the small, bedroom window. Wrapping her arms around her center, she thought of Matt and wondered how she'd let things get so messed up.

Through the years, she'd imagined having that same conversation with him. Over and over, she'd pictured what it would be like—how he would react—if she ever got the chance to tell him the truth.

She would explain everything, and when he realized she'd broken his heart in order to protect him, her mind's eye always created a scene like that from a movie. One where the man forgave the woman's mistakes and went rushing back into her arms.

In Kat's fantasies, they always ended up living happily ever after...forever.

But it never lasted. Reality had a way of seeping back in, and eventually the pointless fantasies stopped. Now she knew why.

Matt hadn't run to her. He'd run *away* from her. As fast

ANNA BLAKELY

and as far as he possibly could. The disgusted look in his eyes still played behind her own. God, he couldn't even stand to look at her anymore, let alone be locked away with her.

Thankfully Zade had given her the time and space she desperately needed. Other than to ask if she was hungry or bring her some ibuprofen for the splitting headache she'd woken with earlier this morning, he'd allowed her to hide away in here. Alone with her torturous thoughts.

For a good while after Matt left, she'd cried. And cried...and cried. Then, she'd slept.

Long and hard, her body and mind had finally shut down for several hours. She hadn't even dreamed, thank God.

Instead, she'd cried herself to sleep only to wake up with the beginnings of a painful migraine. The aching had eased some now, but it was still present. Hovering in the background, along with her guilt and shame.

She shouldn't have yelled at Matt like that. Couldn't believe she'd actually blamed him for any of it.

Sure, it would've been nice for him to at least try and fight a little bit, but he was right. It wouldn't have changed anything.

In fact, if he *had* continued to stand there on the pier that day, had begged her to stay with him like part of her wished he had, she very well may have crumbled. If that had happened, she would've broken down and told him everything.

If that were the case, he may still be in prison to this day.

So no, she shouldn't have put any of the blame on him. This was all her doing. Hers and her father's. And here she was, ten years later, dealing with the consequences all over again.

*Suck it up, Marsh. Time to put your big girl panties on.*

Deciding to take a shower to help wash away her sorrows, she was standing under the warm water when she realized that tiny voice was right.

Kat had made her bed a long damn time ago. Or rather, her father had. Regardless, she wasn't the only one in the world to have been dealt a shitty hand, and she needed to get over it already.

As she rinsed the conditioner from her hair and the soapy suds from her body, Kat finally acknowledged that which she couldn't change. Apparently, this was the way things were supposed to be, and it was high time she accepted Matthew Turner was not the man for her.

Committed to making her heart believe that, she was about to shut off the water when the shower door swung open. Gasping from the unexpected intrusion, Kat didn't even have time to react before Matt stepped over the metal threshold, joining her in the small, wet space.

"Matt? W-what are y—"

He kissed her.

With his hands framing her face, he paid no attention to the water pouring down over them both—or the fact that he was still fully dressed, boots and all—as he pressed the tip of his tongue against the tight seam of her lips.

All thoughts of forgetting this sexy, confusing man vanished the second his mouth took hers. Kat opened herself up to him in every way possible. Because in that exact moment, she knew…

*I'll give this man anything he wants.*

Ending the rough, possessive kiss too soon, Matt

pulled himself away enough to look into her eyes. Blinking against the falling water, his eyes darkened with a level of determination far exceeding her own.

"I'm sorry, baby. So. Fucking. Sorry."

"I-I...I don't..."

"I know." He smiled again. "But you will. I promise, I will do whatever it takes to make you understand."

Kat's head was spinning. "Understand what?"

"That you're mine." He rested his forehead against hers. "You belong to me, Katherine. You always have."

She gasped, her breath hitching from confusion and surprise. From hope. God, she felt more hope than she had in so very long.

*Please don't be messing with me.*

"I can see those brilliant wheels of yours turning. You're probably wondering what the hell I'm doing in here with you. Trust me, we'll get to that in a minute. I can also see the hesitation behind those mesmerizing eyes of yours, and I don't blame you. But I swear with everything I have, this is *not* some sort of ruse to get close to you in order to dig up more intel. This is me, standing here, telling you I love you."

Kat's knees gave out, but Matt was ready to catch her.

"Easy, sweetheart." His strong arms held her naked form securely. "I've got you."

"Y-you...*love* me?"

She had to hear it again. Needed to look him in the eyes and see his mouth form those precious words again. Otherwise, she'd convince herself this was all a dream.

"Look at me, sweetheart." Keeping an arm around her waist, Matt used his thumb and forefinger to tip her chin upward.

She knew he was doing it so she'd look up at him but he didn't have to. There wasn't a force strong enough to make her tear her eyes from his.

"I'm listening," she assured him.

"Good." A corner of his mouth rose in the same sideways smirk he used to wear, her chest filling with wild palpitations. "I need you to really hear me this time." Dark eyes reached into her soul, his words like gentle tendrils wrapping themselves around her heart as he repeated, "I love you, Katherine. I never stopped. Even when I thought I hated you, I still loved you."

Tears mixed with water as Kat became so emotionally overwhelmed she had to fight against the dizzying effects to keep from passing out.

For years, she'd dreamed of hearing him say those same words, yet...

"The things you said." She swallowed hard. "I know I hurt you, Matt, but you hurt me, too. Those things you said...knowing you thought I could ever be that cruel to anyone, let alone you..."

"I know I fucked up." Shame filled his expression. "And I'll never forgive myself for the way I've treated you. But I swear, Katherine. If you'll just give me a chance, I'll spend the rest of my life making it up to you."

She wanted to believe him so badly.

"I know I've been a Grade-A prick, but please, baby." His voice cracked. "I'm not me without you. You make me better. You make me the man I *want* to be." Twin tears fell down his cheeks. "I love you so much, Katherine. So much."

"I love you, too," she heard herself whisper back.

Barely keeping herself together, she added, "I love you so much it hurts."

Through his tears, Matt smiled wide. An honest to goodness, light-up-his-face smile. He looked instantly younger, more like the boy she used to know. The sight was absolutely breathtaking.

"Thank Christ." He kissed her forehead before leaning his against hers once more. "I know I don't deserve it. I don't deserve you. But I swear to God, I will do everything I can from here on out to prove myself worthy of you."

She understood his previous words and actions toward her were merely his defense mechanism. A way to protect his damaged heart.

Justified or not, it was a heart *she'd* damaged, yet here he was...offering it to her again. How could she say no?

Kat lost the battle, then. Hot tears poured from the corner of her eyes as she attempted to say, "Y-you already a-are, Matt. Always h-have b-been."

"I'm so sorry, baby." He pulled her against his chest. "I never should've doubted you."

"I'm sorry...too." Kat's words spurted out with hiccuping breaths as she fisted the back of his soaked shirt. "F-for every...thing."

"No." He pulled back, his hands steady on her bare shoulders as he shook his head fiercely. "You don't ever apologize again. Not for that. You hear me?"

"B-but—"

"No buts. You did nothing wrong. If anyone needs to apologize, it's me. Jesus, the things I said to you. The way I treated you..."

"But I l-lied."

"To *protect* me. I get that now, so you need to let that shit go."

Kat nodded. "We both do."

The corner of his eye twitched from her comment, and she knew a part of this man would carry that burden for the rest of his life.

"I can't believe this is really happening." She stared up at him in awe.

"Believe it, baby. From now on, you're stuck with me." A flash of vulnerability shone behind his confident eyes. "As long as that's what you want."

"Oh, it's what I want." Kat raised up on her tip toes and pressed her lips to his. "It's all I've ever wanted."

She'd worry about the what and why of it all later. For now, all she wanted to do was relish in the miracle that was currently in her arms.

Matt must have felt the same way because in less than a second, he'd stripped off his sopping clothes and began showing her how much he truly did love her.

Hours later, after a second—and third—round of mind-blowing sex, Kat found herself lying in the comfort of Matt's arms. Nothing in the world felt better than that.

"I'm assuming you sent Zade home?" she finally thought to ask. They hadn't had much time to actually talk since he came back. Not that she was complaining.

"The second I walked back through that door."

His deep voice rumbled through her ear as she traced a finger across his chest and down the valley separating his well-defined six-pack.

"You think he knows why?"

Matt chuckled, the sound reverberating through his chest. "Oh, yeah. I'd say my intentions were pretty clear."

Kat felt her cheeks become flush, but she really couldn't bring herself to care.

"Hey." He shifted to his side in order to face her. Tucking some hair behind her ear—a gesture she'd come to cherish dearly—he grinned. "For the record, those guys were rooting for us from the start."

Kat's brows rose. "Those *guys?*"

He shrugged one of his broad, bare shoulders. "Zade and Gabe. Oh, and Jake and Trevor. Hell, I'm sure Kole and Derek have been, too. They just didn't say it."

"Your boss was *hoping* this would happen?" She lifted herself onto an elbow. "Wait, who's Trevor?" She would have remembered the name had she heard it before now.

Matt simply smiled. "He's a member of Alpha Team. And yes, my boss was hoping this would happen. He tried to play it off as sympathy hormones from his pregnant wife, but in truth, the guy's as romantic as they come."

"So that's why he assigned you to me."

"In part."

"Oh." Her shoulders fell slightly.

Picking up on her unspoken concern, Matt said, "Don't worry. He and the others know you're in the clear as far as the explosion and all that goes."

She let out a breath. "That's good, but how?"

"Shit." Sitting up, Matt adjusted his pillow behind him and leaned his back against the headboard. Running a hand over his handsome face, he shook his head. "I was so focused on…you…I forgot to tell you."

Scooting up to join him, Kat listened as Matt filled her in on what they'd found out about Todd. Fresh tears formed from both the realization that he'd been in on the scheme to steal the formula and from finding out about his wife's illness.

"I had no idea."

"He never said anything?"

She shook her head. "Todd was a very private person. He never really talked about anything in regards to his personal life. None of us did, really."

With his arm holding her snuggly against him, Matt kissed the top of her head before resting his cheek there. "I'm sorry, sweetheart."

"Thanks." She waited a beat before talking again. "I take it Derek hasn't found the person who paid him off?"

"Not yet. He did call me while I was on my way back here to say they'd recovered some of the text messages from Todd's damaged work phone. There were a handful back and forth between him and whoever it was. Unfortunately, they were from a number D traced back to a burner. Records show it bouncing off several different towers in and around Dallas. Whoever it was used a program to ghost it, which means Derek couldn't pinpoint a specific location from where the texts originated."

"This is all so crazy."

Matt's chest rose and fell with a deep breath. "There's more."

Great.

"I, uh...I went to see your father yesterday."

This bit of news had Kat sitting straight up. "You went to Long Beach?"

"I needed to confront him."

Kat blinked quickly, both loving and hating the fact that Matt had called her father out.

"So…what happened?"

"We talked."

"About?"

He gave her a look. "What do you think?"

Okay, so yeah. That was a stupid question. "I meant, what did you say? What did he say?"

"In short, I let him know what he did to us was a total dick move. That I would have done anything to give you a good and happy life."

Kat's heart swelled, even as she bit her bottom lip nervously. "And, Dad? What did he say to that?"

"Surprisingly, your father admitted blackmailing you to keep you away from me was a mistake. One he'd never make again. Said he was only trying to give you the best the world had to offer. At the time, he believed that meant financial security."

"Meaning, I needed to marry rich."

"Pretty much."

She thought for a moment. "So how did you two end things?"

"I made sure he knew it was in his best interest to never even think of hurting you like that again. And if he did, it wouldn't end well for him." Matt shrugged again. "He swore he wouldn't."

Kat was stunned. "Do you think he was telling the truth?"

"Honestly?" Matt looked back at her. "Believe it or not, I do. I think in his own, twisted way your father thought he was doing what was best for you."

"He was wrong."

Matt's jaw muscle bulged. "Fuck yeah, he was."

Kat looked back up at Matt. "Thank you."

"For what?"

"Everything. For believing me when I finally told you what happened. For standing up for me...for us...with my father." Kat slid up his body and took his mouth in hers. "And for still loving me, after all this time."

He caressed her cheek with his thumb. "Lord knows, I tried not to." His Adam's apple bobbed up and down with an audible swallow.

The look in his eyes was beginning to scare her. "What is it?"

"If we're really going to do this, we need to start fresh. Lay it all out on the table, so to speak."

"O-okay." Nervous butterflies began to swirl around in the pit of her stomach.

"After we split, I swore I'd never allow myself to get that close to anyone ever again. And I didn't, but..."

His voice trailed off, his rugged face frowning with indecision.

"Matt, you're starting to scare me. Just spit out whatever it is you're trying to say."

He filled his lungs to the brim before releasing the air with a single, loud exhale. "Okay, so here's the thing. I've been with a lot of women these past ten years. It's not something I'm proud of, but I thought you needed to know. I don't want any secrets between us from here on out. None."

"Okay." Kat breathed the word.

That pit in her stomach was suddenly chalked full of those damn butterflies. Though it shouldn't have been.

It was only natural for a healthy, grown man—especially one as sexy and desirable as Matt—to have an active sex life. He'd been single for a long time, and until now, had no way of knowing why she'd ended their prior relationship. As much as the thought made her physically ill, he'd been free to sleep with whomever he wanted, as many times as he wanted.

But there was still one thing she needed to know.

"Did you love any of them?"

"No." His answer was so immediate, it was like a hand swatting the fluttering creatures away. "It was just sex. No strings, no commitment. They knew where my head was going in and they all felt the exact same way. I think." He licked his lips. "I think somewhere inside my subconscious I thought I could, I don't know…"

"Fuck me out of your system?"

His eyes widened a bit with surprise. "I wasn't going to put it like that, but yeah. I think that's exactly what I was trying to do."

"I'm glad it didn't work."

Matt smiled. "Me, too."

He started to lean in, but she put a hand on his chest to stop him. "In the spirit of honesty, you should know I haven't been with anyone else but you."

"I know." His eyes darkened with a mixture of pride and desire.

"How could you possibly know that?"

"I could feel it." He did kiss her then, his hand trailing down her flat stomach. "Your body's so tight. So snug." Matt brought his lips to her neck. "Like it was made specifically for me."

Moaning, she smiled lazily. "Again? Already?"

Kat leaned her head to the side while simultaneously letting her outer leg fall open. The man had given her multiple orgasms over the past few hours, yet she was already feeling primed and ready to go again.

"I can't get enough of you," he whispered against her ear. "Never enough."

Matt's fingers had only just brushed against the top of her bare sex when a loud pounding startled them both.

Without missing a beat, Matt jumped out of bed, grabbed his gun from where he'd placed it on the nightstand after round one, and threw on the clean jeans he'd worn during a quick, re-charging meal before round three.

"Stay here," he ordered brusquely.

Gone was the sweet, loving man she'd spent the afternoon reacquainting herself with. In his place was this serious, hardened warrior.

"Okay."

Though Kat doubted the bad guys would announce their presence with a knock to the front door, she wasn't stupid enough to take the chance. She also wasn't going to remain naked and in bed, just in case.

Dressing faster than ever before, Kat quickly pulled on the black leggings and oversized sweatshirt. She finished slipping on the last of her two socks when she heard Matt answer the door, followed by another man's low voice.

She couldn't hear what was being said, but the lack of gunfire and yelling led her to believe it was safe to come out. To be safe, she carefully peeked around the door's edge.

Her tense body relaxed when she saw Gabe—the silver fox she'd met at R.I.S.C.'s office—standing inside the cabin's small entryway. Both men noticed her right away, and from the looks on their faces, their conversation was more than a little serious.

"It's okay, Kat. It's Gabe."

Pushing away her embarrassment from having been caught spying, Kat straightened her shoulders and joined them.

"Hi, Gabe. Good to see you again."

"Hey, Kat."

The other man tipped his head in a single nod. He'd seemed serious when she'd met him before, but the expression on his face as he looked back at her this time was different. Kat couldn't quite put her finger on it, but it was almost as if he felt sorry for her. Which made absolutely no sense, whatsoever.

She slid her gaze to Matt, who definitely looked remorseful. *What the hell?*

Kat took a step closer. "What's going on?"

He opened his mouth but shut it before any sound escaped. She watched as he swallowed in the same, nervous way he had in the bedroom a few minutes before. Oh, this couldn't be good.

"Matt?" Her eyes bounced back and forth between the two men. Hugging herself, she did her best to stay calm when she asked, "What's wrong?"

It was Gabe who answered.

"Jake got a call about an hour ago. It was a detective with the Long Beach Police Department."

*Oh god!* "My dad?" She rushed to Matt's side. "Is he okay? What happened?"

"Sweetheart, why don't we sit down."

With a gentle hand to her elbow, he tried to guide her over to the couch, but Kat jerked herself free.

"I don't want to sit down. I want you to tell me what's going on."

The two men shared a look before Matt said, "I'm so sorry, Kat. Your father..." Matt couldn't seem to find the words, so Gabe finished for him.

"The Long Beach Police were notified of a car that had been found at the bottom of a ridge. It was your father's car."

Gasping, Kat covered her mouth with her hand before promptly dropping it to ask, "Is he okay? How badly was he hurt?"

"When the first responders arrived, they found him bleeding and unresponsive. There was a lot of damage to the vehicle, and it took over two hours to get him out."

Despite her earlier protests, Kat stumbled over to the arm of the couch and sat down. "Oh, my god," she whispered. Her head had begun to pound, and suddenly, she found it very hard to breathe. "B-but he's okay. They got him out and to the hospital, so he's going to be okay. Right?"

She stared back at the two men, Matt's entire face filled with an emotion she refused to accept.

*I have to go. Now.*

Kat shot up from where she'd been sitting and started for the bedroom. "I need to be with him."

"Kat, wait."

Matt hurried to follow her, but she ignored him. Already in the bedroom, she grabbed her bag from the closet and tossed it onto the mattress. Her head spun, adrenaline rushing through her body as she tried to think clearly. To remain calm and gather only the items she really needed.

"Kat, stop."

"I know you hate him, Matt." She continued packing. "I don't blame you. Part of me hates him for what he did, too, but he's still my dad. I'm the only family he has left." She ripped a blouse from one of the hangers and shoved it into the small suitcase. "He doesn't have anyone else. I should be with him."

"Baby, stop." Matt gripped her shoulders gently yet sternly.

With her voice raised, she tried wiggling out of his grasp. "I can't! My father needs me!"

"Your father's dead!"

Kat's breath froze in her lungs as her world stopped. "W-what?"

The sympathy pouring from Matt's eyes crushed her. "He broke his neck in the accident. I'm so sorry."

Her body went numb, and though she could tell Matt was saying something else, she couldn't hear him over the loud buzzing in her ears.

Concern began to filter through his expression as the room—and everything in it—tunneled down to the size of a pinpoint. The last thing Kat heard before everything went black was Matt's muffled voice, screaming her name.

# CHAPTER 11

Matt scanned the immediate area surrounding Thomas Marsh's final resting place. Then, from behind his dark, polarized lenses, he watched Kat as she stared down at the solid mahogany casket adorned with a large splay of red roses.

Other than to thank her father's so-called friends and acquaintances for coming to pay their respects, she hadn't spoken much today. Though he'd made multiple attempts to strike up a conversation, she'd pretty much been locked away in her own thoughts all afternoon. Not that he could blame her.

Still, knowing she was hurting was like a punch to the gut, and Matt hated that he had no idea how to help her. She'd scared the hell out of him when she'd passed out after hearing the news of her father's death. Thanks to his medical training, he'd understood it was her mind's way of protecting itself.

She came to a few minutes later, and he'd held her as she sobbed. After that, they packed all her belongings and

ANNA BLAKELY

left. With a quick trip to Matt's place for a few more clothes, they met Zade at Jake's private hangar on his ranch.

With permission from their boss, the two men and Katherine had flown here, to Long Beach, so Kat could begin making arrangements for her father's funeral. That was four days ago.

In that time, she'd been quiet and distant. While Matt understood why, he wished like hell he could find the words to make it all better for her. Unfortunately, he knew they didn't exist.

Not only was Kat struggling to deal with the loss of the only parent she had left, she was also heartbroken by the fact that she and her father's strained relationship hadn't ever really had a chance to fully heal.

Upon Kat's insistence, they'd all stayed at her dad's estate, rather than a hotel. Matt was more than a little okay with that, but only because it was more secure.

No further action had been taken against her in regard to the formula, but she'd also been under R.I.S.C.'s protection in the middle of the woods. Matt refused to take any chances with her safety. Especially now.

If he had it his way, they wouldn't even be here. Having her out in the open like this left him anxious as hell. But it wasn't like he could order her to miss her own father's funeral, which is why Jake had instructed Zade to accompany them on the trip as backup.

Matt turned his head on a swivel again, his gut tight as Zade stepped up beside him.

"Uh, oh. I know that look. What's up?"

With the crowd nearly gone now and Kat busy speaking to a very non-threatening, elderly woman, Matt felt it safe enough to move a few feet away, so the two ladies wouldn't overhear.

"Something about this whole thing feels…off."

Zade's brows furrowed behind the rim of his sunglasses. "Off, how?"

"That's the thing. I don't know."

"So talk it out."

That was one of the things Matt loved about Zade. The man was a badass in his own right. A former SEAL who'd seen and done things most couldn't even imagine. Yet there was still a sort of tenderness about him that brought with it a fresh outlook to the team.

Matt had teased him once about being the kind of guy girls left in a perpetual friend zone because he always wanted to talk about shit. Truth be told, Zade's uncanny way of knowing when someone needed a sounding board was one of the things Matt liked best about the guy.

"Maybe I'm seeing shit that isn't there, but this whole situation has been nagging at me."

"What's eating at you?"

"For starters, I don't like Kat being out in the open like this."

Zade gave a slight shrug. "It's her dad's funeral, Matt. Not like she'd miss it."

"My point exactly."

The other man frowned before looking out around them. "You think someone's going to try something here?"

Shoving his hands into the pockets of his black suit pants, Matt sighed. "I don't know. All I do know is I haven't talked to Marsh in over ten years. Suddenly, I go to confront him about what he did to Kat and me, and he ends up dying hours later, that very same day?"

Zade thought a moment. "The timing does seem a bit odd."

"My thoughts exactly."

A raspy female voice had both men's heads turning. With a casual, yet guarded step, a woman and a man—both appearing to be in their early-to-mid thirties—approached them. Matt immediately noticed their matching badges and guns.

"You Matthew Turner?" the man asked Matt.

"Do I know you?"

"Not yet"—the female answered—"but you will. I'm Detective Casey. This is my partner, Detective Holloway. We're with the Long Beach Police Department's homicide division."

The tightening in Matt's gut worsened. "Homicide?"

"That's right." Holloway looked back at him. "We'd like to ask you a few questions about your relationship with Mr. Marsh."

With a quick glance to make sure Kat was still preoccupied, Matt told the two detectives, "Pretty sure someone in your department got their wires crossed. Thomas Marsh died in a car accident. He wasn't murdered. Sorry you wasted a trip out here."

He and Zade had only just turned around when the woman said, "That's what the M.E. thought, too. At first."

Matt closed his eyes. *Ah, fuck.* Facing the detectives again, Matt said, "As you can see, Marsh's body was released for burial days ago. So, if there was some confusion in the paperwork or something—"

"Oh, there's no confusion," the woman said confidently. "We know for a fact the man in that casket was murdered."

A soft gasp hit Matt's ears, and he spun around to find Kat looking back at the two strangers, her jaw having dropped.

"Murdered? W-what are you talking about? There must be some mistake. My father was killed in an automobile accident."

"Ah, hell," Zade muttered under his breath.

"Someone went to a lot of trouble to make us think that, Miss Marsh." The woman stepped forward and offered Kat her hand. "Detective Casey, Long Beach Homicide. I'm sorry for your loss."

Woodenly, Kat took the woman's hand. "I don't understand. The police officer I spoke to the other day said my father lost control on a sharp curve, and his car rolled down an embankment. They said he...broke his neck."

"Three discs in your father's neck were broken," Casey confirmed. "However, after a review of the x-rays and autopsy notes, it was determined that the spinal cord injury your father sustained the day he died wasn't from the car accident. In fact, the reviewing doctor is quite certain your father was already dead when his car rolled down that embankment."

Kat reached for him, her delicate fingers digging into his bicep. "Someone k-killed my dad? Why...why are we just now hearing about this? Why wasn't this caught sooner?"

"We'll explain all that once we're able to sit down and talk."

The tremor in her voice pissed Matt off. "What's the matter with you two?" He took a wide step forward. "This couldn't wait until tomorrow?" Glancing behind him and back again, he glared down at the pair. "The man's not even in the ground yet."

A soft whimper met his ears, and Matt couldn't keep from pulling Kat into his arms. "It's okay, sweetheart. We'll figure all this out later."

"Actually..." Holloway began. "We need to figure it out now." To Kat he said, "I apologize for the timing, but as I'm sure you can imagine, we'd like to find whoever did this to your father as soon as possible. It would be a big help if you two could come down to the station with us to answer a few questions."

"Go to hell," Matt told the man bluntly. "We've done nothing wrong, and you have no cause to detain us." To Zade he said, "We're leaving. Now."

With a nod, Zade began making his way across the freshly cut grass to the paved road where they'd parked but stopped when the pushy woman began talking again.

"Mr. Turner, while I understand your hesitance to speak to us, it's really your best interest if we take care of this now rather than later." Detective Casey gave him a tight smile.

*Mr. Turner?* His gut was screaming now.

"How the fuck do you know who I am?" he demanded to know.

"Oh, we know a lot about you, Matthew. Who you are. What you do for a living." Holloway, the bastard, smirked. "What you and your team are capable of."

*Shit. Fuck. Shit.*

The whole scene stunk to high heaven. It also reminded Matt of a time not long ago when Derek had been pulled in by the DPD under the suspicion of murdering his now-wife's abusive ex.

Like Matt, D had been innocent, but while they'd questioned Derek about the supposed murder, his woman had been kidnapped. By the time anyone realized what had happened, Charlie—Derek's wife—had nearly been beaten to death.

*The fuck if something like that was going to happen to my woman.*

"I'm not leaving Katherine."

"See, that's where you're wrong." Casey pulled out a set of cuffs. "I don't want to do this here. Like this. But I will, if I have to."

"We got a report of a man matching your description being inside the house with Thomas Marsh the day he died."

"A report?" Matt raised a brow.

"Eyewitness places you at the residence. Said they knew who you were and described you to a T. They also said you and Marsh were involved in a pretty heated argument."

Matt didn't react, but his memory was working overtime. He didn't recall seeing anyone else in the house that day, other than Kat's dad. The only other person he'd spoken to was the guy who'd answered the intercom.

The house was large, however, so it was possible that man had been around, in the home's shadows. He could've been someone who worked for Marsh back in the day.

Matt should've been more aware of his surroundings, but he hadn't been thinking of that at the time. His total focus on confronting Marsh had overridden everything else that day.

Matt had been a man on a mission, determined to put

the guy in his place and not the voice on the other end of the speaker.

"I don't understand what's happening right now." Tears fell from Kat's eyes, her voice sounding as desperate as he felt.

"Miss Marsh, your boyfriend is the last known person to see your father alive. It's standard policy for us to question him in a case like this."

"And since you're the sole heir to his estate, Miss Marsh, we need to speak to you as well."

"You think I killed my own father?" Her voice raised into a high-pitched tone that had the handful of guests still in attendance glancing in their direction.

"You son of a bitch." Matt covered several inches of ground.

As they'd been trained, the detectives took a cautionary step back, their hands immediately going to the butt of their guns.

"I'd advise you to keep your distance, Mr. Turner," Holloway warned.

"And I'd advise you to kiss my ass, *Detective*."

"Everyone stop! Please." Kat stepped between them all and put a hand up. With a weary sigh, she set her gaze on Casey and Holloway. "Look, Detectives. I know you have a job to do, but Matt did not kill my father, and neither did I."

"If that's true, you two should have no problem coming to the station to talk with us."

Though he could tell it was the last thing she wanted, Kat nodded hesitantly. "Fine. We'll go. You can ask your questions, and we'll answer them. After that, you can quit wasting your time with us and find the real killer."

Damn. Not only was she smart, she was tough. *As tough as they come.*

"I'll go to the station, but you're not putting her in a goddamn interrogation room like some fucking criminal. You want to question Katherine, you can do it at her father's house." Not waiting for their response, Matt turned to Zade.

"I want you to drive Kat and..." He looked to the two detectives. "Which one of you will be questioning Katherine?"

It was clear neither one was happy about the way Matt had taken over, but he didn't give a flying fuck. If they wanted answers to their pointless questions, this was how they were going to get them.

"I'll go with Miss Marsh," Holloway told his partner. "You drive Turner to the station. When you're done with him, you can come by the Marsh estate and pick me up."

Still hesitant to concede to Matt's plan, Casey finally gave the other man a curt nod. "Fine. I'll text you when we're on our way."

Kat's eyes rose to meet his, her grief and anxiety-driven fear prevalent. Matt hated being separated from her, but knowing Zade had her covered helped some. Plus, even though he thought the guy was a dick, having Detective Holloway as an additional escort didn't hurt, either.

"I don't want to leave you," Kat told him softly.

"I know you don't, sweetheart." Matt cupped her cheek. "It's going to be okay. Zade will be with you the entire time, and I'll be back with you before you know it."

"They shouldn't be doing this to you." He caught a tear with his thumb. "I know you didn't hurt Dad."

That she trusted him so completely after everything they'd been through floored him. "You're right. Thank you for believing me. They will, too, as soon as I do their little dance." Wanting to end this shit show as soon as possible, he leaned in and kissed her forehead. "Go. Be as open and honest as you can be with them. I'll be with you again, soon."

With a squeeze to his wrist, Kat worried her brow but nodded. "Okay."

Pressing his lips against hers in a brief but meaningful kiss, Matt watched as she, Zade, and Detective Holloway walked away.

The second they were out of earshot, Matt looked down at Casey and said, "He upsets her any more than she already is, it'll be both your badges." Then, using his height to his advantage, he moved even closer to the pretty detective before adding, "And since you're so...*familiar* with what me and my team are capable of, I'm confident you know I can make that happen."

A slight twitch of her hazel eyes was the only sign his intimidation tactic had worked. It was enough.

"Follow me."

Detective Casey lifted her chin as she led Matt to her department-issued sedan. Within minutes they were on the road and headed to her district's station house.

They'd been on the road about ten minutes when the mounted police scanner crackled through the car's tense air.

"All units be advised, we have a ten-thirty-eight in progress. I repeat, we have a ten-thirty-eight in progress. Officer needs assistance, traveling northbound highway two-forty-one, west of Loma Ridge. Officer reports two vehicles attempting to force them off the highway. The vehicle the officer is in contains two civilians. All available units in the vicinity report to the scene, post haste."

Matt's stomach dropped as his head swung to face the detective. "Two-forty-one is the way to Marsh's estate. An officer and two civilians? It has to be them."

Thankfully, she didn't try to placate him by acting as though it could be someone else. Instead, she grabbed her phone from her pocket, he assumed so she could call her partner. The phone began to ring before she got the chance.

She shot him a look. "It's Holloway."

"Put it on speaker."

Fully aware he'd barked the order, Matt was more than grateful she hadn't started bitching about him not being in charge. Thankfully, she did as he asked.

"David? Are you guys all right? We heard the—"

"We're under attack!" the man's loud voice boomed through the phone's speakers. "Twin SUV's, black, no license plates. The windows are heavily tinted, so I can't tell how many suspects we're dealing with."

Casey's eyes widened slightly before becoming laser focused. Flipping a switch to activate her lights and sirens, she asked Holloway, "Where are you? Exactly?"

"Northbound Two-forty-one. At the northern edge of Loma Ridge, coming up on the Two-sixty-one overpass. King's doing his best to evade them, but they're boxing us in."

While her partner gave her their general location, Matt was already pulling up the tracker app he and every other R.I.S.C. operative had access to. It allowed them to locate each other's phones at any given time, in case of emergencies such as this.

"I've got 'em," he practically yelled. "According to this, they're ten miles ahead of us."

Because of the different routes they'd taken, Zade had hit the interstate a couple of minutes after leaving the cemetery, whereas Matt and Detective Casey had been stuck going through stop signs and stoplights on their way to the precinct. They'd been forced to make a U-turn and weave in and out of traffic, putting them even further behind the others.

Before Detective Casey could respond, a loud crashing sound like metal hitting metal came through her phone. It was immediately followed by a quick, high-pitched yelp.

"Katherine!" Matt yelled, terrified she'd been hurt.

"She's okay," Holloway hollered back. "Bastard slammed into us."

Though it was somewhat muffled, they could hear Zade's angry voice in the background.

"Fuck this defensive shit. I'm taking the shot!"

Matt held his breath as he heard several loud pops, tires squeal, and Zade's triumphant, "One down, one to go!"

*Come on, Zade. Keep her safe, man.*

A few silent, torturous moments passed before Holloway announced, "I think the other one's pulling back." The man sounded relieved. "Jesus. That was close."

"Take the next exit and get to the nearest public place." Matt thought of the tinted windows Holloway had described. "These guys aren't going to be seen."

He no more got the words out when Kat screamed again. "Zade, look out!"

A second crashing sound echoed from the other end of the phone, this one sharper. Louder. And then...nothing.

"David!" Detective Casey yelled for her partner, her face falling when she looked down at the screen and up at him. "The line just went dead."

"Call him back!" Shoving his hand into his pocket, Matt immediately tried Zade's phone. A powerful, tight pressure began pressing down his chest, right above his heart when his teammate didn't pick up.

"No one's answering," Detective Casey's eyes began to well.

He could barely breathe. "Fuck!" Matt slammed his hand down onto the dash. He checked the app again. "We're still seven miles out. Get us the fuck there, now!"

As she drove, the detective radioed dispatch to give them an update. Matt kept his focus on the flashing red dot on his phone. Before, it had been moving along the highway at higher-than-normal speeds. Now, it was showing Zade's phone off the road's shoulder, several yards away, in the grass.

For the first time in a very long time, Matt found himself praying.

*Please, God. Let them be okay.*

That last mile was the longest of his life.

"There!" His heart rate kicked into high gear as he pointed to a set of flashing lights. The responding patrolman had stopped near a portion of railing that had been damaged.

The metal was bent away from the road, as if it had been struck by a vehicle, and there were large ruts in the grass from where a set of tires had ripped it from its roots. Matt's blood turned cold when he spotted the car he'd rented in the grass, several yards away.

"Shit!" Detective Casey cursed as she slid to the shoulder before bringing the car to a skidding stop behind the other emergency vehicle.

Guns drawn, both she and Matt gave the area a quick scan, both re-holstering their weapons when they found no trace of the black SUV Holloway had described.

"Kat! Zade!" Matt took off on a sprint. Neither responded.

The car had evidently spun around, its front now facing the direction opposite the flow of traffic. The officer on scene was leaning down by the driver's door. He glance up at them from over his shoulder.

Matt opened his mouth to identify himself when Casey beat him to the punch.

"Detective Laurie Casey, Long Beach P.D. My partner, Detective Holloway is in that car!"

"He's...on the other side," the officer said hesitantly. "I'm sorry."

"What the hell do you mean, you're sorry?" The woman rushed around the car to the side her partner was on. From the loud cry of denial, Matt knew the man was already gone.

Focused on getting to his own people, his dress shoes slipping in the grass as he went. The other officer moved out of the way, and the second Matt saw Zade, he knew something was wrong. Very wrong.

"K-Kat...gone," his injured teammate stuttered, his voice strained with obvious pain. "Took her. C-couldn't... s-stop."

"He was more alert when I got here," the officer

explained from behind where Matt was now standing. "Said they were forced off the road, the car rolled. A man approached them when they came to a stop. Shot the officer in the head, shot your guy in the shoulder, and pulled a woman out of the back seat and took her. I tried getting him out, but the door's jammed shut. Fire's gonna have to pry it open."

*Ah, Jesus. They took her.*

Matt's legs damn near went out from beneath him. His world began to spin, but as hard as it was, he forced himself to remain focused. He had to stay strong. For Zade. For Kat.

Reaching inside the car, he put pressure on his teammate's wound to help stop the bleeding. Zade groaned loudly, the sound escaping through his clenched teeth.

From what he could tell, the bullet appeared to have missed anything major, but that didn't mean his teammate wasn't at risk for bleeding out.

"Sorry, man. But we need you to quit losing so much blood."

"S'okay," Zade whispered weakly. The man was pale and beginning to fade. Fast.

Tuning out Detective Casey's quiet sobs, Matt shot a look at the other officer and growled, "Where the hell is that ambulance?"

Just as he said it, they heard sirens approaching. While waiting for the paramedics to get the stretcher to them, he tried to get as much information as he could.

"Okay, man. The medics are here. They're gonna get you fixed up, good as new, but I need to know as much as you can remember before they take you. Did you see the man who shot you or who took Kat?"

The other man nodded, sweat beading on his creased forehead. "W-walk...er."

It took Matt a second to realize what Zade had meant. Once it clicked, his blood turned to ice. "Adrian Walker? *He's* the one who shot you and took Kat?"

Zade's eyes closed, but he gave another slight nod. "B-bastard said...tell...you...h-hi."

Matt felt like he was going to be sick.

"S-sorry." A tear fell from the corner of Zade's eye. "Tried...s-stop."

Wanting to cry himself, he held back for his teammate's sake. "Hey," Matt said sternly. "Not your fault, man. We're going to find her. You just worry about getting better."

"Okay," his teammate whispered. He closed his eyes again, having lost the battle to stay conscious.

Matt moved out of the way so Fire and EMS could work to get Zade extracted from the car and onto the stretcher. As they loaded him into one ambulance, Detective Holloway's body was transported in another.

At the top of the hill, a distraught Casey quickly gave her statement to a different detective who'd arrived on the scene. When she was finished, she slid a glance to Matt before climbing into the back to be with her partner as they took him to the county morgue.

In his own statement, Matt told the questioning detective how he and Zade had been hired to protect Katherine. Though he didn't go into specifics, only that she'd felt threatened after the break-in at her apartment, he shared everything he knew about Marsh's death—which pretty much nothing. And Matt also told the man the cliff notes version of what he knew about Adrian Walker.

After giving the man Jason Ryker's direct extension at Homeland and instructing him to call for further questions regarding Walker, Matt was driven to the hospital by yet another detective.

Every cell in his body burned with the need to be out there, searching for Kat. But as much as his heart screamed for him to do just that, Matt knew he couldn't find her on his own. Not without more intel.

Knowing exactly who could help with that, he'd called Jake on the way to the hospital and filled him in on what had happened. Since the company jet was still here, in California, Jake promised he and the others would be on the next flight out.

For the rest of the evening, while he waited for the doctor to come out with news on Zade, Matt plotted his revenge. Adrian Walker was a no-good fucking traitor to his country. Not long ago, he'd shot and damn near killed Nate, Matt's other friend and teammate. Walker had also kidnapped Gracie, the woman Nate was protecting—now his wife—and the bastard had delivered her to an even worse man for a profit.

Now the motherfucker had done it again. Only this time, Walker had taken Matt's woman. Where and why, he didn't know yet, but he would. And when he did... when he finally got his hands on Walker...

*I'm going to fucking kill him.*

# CHAPTER 12

Kat sat in one corner of the cold, empty room. With her knees pulled to her chest, she kept her arms wrapped tightly around her legs as she continued to pray.

Her head was pounding, from both the stress of the situation and the fact that she'd banged it pretty hard when they'd wrecked. The bleeding had finally stopped, the hair on the right side of her head caked with dried blood.

She couldn't see it, obviously, but Kat was pretty sure she could feel a nice gash hiding in the swollen flesh beneath her matted hair.

Her butt had gone numb long ago, which was the least of her concerns. She was too afraid to move. Afraid they'd hear her and know she was awake.

She had no idea what the man who'd taken her wanted. Did it have to do with the formula? Her father's death? Both?

The only thing she knew for certain was his name was Walker. And he was a ruthless, cold-blooded killer.

Blinking, Kat sent another tear down her already damp cheek. It seemed as if she'd done nothing but cry since she'd regained consciousness, and she hated it. Hated feeling so weak. But the tears didn't care. They simply kept coming.

As she held herself even tighter, Kat cried for her father. She'd been so confused by the detectives' claims that he'd been murdered. Still was. Now that she'd been brought to this place by that horrible, awful man, Kat understood she may never find the answers, she desperately needed.

More tears fell for Detective Holloway. The poor man had been completely defenseless when he'd been brutally gunned down. He wasn't even the slightest threat to the man who'd shot him. Who'd then taken and drugged her before shooting Zade.

It was a memory she knew would last a lifetime, however long that lifetime may be.

The metallic smell of blood continued to fill her nostrils as the horrific scene played over and over in her mind. Like a sadistic video set on loop.

They were all forced to sit there, trapped in the crushed and mangled car. Holloway's gun had flown out the window when they'd rolled, and he'd clearly become injured in the crash. None of that mattered. Not to the guy named Walker.

The man had simply walked up to the car, pointed his gun at Holloway's head. She could still hear Holloway begging for his life. Could hear herself and Zade pleading for Walker to stop.

Worse, she could still hear the deafening gunshot as

the gun's trigger was pulled—twice—ending Detective Holloway's life in an instant.

Kat squeezed her eyes shut in a feeble attempt to make the memory disappear. It didn't work. She'd never been more terrified than the moments immediately following, knowing with absolute certainty, she would be next.

As if it were happening right then, Kat could see the man coming toward her window. She knew he would shoot her in the head, the same way he had Holloway. But he hadn't.

Instead, for reasons she still didn't understand, Walker had leaned in so he could look at her through the back seat's shattered window. The maniac had actually smiled at her with a greeting that still chilled her to the bone.

*Hello, Doctor Marsh. It's great to finally meet you.*

When he pulled a large knife from a leather sheath at his belt, Kat had screamed.

Seeing the sharp, shiny blade coming at her, she'd wholeheartedly believed he was going to use it, rather than a bullet, to end her life.

Shock had reverberated through her entire body when the man sliced through her seatbelt, first at a spot across her chest and then at her waist, in order to free her. After sliding his knife back in place, he'd unceremoniously reached in, grabbed hold of her tightly, and pulled her through the broken window.

Kat had tried to fight back. She'd kicked and screamed, but it hadn't helped. Even so, the second her legs were free from the car, Kat had begun fighting again. That's when she felt the stinging sensation on the side of her neck.

She remembered hearing Zade shouting for her and cursing Walker's name. The former SEAL's voice had turned deadly. His tone deep and dark as he gave Walker a warning.

With utter confidence, Zade had told the evil man his team would hunt him down and kill him. Kat remembered praying he was telling the truth. But the thing that stuck with her the most was Walker's calm response.

*Ah, yes. Your team. Be sure to tell Turner I said hello.*

Another, ear-piercing gunshot blasted through the air. Kat had screamed and cried, certain he'd just shot Zade in the head like the other man.

But as the drugs kicked in, the last thing she remembered seeing was Zade's apologetic and pain-riddled face as he sat helpless in that car, bleeding and calling her name.

God, she hoped Matt had found him, and he was going to be okay. She couldn't bear the thought of the sweet man dying, too.

Later—she had no idea how much time had passed—she'd woken up here, in this room. The industrial-looking space wasn't overly large. About twenty by twenty if she had to guess. And minus her, it was completely bare.

As she sat there, fighting a migraine and staring at the concrete block walls, Kat covered her mouth to stifle her forceful sobs. Her shoulders shook as more tears fell. This time, they were for Zade. For herself. And for the life she and Matt never had the chance to explore.

Mostly, she cried because she knew he'd blame himself. The brief conversation between Zade and Walker ran through her aching mind again.

*My team will find you, Walker. And they will kill you.*

*Ah, yes. Your team. Be sure to tell Turner I said hello.*

The fact that Matt knew who this man was somehow made the situation even worse. Kat didn't understand how, but she knew in her gut the two had a history. A bad one.

By the time her cheeks had dried and she couldn't cry anymore, Kat thought her head would explode right off her shoulders. She'd finally said screw it and had gotten up a few minutes ago to check the room's only door. It was solid steel and, no surprise, was locked.

The one good thing about the cool, dank space...it was dark. Light was the worst thing for a migraine, so she was grateful for the silence, at least. Not much of a silver lining, but at this point, she'd take what she could get.

Though it was hard to think past the pain, Kat did her best to remain calm. When that man came back, she wanted to be alert. Focused. Ready to take advantage of any opportunity that might present itself. The opportunity to be free.

An hour or so later, the door opened, and the man called Walker returned. For the first time since he'd taken her, Kat got a really good look at him.

He wasn't the monster her mottled mind had created. Actually, wearing jeans, black boots, and a black t-shirt, he looked quite...normal. Handsome, even.

The cotton t-shirt strained as it covered a muscular chest and set of large, defined biceps. Standing a little taller than Matt, his sharp, symmetrical features, light brown hair, and a close-cut beard covering a strong jaw made Kat think this was a man most women would swoon over.

*Not this woman.*

"Hello, Doctor Marsh." He slowly moved closer. "Or, may I call you Katherine?"

Seriously? The guy kills one man, shoots another, and kidnaps her, and he's worried about pleasantries?

Standing, Kat pressed herself as far back against the wall as she could. "I don't give a shit what you call me, as long as you let me go."

Walker's light blue eyes glimmered as he smiled. "You've got spunk. I like that. I'm Adrian," he introduced himself as he made his way closer. He stopped directly in front of her.

"Adrian," Kat tried it on her tongue. "That's a fairly normal name for someone who is anything but."

He tilted his head to the side and smiled. "You remind me of another woman. One I met not long ago."

"Lucky me." Kat didn't bother asking what happened to that poor girl. She didn't *want* to know. One thing she did have the desire to learn, however, was, "Where am I?"

"Iran. Tehran, to be exact."

The man's matter-of-fact answer was like a punch to the gut. "I-Iran?" she stuttered. Holy shit. She was in even more trouble than she thought.

Rather than answer the redundant question, Walker raised his hand toward her face. Kat jerked her head away quickly to avoid his touch. She grimaced from a particularly painful throbbing the movement caused.

Adrian frowned. "I wasn't going to hit you." He almost sounded offended she'd think otherwise. "You were hurt in the crash. I can tell you're in pain, and I wanted to check to see if you needed medical attention."

Kat's heart thumped unforgivingly inside her chest as

she forced herself to remain still while he examined the wound. She watched him closely, his blue eyes assessing the damage to her scalp as if he actually gave a damn.

"W-why do you care?" She struggled to keep her voice steady. "You're just going to kill me, anyway."

His brows turned inward as he brought his gaze to hers. "I have no intention of killing you, Katherine. If I were going to do that, I would've left you in that car with the other two."

The image of Zade and Holloway in the car as she was being dragged away flashed behind her eyes. Nausea rolled in her gut from the knowledge that it was an image she'd literally never be able to forget.

"Then why am I here?"

"Come with me." He took a step back and gestured for the door. "I'll get you some medicine for that headache of yours. After that, we'll get you cleaned up and fed, and then I'll show you exactly why you are here."

Kat's eyes slid to the open door and back to Walker. Her mind whirled with the possibility that this was some sort of test. That he was trying to see if she'd run so he could chase her down.

He must have caught on to what she was thinking, because he lowered his hand and sighed. "This isn't a trick, Katherine. That cut on your head needs to be treated before it becomes infected, and you'll be of no use to us if you pass out from pain or hunger. At the very least, you have to be dying of thirst."

Well, crap. She hadn't really noticed it until he said something. Now it was all Kat *could* think about.

Swallowing against her dry throat, she lifted her chin.

"Fine." She started for the door. "But you should know people are out there looking for me. And they won't stop until they find me." God, she prayed that was the truth.

"People like Matt?"

Kat's chest tightened, her steps faltering before she turned to face him. "H-how do you know him?"

Walker smirked. "Oh, Turner and I go way back. And, unless he's changed a whole hell of a lot, I'm sure he'll do everything he can to find you."

Something flickered behind his eyes, but Kat couldn't decipher what it was. She was also confused by the tone in Walker's voice. He almost sounded hopeful, which made absolutely no sense, whatsoever.

At this point, she was just praying Matt found her before this man—and whoever else was part of the 'us' he'd referred to—did whatever it was they were planning to do.

"Let's go get you taken care of. After all, you've got a lot of work to do."

* * *

MATT SAT IN THE HOSPITAL'S EMERGENCY SURGICAL waiting room, out of his mind with worry.

Zade had been in surgery for hours. He was still in there. Lying on that goddamn table, fighting for his life. And Kat...

Christ, Matt could barely breathe for the fear he felt for her. Knowing Adrian Walker—of all fucking people—had even laid a finger on her filled him with more terror than Matt had ever known.

And all he could do was sit here and wait. Wait for the

doctor to come out and tell him whether or not his teammate and friend was going to make it. Wait for Jake and the others to arrive so they could put a plan of action together. Wait and wonder if he'd ever see Katherine again.

He was tired of fucking waiting.

Matt started to run a hand over his face when he realized he still had Zade's blood on him. He'd been so out of it since the detective had dropped him off he hadn't even noticed.

Staring down at the rust-colored stains, he noted they were darker where the blood had settled in the creases. When Walker shot Nate a while back, Matt had been worried then, too. Nate was every bit as important to him as Zade. As much a brother as any of the other Bravo or Alpha Team operatives.

The difference was Matt hadn't been on the scene minutes after Nate was shot. He hadn't put pressure on the guy's wound like he had Zade's. Nate's frantic pulse hadn't been beating beneath Matt's palms the way Zade's had.

His frantic thoughts turned to Kat, and for the millionth time, he wondered what she was going through. Was she okay? Had she been hurt?

They had to find her. They *had* to.

"We will."

The confident voice broke through Matt's thoughts. Startled, he looked up to see Jake standing over him, along with Derek and Gabe. He'd apparently been so lost in his own thoughts he hadn't realized they'd arrived. Or that he'd said those words aloud.

"Boss." Matt stood. "This is all my fault. I'm the one

who told Zade to take her to her dad's place instead of us all going to the station together."

"But you weren't the one who pulled the trigger." Jake stared back at him. "So put that shit away. There's no place for it here."

Swallowing hard, Matt nodded. "You're right. Sorry."

"Any news on King?" Gabe asked anxiously.

Matt shook his head. "Not yet."

Gabe tipped his chin to Matt's hands. "That his?"

He glanced down at his palms once more. "Yeah. I held pressure until the paramedics took over. I tried to stop the bleeding, but...I'm not sure it was enough."

"It was."

All four men turned to see a weary doctor had entered the room. Matt pushed his way through the others. "You Zade's doctor? How is he? Is he okay?"

Removing the thin, paper cap from the top of his head, the older man looked down at Matt's hands . "I assume you're Matthew Turner?"

"Yes."

"Thought so. Mr. King said you'd kept pressure on his wound. He's been asking for you."

"So, he's okay?"

The doctor's mouth turned up slightly. "Not sure I'd use that particular term to describe your friend's condition, but yes. Rather, he will be."

There was a collective sigh amongst the group. Matt's legs shook with relief as the doctor eyed them carefully. "You Mr. King's...family?"

"As close as." Jake stepped forward. After making a quick introduction and explanation as to how they knew

Zade, the doctor nodded. "Thought you all looked military."

"Used to be," Derek drawled.

"Tell us what you know about Zade," Matt ordered gruffly.

"Well," the exhausted doctor exhaled loudly. "The bullet missed all major organs, but it nicked one of his arteries." His knowing eyes filled with empathy. "That's why you had such a hard time getting the bleeding to stop. Anyway, as you can probably guess, repairing it was a delicate procedure. The bullet also hit his right clavicle. That damage to the bone was fairly extensive, but we managed to piece it back together. He's in a brace to keep the bone immobile, which he'll need to wear for six to eight weeks. In addition, he'll need physical therapy to help regain the strength in that shoulder and his surrounding muscles before resuming normal activity."

Matt thought of Zade's job as one of the team's snipers. The guy was going to go stir-crazy waiting to get back in the game, but at least he was alive to play it.

"Can we see him?"

The doctor looked at his watch. "He should be in his room shortly." He gave them the number. "I do warn against staying too long. Mr. King has been given some pretty strong pain medications and needs his rest in order for his body to begin healing."

"Understood." Jake shook the doctor's hand. "Thank you."

Matt nodded to the man, too. "Thanks."

With a tired nod, the man went about his business while Matt and the others made their way up to the floor where Zade had been admitted.

After a quick stop at the restroom to wash his hands, the four men entered their friend's room.

"Man, King." Derek shook his head at Zade before smirking. "You look like ass."

With a drowsy smile, Zade lifted his left hand and flipped Derek the bird. "Fuck you...too," he slurred weakly. His eyes turned to Matt's.

"Kat?"

"We, uh…" Matt swallowed hard, hating that he'd let both his teammate and Kat down. "We don't know yet. Jake and the guys just got here when the doctor came to tell us you're going to be okay. We came straight up here."

"I called Homeland as soon as Matt told me what happened," Jake informed Zade. "Ryker's working on pulling shit together for us as we speak."

"Walker." Zade's voice sounded dry and scratchy as he said the bastard's name.

"We know." Gabe stepped a little closer to the bed. "We're on it, Z. Don't worry. We're gonna catch the bastard this time. The only thing you need to focus on is getting better."

"I've made arrangements with Long Beach P.D. to have an officer stand guard outside your room," Jake spoke up again. "Just as a precaution. I don't think Walker will come after you. If he wanted you dead, we'd be visiting you in a totally different kind of room."

Matt flinched at the thought of how easily his friend could've been killed.

"And on that pleasant note"—Derek tipped an invisible hat to Zade—"We should probably let you get some rest. Take it easy, King."

"D's right." Jake nodded. "We'll check back in later with an update."

"Take care of yourself, brother," Gabe instructed Zade. "The team won't be the same until you're back."

Zade gave them all a dazed smile. "Thanks."

Matt started to follow the other three out but stopped just inside the door. "Give me a minute?"

Jake gave him a knowing glance. "We'll be in the hall."

Waiting until the door shut to turn back around, Matt faced the man he'd almost gotten killed.

"Stop."

Zade's order surprised him. "Stop what?"

"Blaming yourself."

The other man cleared his throat before licking his dry lips, the actions kicking Matt's ass in gear.

"Shit. Sorry." He rushed to the wheeled tray where Zade's nurse had placed a pitcher and cup, both filled with ice water. "Here."

After helping his friend take a good, long drink, Matt set the lidded cup back down, making sure it was within Zade's reach.

"Thanks. Feels like I've been swallowing fucking rocks."

Matt grinned, but his lips fell quickly.

"I said, stop," Zade ordered again.

"Can't help it, man." Matt looked down at him. "I put you in that car. If we'd all gone to the station together—"

"They would've found us on the way." Zade blinked slowly, his speech becoming more slurred. "Walker wanted Kat. Would've followed her wherever she went."

Logically, Matt knew his friend was right. Didn't make it any easier to stomach, though.

"He say anything else? Give you any indication of where he might be taking her?"

Zade shook his head. "No. Sorry. I tried to get to my gun, but it was knocked out of my hand. Flew to the floorboard. Couldn't reach it."

Picturing the image Zade's words created made Matt sick. "Nothing to be sorry for. I'm the one who screwed up. But I promise, I'm going to find Walker and make him pay for what he did. To you and Holloway. To Kat." His voice cracked, but he cleared it away. "You're lucky as hell, you know that, right?" He blinked against the sudden burning in his eyes.

"I know." Zade's head swished against the rough, white pillowcase as he nodded, but then he frowned at Matt's expression. "What?"

"Don't get me wrong." Matt shook his head. "I'm glad as fuck that you're alive and, for the most part, okay. But I don't get why Walker killed Holloway but let you live."

Zade swallowed and took a breath. "Needed me alive."

"Why?"

"So I could give you his message."

Matt thought of those infuriating words again. *Tell Turner I said hello.*

His blood boiled. "The bastard's toying with me. He wanted to be sure I knew *he* was the one who took Kat. That he's involved in this."

Zade nodded again, this time barely able to keep his eyes open.

The guy needed to sleep. "Listen, man. I'm gonna go. Get some rest and don't give the cute nurses a hard time."

A weak chuckle escaped the back of Zade's throat, but

then he winced. "If you see any...let me know. Now go. Get your ass...out of...here. Find...your girl."

"I will," Matt promised his friend. Because for him, there was no other option.

## CHAPTER 13

Kat waited anxiously for Walker's return. Not that she really wanted him to. She just needed to figure out why she was here.

Pacing the empty room she'd been brought to over an hour ago, Kat wracked her brain to figure out what the hell was going on. First, she's drugged and kidnapped, then the same man who'd shot Zade and left him for dead had been incredibly gentle while seeing to her cut.

The maniac had even taken her to a bathroom first, allowing her to shower so she could wash the blood from her hair. After she'd gotten dressed, he'd instructed her to sit on the closed toilet while he numbed the area up with lidocaine. Once she could no longer feel the poke of the needle, he proceeded to give her eleven stitches.

It was hard as hell to sit still when he'd come at her with that damn needle, but it wasn't like she'd had much choice. He'd stood between her and the bathroom door, and she knew from experience he was much too strong for her to take on by herself.

Part of her wanted to ask where he'd learned to administer sutures, but she didn't. Instead she'd kept her mouth shut, praying he knew what the hell he was doing.

*I'm so over getting poked in the head. Twice in less than two weeks was two too many.*

When that was taken care of, he brought her here, to this room. It was almost identical to the one she'd woken up in. Except this one housed a small, square table—like the ones people used for playing cards—and a metal folding chair.

Sitting on the table was a Styrofoam container, still half-full of the dinner he'd provided. It was some sort of chicken and rice dish, the seasonings on it good, but unfamiliar. He'd also given her a large cup of ice water.

Like with the lidocaine, Kat had been leery to try the food and water at first. Sensing her suspicions, Walker had opened the container and used the plastic spoon inside to scoop up a good amount before taking a bite.

Assuming the man wouldn't drug himself, she'd felt fairly safe to eat a few bites after that. Truth be told, her stomach needed it to help with the digestion of the over the counter, extra-strength migraine medicine he'd somehow managed to obtain.

The entire scenario was bizarre, to say the least.

While being escorted to the different rooms, Kat had committed every detail she could to memory. From what she could tell, she was in some sort of warehouse. The question was where.

She was still pacing the small room when the door opened, and Adrian Walker stepped back in.

"I trust you've eaten your fill?"

Kat stopped moving and nodded. "Yes. Thank you."

It went against everything inside her to be nice to this man, but after the hospitality he'd shown her—god, it was hard to even think that way without choking—Kat figured it was in her benefit to be polite. At least, for now.

Her appreciation made him smile. "You're welcome. Follow me, it's time to show you why you're here."

Fingers and toes tingling with fear and adrenaline, Kat did her best to remain calm, as she followed Walker out of the room and down the long hallway. After crossing a large, spacious area with rows of windows up high, near the ceiling, he took her to yet another room.

When he opened this one, however, Kat's blood turned cold.

"What the hell?" she muttered as she slowly stepped inside. She blinked, her mind trying to make sense of what she was seeing.

"It's…my lab."

"As close as we could get to it, anyway."

Kat absentmindedly ran her fingertips across the familiar, metal countertops. Her eyes scanned the sizable room and all the equipment in it. With a few minor exceptions, she was staring at an exact replica of the lab she worked in at Anderson Biomeds.

"H-how?" She faced Walker. "How did you do this?"

"We had some help."

Kat's memory flashed back to the conversation she'd had with Matt the day they'd first made love. As adults, that is. Her heart had broken as she sat in his arms, listening to him explain the evidence Derek had found against Todd.

"Todd helped set this place up?"

"In a manner of speaking." Walker nodded. "Kennedy

sent us pictures, along with a list of essential equipment and supplies that would be needed for the job."

"I can't believe he associated himself with you."

The man shrugged. "People do all sort of things you wouldn't expect them to when they're desperate. Make them an offer they can't refuse, and they'll do just about anything you want."

Kat thought of the explosion. "Did he set the explosion in the lab on purpose?"

"He did."

"Why?"

"Why do you think?"

She felt sick. "To kill me?"

Walker gave her a single nod.

"The text?" she asked, knowing he'd understand.

Again, Walker nodded. "My boss is a little…inept when it comes to using modern phones. He also tends to rush things."

"That's why he sent the go-ahead to steal the formula to my phone by accident. He transposed the last two numbers."

"I'm afraid so. After that, the job became more about damage control. And when that happened…"

"I became a target."

"Yes." Walker shoved his hands into his jeans. "Kennedy explained how, since you were the head engineer on the project, your computer was the only one with full access to the entire formula, notes, and data. You were also the only one with the access codes needed to obtain it all. He was supposed to get you out of the way so he could take your place."

Todd was the next one in line for the position. If she'd

died, the job automatically would have gone to him, along with all the access codes.

"We were hoping to wait until the formula was stable enough to be fully effective, but my boss is also very impatient. He took it upon himself to text Todd, or rather you, which set off the unfortunate chain of events. When Todd blew himself and the entire lab to pieces, he also inadvertently destroyed the one thing my boss wanted."

Kat studied the man a moment. "Were you the one in my apartment?"

"Yes. I'd hoped to find instructions on how to create the formula to avoid all...this." He gave her a sad smile. "Unfortunately that didn't happen."

"I'd never bring something like that home with me," Kat told him. "It's too dangerous. If something like that were to fall into the wrong hands—"

She cut herself off when she realized how stupid she sounded, given her circumstances.

Walker continued on with his explanation. "Since the lab and all the data was destroyed in the explosion, and you didn't bring it home with you, that left one other option." His knowing eyes stared back at her.

"You want me to recreate the formula here." She glanced around the room. "That's why your boss constructed this lab. You know about my eidetic memory."

The man smiled before looking over his shoulder. "See? Told you she was as smart as they said."

"She'd better be."

A second man entered the room. One she'd never seen before. *Walker's boss.*

Older than her by several years, Kat guessed him to be

in his late fifties or early sixties. In a black button-up shirt and khaki dress slacks, he reminded her of a modern-day grandpa. Somewhat elderly yet stylish.

He was olive-skinned with white hair that was parted neatly to one side. His matching beard was short and well-groomed, and his dark eyes oozed of intelligence.

As he stood there, staring back at her with the same assessing glance she'd been giving him, Kat noted an air about him. One that said this was a man of power.

*The guy orchestrated this entire, crazy situation in order to replicate a super-soldier formula commissioned by the U.S. government. So, yeah...he's powerful.*

Resisting the urge to roll her eyes at herself, Kat kept her head held high, refusing to allow this man to see the fear threatening to destroy her.

"Doctor Marsh." The other man greeted her. "It's a pleasure to finally meet you."

Recognizing his accent as Middle Eastern, she gave him a tight smile. "Too bad I can't say the same of you."

Though he didn't react with anger, Kat could see it brewing behind those terrifying eyes. Walker, however, didn't bother to hide his smirk.

"Gonna have your hands full with this one, Bukhari."

*Bukhari. Why did that name sound familiar?*

"I see you recognize the name," the older man surmised.

Kat shrugged. "Sounds vaguely familiar."

"As it should." He came closer. "I am General Rajif Bukhari, leader of the most feared Iranian military force in existence."

Of course, he was. Kat half expected a round of

dramatic music to start playing in the background. *Duh... duh...duhhhhh.*

"I won't help you," she told him bluntly.

He smirked. "Yes. You will."

"No." Kat shook her head. "I won't." She was telling him the truth. She'd rather die than help this man do anything that could harm American lives. Especially those of American soldiers.

Bukhari continued closer until he was standing directly in front of her. His dark eyes smoldered with anger as he glared. "You will do exactly what I say, when I say it. Starting with making a list of chemicals or whatever else you need to make the serum."

Though her knees shook with fear, Kat called upon her inner strength to keep him from seeing it. This man had manipulated Todd into helping him by using his wife's horrible situation against him. He'd also ordered Kat's murder.

When that failed, he'd then orchestrated a plan of attack on the day of her father's funeral. His hired gun had killed a police detective, shot Matt's teammate, and taken her hostage.

Kat wasn't naive enough to think this ended with anything but her death. Because of that, she wasn't going to play nice.

Lifting one corner of her mouth, she formed her best smart-ass smirk. "Or what?" she asked the arrogant prick "You'll kill me? You do that, you'll also kill your chances at the serum. Of course, you may be able to find another scientist to create something similar, but it will be years before that happens." She looked up at his white hair and back at him. "Not sure you'll still be around to see it."

A muscle beneath his white beard bulged, his tanned skin becoming red with anger. "This is the problem with you American women. You believe you have the right to speak to a man this way."

She resisted the urge to roll her eyes at the man's ridiculous way of thinking.

"I also believe I have the right to not be kidnapped and held against my will," Kat shot back. "This formula was created with the sole purpose of saving American soldier's lives. If you think I'm going to help you use it *against* the United States, you're not as smart as *you* claim to be."

Moving quickly, Bukhari grabbed her jaw in a painful grip. With his nose nearly touching hers, his hot breath hit her face as he said, "You will learn to watch your tongue while speaking to me, Doctor Marsh."

Without thinking, Kat gathered as much spit in her mouth as she could and let it fly. Rearing back, the misogynistic asshole released her chin to wipe the moisture from his face.

Enraged, he swung his hand toward her head, the movement so fast and unexpected, Kat didn't have time to move out of the way. Fire erupted in her left cheek and eye as he backhanded her. The force of the blow sent her flying to the side.

Her hip slammed into the edge of the metal counter, her body ricocheting down to the concrete floor. Kat groaned as she tried to regain her bearings. White stars flashed before her, and the headache that had started to dissipate returned with a vengeance.

"You will help me, or your father won't be the only man in your life to die."

Her father? She looked up at him, his image blurred from the tears in her eyes. "You k-killed my father?"

"I had him killed." The monster shrugged. "I needed a way to bring you out into the open again."

Dizziness struck, making Kat feel as though she were going to be sick. Through the ringing in her ear, she heard Bukhari's command as he walked past Walker on his way out of the lab.

"Make sure she understands the choice is not hers to make and then put her ass to work."

Kat was still on the floor when Walker crouched down beside her.

"You shouldn't have done that," he stated quietly.

Tears covered her cheeks. "I won't help you," she choked out. Pushing herself to her feet, she wiped her face, wincing when her fingers brushed against the already-bruising skin. "I won't."

Rising with her, Walker started to raise his hand to her face but stopped when Kat flinched out of the way. He looked back at her with disappointment. "He will kill you if you don't."

"The second I put that formula together and create the serum for him, I'm dead anyway."

Walker nodded. "At least that death will be swift. Painless. But if you continue to fight him, he will do things to cause a level of pain you can't even imagine. Trust me. I've seen it happen."

"I don't care."

He studied her more closely. "I believe you. However, you *do* care about Turner, yes?"

*Your father won't be the only man you care about to die.*

"Oh, god." Kat held a hand against her mouth, forcing

223

her throat to work the rising bile back down into her stomach. "Was it you? Did you kill my father?" His silence was his answer. "You son of a bitch!"

Her hand swung at his face, but Walker avoided the blow easily by grabbing hold of her wrist. When she tried beating him with her other fist, he held onto that arm as well.

"Why?" She sobbed while trying to pull herself free. "He had nothing to do with this!"

Keeping his grasp firm, he answered her honestly. "You have your orders from Bukhari. So, do I. And if you don't make that serum, I'll have no choice but to kill your boyfriend."

He released her wrists and took a step back. Kat wanted to go after him again, but knew it was pointless. Physically, she was no match to this man.

"Why are you doing this?" she demanded to know through her tears. "For money?" Kat spit the word out as if it were a curse.

Walker shrugged. "Why else?"

"But you're an American!" She shook her head in disbelief.

Something flashed behind his eyes. "I *used* to be an American. Now, I don't belong to anyone but myself."

Kat stared back at him, dazed from both the pain in her head and the unbelievable situation. The man started for the door.

"For the record," he spoke while keeping his back to her, "I don't want to kill Matt. But I will, if I have to." Walker stopped at the room's entrance to face her again. "Figure out the formula, Doc. Make the serum and give it to Bukhari. Sooner you do, the sooner this is all over for you."

With those parting words of devastating wisdom, the man who'd taken everything from her walked out, locking the door behind him.

*He hasn't taken everything. Not yet.*

But he would. If she didn't do as Bukhari ordered, Kat had no doubt the man would make good on his threats. Walker would kill Matt without so much as blinking an eye. She believed that wholeheartedly.

"Oh, god."

Kat raced to the nearest trashcan, barely reaching it in time to empty the contents of the meal she'd consumed earlier. When the painful retching ended, she stumbled over to one of the metal stools brought in as part of Bukhari's sick twisted recreation.

What was she going to do? If she refused to help, she and Matt would both die, and the psycho would find another scientist who would eventually recreate the serum, anyway.

If she did go along with his plan and made the serum, he'd kill her the second she handed it over.

"Either way, I'm dead."

In her heart, Kat knew this to be true. But at least with that last scenario, there was a good chance Matt would stay alive.

He'd be crushed by her death, but at least he'd have a life. He could go on working with Bravo to save who knows how many innocent lives. Maybe, over time, he'd even find love again.

Fresh, hot tears poured over her bottom lids as Kat realized what she had to do. Once again, she was in an impossible position, forced to make a choice that wasn't really a choice at all.

Though she'd buy herself as much time as she possibly could, Kat would begin working to recreate the super-soldier serum for Bukhari. Not because she was afraid of what he'd do to her if she refused. But because she was terrified of what Adrian Walker would do to Matt.

Kat made her decision. She had to protect Matt again. There was no other way. This time, however, instead of giving up her hopes and dreams in order to keep him safe, she'd be paying for his protection with her life.

# CHAPTER 14

Two days. It had been two fucking days and there was still no trace of Kat.

Sitting on Gabe's couch, Matt looked through the Homeland file they still had on Adrian Walker from when the bastard had shot Nate and taken Gracie a few months back. He'd read it forward and backward a dozen times over the past two days, as if something new would magically appear.

With a growl, Matt closed the folder and threw it across the room.

Sitting in an overstuffed chair across the room, Derek looked at him from over his laptop and drawled, "I take it you're done with that one?"

Matt shot up from the couch and glared at the former SEAL. "Kat's been missing for two goddamn days, Derek. This isn't the time for fucking jokes."

"Easy, man. Just tryin' to lighten the mood."

"There isn't a way to lighten the fucking mood." Matt began pacing the small, open living room.

"I'm just glad Nate doesn't know what's going on," Kole muttered from Gabe's kitchen table. "That shit with Walker taking Gracie is still too fresh for him. He'd be going about as apeshit as you are if he were here."

With Zade out of commission and Jake taking some time to check on his pregnant wife, Kole had stepped out from behind the scenes to see what, if anything, he could do to help. Matt was more than grateful for the extra set of eyes. He only wished they'd see something that would help them find Kat and bring her home.

"I feel like we're wasting our time." Matt ran a hand over his growing scruff. "This is all shit we already knew. There's nothing here to help us find Walker or who hired him."

Gabe came into the room. "Yeah, well…until we get something new, it's all we've got to go on." He used his thumb to point behind him. "I put shit out for sandwiches in case anyone wants something to eat."

"I'm game." Kole stood and stretched. "Haven't eaten since breakfast this morning. I'm starved."

The young sniper walked into the kitchen, but Matt remained where he stood. His gut had been churning like crazy with worry for Kat. Last thing he wanted to do was eat.

"You should get a bite, too, Matt," Gabe suggested. "I don't remember the last time I saw you eat something."

"I'm good."

Gabe's intense gaze locked on his. "You're no good to her if you don't keep your strength up."

"Appreciate what you're trying to do, Dawson, but I don't need a fucking mother hen telling me when to eat."

"I get it, man, but you can't let yourself—"

"You get it?" Matt crossed the room until he was in his team leader's face. "Really? Your woman's been kidnapped and held against her will by a sadistic fucking killer? You've had to listen to her screams as she was under attack, and then sit around with your thumb up your ass for days on end because you had no idea where the fuck your girlfriend was or how to even start looking for her?"

"No," Gabe admitted. "I don't know what it's like to have my girlfriend taken and held hostage."

"Exactly." Matt stared him down. "So, until that day comes—"

"I do know, however"—Gabe cut him off— "what it's like to have my *wife* taken hostage. To know she was being held at gunpoint by a group of punks spazzed out of their minds on drugs and not be able to do a fucking thing to help her."

The room went silent.

"Your wife?" Matt frowned. "I didn't think you were married."

"I'm not." The formidable man's face fell slightly. "Not anymore."

Matt blinked and took a step back. "Shit, Gabe. I'm... sorry. I didn't know."

"Not many people do."

"What happened?" Kole asked as he stood in the kitchen entryway finishing what was left of his sandwich.

Gabe sighed, resting his hands on his hips. "It was a long time ago. I was away on an op. It went flawlessly, and on the plane ride back, we made plans to celebrate." He shook his head and let out a humorless laugh. "We were halfway over the Atlantic Ocean when my commander called me on the sat phone. Said the bank where my wife worked at the time was being robbed. Guys had automatic rifles. They'd already taken out the bank manager, the security guard, and two customers."

"Ah, shit."

Their team leader nodded. "Those were my first words to him when he called. Later, when I asked why he didn't wait until we were home to tell me, he said he made the call because, if it were his wife, he'd want to know."

After several seconds of silence, Matt swallowed and started to ask the hard question. "Did they…"

"SWAT breached before they could hurt anyone else. Ellena made it out unharmed. Physically, anyway."

The other men's relief was palpable. "That's good."

"Very good." Gabe smiled sadly. "Elle survived, but unfortunately our marriage didn't." He looked around the room. "I only shared that with you, so you'd understand I do know what you're going through. Maybe not the exact same scenario, but—"

"Close enough." Matt gave his friend an apologetic look. "Sorry, man. I'm going out of my mind sitting around, waiting for something new to pop up."

"It just did!" Derek announced excitedly.

All heads turned in his direction.

"What is it?" Matt rushed over. "Did you find Walker?"

"No, but I found the next best thing. Remember I told you I've been working trying to locate the holder of the account that Todd Kennedy's payoffs originated from?"

He nodded, his excitement matching the other man's. "You found the guy?"

"Took a hell of a lot longer than I thought it would. Whoever set this account up was good. Like, almost better than me, good. They knew how to encrypt and reroute... I've been chasin' my tail for days tryin' to—"

"Derek!" Matt purposely raised his voice. "Who's name is on the account?"

With a sly grin, Derek turned his computer around for Matt to see. "Sloane Anderson."

"Kat's boss?" Kole asked from behind Matt's shoulder.

"And her former father-in-law." Matt nodded. "That son of a bitch."

"Wait." Kole sat his paper plate down onto the table. "Why would the guy steal from his own company? Wouldn't that destroy his business?"

"Wouldn't matter," Derek explained. "I've seen his company's financials. Selling that formula to the right people would make him a hell of a lot more money than he's making now."

"What about the government contract?" Gabe asked.

Derek snorted. "You know how our government works. They're not going to pay any more than they have to. Another country's a different story."

Matt agreed, "Especially if that country hates the U.S. and plans to use the serum to have stronger forces against us. Countries like that have almost zero regulations when it comes to spending. Even if they didn't, they'll fork over the money if it means taking down our military."

"Anderson must be slated to make fucking bank on this deal," Kole surmised.

Derek nodded. "That's my guess."

"You got an address?" Gabe asked in full team leader mode.

"Already entered into my phone's GPS app."

To Gabe, Matt asked, "When do we leave?"

Three hours later, under the cover of the night sky, Matt and the others made their way across Anderson's vast back yard. Dressed all in black, they kept their guns at the ready as they prepared to breach the private residence.

According to Derek, shutting down Anderson's security system had been child's play. Seeing how it took the guy less than two minutes to hack in and disable the property's entire system, Matt believed him.

Kole had laughed, commenting on how Anderson should've paid as close attention to keeping his home secure as he had hiding the electronic trail that led them here in the first place. Matt was just thankful they were here because that meant they were one step closer to finding Kat.

After a semi-silent entrance through the home's back door, the team walked in the same, straight-line formation they'd use on any other op. Once they'd cleared the spacious main level, the four men spread out as planned.

Kole and Derek took the basement while Matt and Gabe held their positions in the home's entryway. Some may think it unnecessary to take such lengthy precautions but keeping each other safe was never a waste of time.

After all, Anderson was involved in a plot to steal a formula, which if sold to the wrong person, could cost American soldiers' lives. No way in hell would Matt or anyone else enter this bastard's home without being prepared for the worst.

Once those areas were found to be clear, the team made its way upstairs. Brian, Kat's deceased husband, had been Sloane Anderson's only child, and the man had been divorced for several years. According to everything Derek could find on the guy, he wasn't currently involved in a romantic relationship of any kind, which meant he would most likely be sleeping alone. Still, like with everything else R.I.S.C. related, the guys took nothing for granted.

After clearing the other upstairs rooms, the team stopped outside the set of large, double doors. With Derek having already accessed the floor plans to the home, they knew this was the master suite.

With a single nod, Gabe gave him the go-ahead. Matt wrapped his gloved hand around one of the doors' knobs, took a breath, and opened the door. Flipping off the flashlight mounted on his gun to help with the element of surprise, Matt got as close to Sloane Anderson's sleeping form as he could before pressing the end of the barrel to the man's forehead.

Grimacing, it took the drowsy man a few seconds to realize what had woken him. As soon as he saw Matt and the others, his eyes grew round with fear.

"What the hell?" Anderson yelled as he scrambled to get away from Matt—and his gun.

"Don't move, asshole." Matt shifted his gun lower, pointing directly at the man's heart.

"W-who the hell are you?" Anderson stammered. "What do you want?"

"Who hired you to steal the formula?" Matt got straight to the point.

"Formula? W-what formula?"

"Don't play fucking games with me," Matt growled. Pushing the barrel into the guy's chest, he demanded, "Who. Hired. You?"

"I swear, I don't know what you're talking about!"

Not in the mood to deal with this shit, Matt flipped

the safety on his gun, swung it around so it hung off his shoulder, and reached for Anderson. Filling both fists with the front of the asshole's shirt, Matt picked him up and tossed him to the carpeted floor.

"Ah!" Sloane cried out as he landed with a thud. "Stop!" He tried crab-walking backward. "Y-you can't do this!"

"Oh, I can." Matt followed him slowly. "And I will."

"I have money! In a safe in my office downstairs. It's all yours if you'll just go and leave me alone."

For some reason, that pissed Matt the hell off. "You think this is about money?" He towered over the asshole. Using only one hand this time, Matt reached down and dragged him to his feet. "I don't want your fucking money, Anderson. I want the name of the person who hired you to pay off Todd Kennedy."

"I d-don't—"

Matt's tight fist cut the lie off as he threw the man to the floor. Ignoring Anderson's grunts and groans, he lifted him off his feet again, this time shoving the traitorous prick against the bedroom window. The glass cracked from the pressure.

"Stop fucking lying, you sack of shit," Matt growled in the man's face. "You paid Kennedy to steal the formula, and then you paid him to try and kill Katherine Marsh."

"No, I-I—"

Matt pulled his pistol from his holster and shoved the barrel beneath Anderson's chin. "You think I'm playing?"

"N-no." The man swallowed hard.

"Good. We know about the secret bank account and that you made two large transfers into one of Todd Kennedy's. We also know he used that money to pay off most of his wife's medical bills. You found out she was sick and saw that as your in. Didn't you?"

When the man didn't answer immediately, Matt moved his gun away from his face, pointed it at the floor, and pulled the trigger. The bullet hit an inch from Anderson's foot. The man screamed and jumped like a little bitch. Then he pissed all over his expensive silk pajama pants.

"Next one takes off a few toes."

"All right, all right! I'll tell you."

Matt slid a glance to the others who were ready to have his back, if needed, but were also giving him the space he needed to get the answers they'd come for.

Shoulders slumped, the coward folded like a deck of cards. "A-a man named Walker approached me a few weeks ago. Said he had a client who'd pay good money for the formula. Really good money."

Despite already knowing the guy was guilty, hearing him admit it made Matt want to rip the fucker's heart out with a spoon. A rusty, jagged spoon.

"So, you agreed."

"You don't understand." Anderson's desperate eyes pleaded. "The offer...it was more money than every man in this room will ever see in a lifetime. Myself included."

Matt's lips rolled inward as he fought the urge to shoot the son of a bitch. *Don't kill him yet. Don't kill him yet.*

Picking up on his internal battle, Gabe joined in on the questioning.

"Why get Kennedy involved? Why not just hand over the formula and cash in on your payday?"

The guy rolled his eyes. "If that were possible, don't you think I would have?"

"Why couldn't you? You're the company's owner and CEO."

"Which is exactly why I *couldn't*." Anderson sighed before explaining, "Companies like mine have regulations. A lot of very strict regulations. Because I have such a high stake in the company shares, I'm not allowed to have direct access to any of the projects apart from basic data and progress notes. Neither are any of the members on my board."

"Checks and balances," Derek summed it up for the man.

"Exactly."

"So, you found out about Kennedy's wife, using that as leverage to get him to do your dirty work," Gabe recapped. "Why go after Doctor Marsh?"

"The original plan wasn't to kill her. No one was supposed to die."

"Except maybe the American soldiers your buyer's people would kill. But they don't count, right? Their lives don't matter to you?"

A flash of recognition passed behind the guilty fucker's eyes, quickly replaced by an enraged fury.

"My son's life mattered to me," the man shot back. "Brian was my only child, and that bitch took advantage of him."

Matt leaned in, his lips curling into a feral smile. "Call Katherine a bitch one more time, and your toes are going to be the least of your concerns."

Anderson gave Matt a closer, assessing glance. "You're him, aren't you? You're the man Kat was in love with all those years ago."

*What the fuck?* Matt blinked but didn't otherwise react. "What does your son have to do with any of this?"

"Brian has everything to do with this," the man hissed. "Katherine Marsh talked him into marrying her. Made everyone think they had a happy life together and then she destroyed him. She got the job she wanted, the money. Her father and I went into business together because I thought, what better way to bring the two families together? But Brian was so unhappy, he shot himself. In his own home. And then that bi..." Anderson stopped himself. "Then Katherine got all his money. Every dime. And you know what she did?"

"She gave it to the person Brian loved."

Matt's knowledge of the situation took the man by surprise. "That's right. She gave it to a man who led a life unworthy of my son."

"Your son was gay, Sloane. He was in love with Chad Winthrop. *That's* why Kat gave him Brian's inheritance."

"No. My son was confused, maybe, but he wasn't—"

"Brian was gay, and you couldn't accept that. It didn't fit within your perfect life or your perfect appearances. You threatened to disown him because of it."

"No. You're wrong." The man shook his head, continuing on with his denial.

"Your bigotry and hatred for your son's lifestyle is what killed him. Not Kat. The only thing she did was try to help your son. But she couldn't give him the one thing he wanted more than anything in the world." Matt made sure Anderson was listening before saying, "Your love and acceptance."

"His secret lifestyle was a disgrace!" Sloane yelled the ridiculous claim. "An embarrassment to the family name."

This guy made him sick. "He can't embarrass anyone anymore."

A tiny spec of emotion snuck through the ignorant man's expression, but it was gone as quickly as it had appeared.

"Seriously, dude." Kole spoke up for the first time. "You do realize the Dark Ages were over like...forever ago, right?"

"Explain something to me, Anderson," Gabe jumped in again, bringing them back on topic. "If you hated Katherine so much, why didn't you just fire her?"

"You think I didn't want to? I *couldn't.*"

"Why not?" Matt challenged back.

"She's the best at what she does. Her name was the reason the military commissioned my company for the formulation of the serum in the first place. If I'd fired her, I would have lost the project. My company was counting on it to pull us back into the green."

Kole shrugged. "What would've happened if she'd quit? What would you have done then?"

"She was never going to quit. At least not until the project was complete."

Matt couldn't help but ask, "Why not?"

The older man's eyes stared directly into his. "Because of you."

It was Matt's second *what the fuck* moment in as many minutes. "What the hell are you talking about?"

"Think about it, genius. That serum was being created for the military. To give wounded American military members a better chance at survival. You're military, right?"

"Not anymore."

"Katherine worked her ass off on this project. Not for me or the company. She did it for you."

Matt didn't know what to say to that.

"Didn't matter to me why the hell she wanted the project to succeed. As long as she made it happen. We used each other, you see. And it was working fine until..."

"You got an even better offer than the one the military had proposed. One from Walker's mystery buyer."

"Yes," he admitted begrudgingly.

"What happened, next? Todd get greedy? Cold feet? Why did he go after Kat?"

Anderson explained how if Todd took over, he'd gain access to all the information needed to make the serum. He also admitted to telling Walker about Kat's crazy-good memory.

"Okay, that explains why Kat was taken," Matt commented. "There's only one more thing we need to know."

"What?"

"Who's the buyer?"

Anderson shook his head. "I-I don't know."

*The man really is a horrible liar.* "Now, why don't I believe that?" Matt grabbed Anderson's shoulder in a strong grip and squeezed.

"I don't know." The older man's voice became strained as his knees buckled and he attempted to pull away. "Walker never told me his name."

"But you know it, anyway." Matt could see it in the man's eyes. "Come on, Sloane. We've come this far. Walker had to have said it at least once."

When Anderson remained tight-lipped, Matt went

back to his earlier tactic. Pointing his pistol at the man's bare foot, he began counting down from five.

"Five. Four. Three…"

"I don't know!"

"Two…"

"I swear, I don't—"

"One." Matt's finger slid to the trigger right as Anderson hollered out.

"Okay! Okay!"

Matt moved his finger back to its safe position. "You were saying?"

"He'll kill me if he finds out I told you." Anderson's entire body began to shake so badly, if he'd had any shit in his bowels, he probably would've let go of that, too.

*Thank God for small favors.*

"What do you think I'm going to do to you, if you don't?"

Anderson looked back at him with a fear Matt welcomed. "I-I may have overheard Walker talking to him once while we were on the phone. I thought I heard him say 'Rajif.'"

Matt's eyes flew to Gabe's. "Bukhari?"

Gabe shifted his gaze to Anderson. "Did you ever hear Walker say the name 'Bukhari'?"

"No." Anderson shook his head vehemently. "I swear. I heard Rajif that one time. That was it."

Gabe stepped closer to Matt, putting his mouth right next to his ear he whispered, "If Bukhari's involved, this shit's a hell of a lot bigger than we thought."

Matt nodded his head to show his team leader he agreed. "We need to call Ryker."

"I'm on it." Gabe pulled his phone from his thigh

pocket and called the Homeland Security agent's personal cell.

When Ryker picked up, Matt heard Gabe tell him, "You need to get to the office." There was a slight pause before Bravo's team leader said, "Because we're bringing you a present. Homeland's Christmas came early this year."

# CHAPTER 15

After grabbing some clean pants for Anderson to change into—because no one on the team wanted to smell old man piss while driving to Dallas's Homeland facility—they'd used their plastic cuffs to secure their prisoner for transport.

Having transferred him into their custody, Agent Ryker had instructed them to go back to Gabe's place and wait for him. Hours later, as dawn was beginning to break, the four men were in Gabe's living room, drinking some much-needed coffee when there was a knock on the door.

Jason Ryker had shown up, as promised, his hands full of thick manila folders. One for each man present.

Passing them out, as he spoke, Ryker began filling them in on what he knew. "As of an hour ago, Sloane Anderson has officially been charged with treason. Now, we move on to the big fish."

"Bukhari?" Matt assumed.

Ryker went to the table and grabbed the back of one of

the wooden chairs before dragging it into the living room. Sitting down, he shared what he knew.

"As you know, Rajif Bukhari has been considered a high value target to the U.S. government for several years. Until now, he's been untouchable. Too many politics in play. As head of Iran's most lethal military faction, Bukhari knows how to work the system and has a fuckton of people on his payroll. Government officials, local law enforcement...you name it."

"What are you saying?" Matt asked angrily. "We're giving up? Letting the son of a bitch get away with it all?"

No fucking way he'd let that happen. If he had to, Matt would go after Bukhari himself.

"No, Turner," Ryker shot his thoughts down quickly. "That's not at all what I'm saying."

Without giving the man a chance to explain, Matt asked, "How do you suppose we get to him, if he's so goddamn untouchable?"

The cunning agent gave him a sideways smirk. "We call in reinforcements."

Each of the R.I.S.C. operatives shared a look before Gabe said what everyone else was thinking. "You're talking about calling in another team."

Ryker nodded. "One your men are already familiar with."

Matt finally understood. "You mean Ghost and Fletch and those guys?"

Ghost and Fletch were two of the Delta team members that had aided them in Gracelynn's rescue. At first, the team was hesitant to go into an op with a team they knew nothing about. Especially when the op was as important as rescuing one of their women.

Turns out, Ghost and that whole crew were actually pretty cool guys. More importantly, they were kick ass operatives who knew what they were doing.

"Along with a couple other agencies, Homeland has been working closely with this Delta team for the past two months." Ryker leaned forward, resting his elbows on his knees as he explained Delta's play in this particular game. "They've been working various angles, gathering as much intel as possible on Bukhari and his alleged side operations while infiltrating multiple networks believed to be tied to him. A couple weeks ago, Ghost reported hearing chatter about Bukhari's interest in some sort of injection to make soldiers stronger. Less vulnerable."

"Kat's formula," Matt mumbled, more to himself than anyone else.

"We believe so," Ryker acknowledged him. "Sloane Anderson copped to having Kennedy send pictures of the lab from every angle to the same number that accidentally texted your girl. Rumor has it he's ordered the construction of a lab identical to the one at Anderson Biomeds in in a warehouse near the Mehrabad."

"They took her to fucking Tehran," Matt growled. Tossing his folder onto the coffee table, he stood and ran a hand through his hair before pacing the room nervously.

Tehran was the capital of Iran. With a population of over nine million, it was polluted, traffic was horrendous, and it was suffocating as hell.

The idea that Bukhari had taken Kat there, was holding her in a fucking warehouse, filled him with an unprecedented level of hatred and rage. The only thing keeping him from punching a hole in the goddamn wall was the fact that this was Gabe's house. Not his.

"The warehouse was built on a large stretch of unde-veloped land west of the airport, between it and the hospital," Ryker continued with what he knew. "It's on the outskirts of District Ten."

Swallowing a swig of coffee, Gabe sat his mug down and looked at the agent. "No offense, Jason, but if Ghost and the others have been in place for two months and they still haven't found a way in, what makes you think they'll be able go after him now?"

Matt watched Ryker closely, wondering the same damn thing, himself.

"Katherine Marsh is a United States Citizen."

"No shit," Matt popped off impatiently. With his hands on his hips, he barely controlled his rising temper. "You gotta give us more than that, man. We're talking about saving her life."

Sighing, Ryker explained. "Until now, the only thing we've been able to solidly tie to Bukhari are crimes against his own people. Even then, he has so many Iranian government officials in his pocket, any allegations we've tried to make have bounced off his ass like he's made of fucking rubber."

"And this time?" Gabe raised a brow.

"This time, Delta can use their contacts to confirm Bukhari is holding a U.S. citizen against her will. They get photo evidence of that, especially since this particular civilian has the capabilities to help save American lives? That shit opens him up to whatever hell we can bring down on him."

"Then we go in, right?" Matt asked anxiously. "I'm cool working with Delta on this, but I want to be there when they breach."

"I figured you would. Which is why I contacted Ghost before I left the office to come here. He and his men are already on it. The second we get confirmation Katherine's there, we'll fly your team in to join them for the takedown."

"You mean rescue," Matt corrected Ryker.

"Takedown, rescue. Whatever you want to call it."

Needing to make sure the man knew exactly where he stood on this, Matt locked his narrowed gaze with the agent. "Let's get something straight, Jason. Kat's not some goddamn pawn in whatever game Homeland's trying to play. We go in that warehouse, with or without Delta, our primary objective is to locate Kat and get her to safety. Period. Everything else is secondary."

Ryker sat back in his chair and crossed his arms loosely at his chest. "Agreed. Bravo's objective is to get to Kat. Delta, however, is a different story."

"Meaning?"

"Meaning, your teams will work together to locate your girl. Once Bravo has her secure, the two teams will split up. You guys get Kat to safety. Delta takes out Bukhari." The man shrugged. "It's a win-win for everyone."

The room went silent for a beat while Matt and the others contemplated what Ryker was proposing. With perfect execution, a joint op like that could work. Hell, that's pretty much how it *had* gone the last time they'd joined Ghost's Delta team.

They'd gone with Nate to Turkey when the country's crooked—and now dead—president had taken Gracie there. The two teams had come together nicely, working together as if they were one unit.

*This could work.*

"Turner?" Gabe's voice snapped him back to the present. "You good with this?"

"You're the team leader." Matt swallowed. "Decision should be yours."

Gabe shook his head. "Your woman. Your call."

He nodded, grateful his team leader was letting him weigh in. "Ghost and his men did right by Nate and Gracie. I trust them to do the same for Kat."

To Ryker, Gabe said, "Call their commander."

The agent nodded. "I'll make it happen." Standing, the well-connected man walked to the door. "I'll be in touch with the details. In the meantime, I suggest Bravo gets their shit in order." With a parting glance, he added, "I have a feeling it won't take long for Delta to jump on this. You need to be ready."

Matt shared a serious look with the other man. "Don't worry. We will be."

He prayed Kat could hold on long enough for that to happen.

*Hang on, sweetheart. We're coming for you.*

KAT WATCHED THE PLUNGER CAREFULLY AS SHE PULLED THE clear serum into the syringe. With as undetectable a move as possible, she secured the plastic tip over the blunt end before hiding it in the elastic waistband of her pants.

*Too bad I don't have a needle to go along with this. I'd jab it in Walker's eye.* Which was probably the reason they'd only provided the syringe, and not the needle.

Doing her best to avoid the camera, Kat pulled the

edge of the black scrub top Walker had brought her down to conceal the contraband. She knew if she were caught, she'd most likely be killed. Since death was an inevitability for her here already, she figured it would be better to die trying than not.

After Bukhari and Walker had left her alone that first day, Kat had sat down in her 'lab' and cried. Not for herself, but for her father.

Those detectives had claimed he was murdered, but she hadn't had the chance to learn anything more before Walker and his men had ambushed them.

To learn he'd been killed for the sole purpose of getting to her...Kat still didn't know what to do with that. Accepting that wasn't something she'd be able to truly understand or get over anytime soon, she'd pushed it away and did what she had to do to survive.

So far, it was working.

Later, when Bukhari had returned to the lab and demanded a timeline, Kat had called upon her best acting skills in order to fool him. First, she'd downplayed her incredible memory, convincing him it wasn't as fool proof as he'd been led to believe.

The man had gotten angry, but she'd been able to talk him down before he struck her again, assuring him she would remember the necessary research, but it was going to take some time.

When he asked how much time, she'd reminded him she'd had a team of scientists before, and now she was working alone. She'd also used a lot of big, scientific jargon as she began to explain the complicated process needed to create the serum he was after.

The more she talked, the more his eyes had begun to

glaze over until finally, he'd waved his hand in the air impatiently and told her to do what needed to be done.

She promised she'd have it created within the next fourteen days. The dose she'd just hidden in her waist-band had taken three days to create.

Three days. That's how long she'd been stuck in here. Pretending.

Each day, after a meager breakfast of black coffee and two slices of bread, Kat was escorted in here. She'd then go about her day, spending most of those first two days taking scrupulous notes.

Some things she'd written down were real, actual data she remembered from the painstaking research she and her team had completed for this project. Knowing she couldn't simply write her way out of this, Kat had spent the last half of yesterday to actually begin creating that first dose.

Her thought was, if she were somehow able to get free, she'd have it as proof of who she was. It was a shot that was beyond long, but she was in a foreign country known for its hostile treatment toward Americans.

If—and that was a big damn if—she was somehow able to escape, Kat knew she'd need to find someone to take her someplace safe. Preferably, the nearest U.S. military base.

Iran destroyed the U.S. Embassy back in the late seventies, but she remembered hearing about how the country was pretty much surrounded by United States military bases. If she could get out and somehow convince someone to drive her to the border, she may have a chance.

Her stomach threatened to revolt from the fear. As a

woman of science Kat was used to dealing with facts. Relying on maybes and ifs to stay alive was real damn hard for her to swallow. But she had no choice.

Cleaning up the evidence and continuing on with her 'work', Kat prayed her stall tactics would buy her enough time to escape. Or be rescued.

*They can't rescue you if they don't know where you are.*

She ignored the negative thought. Matt and the rest of R.I.S.C. were the best at what they did. If anyone could find her, they could. In the meantime, she'd bide her time and keep up the pretense of following Bukhari's orders.

Walker had been bringing her something small to eat halfway through the day. At night, he'd escort her back to her dark, empty room.

Any time she had to use the restroom while working, Kat had to knock on the door to be let out. Walker would open the door, pat her down, and take her down the hallway to the bathroom.

The bathroom had a small, single window. It was up high, next to the ceiling, and much too small for her to fit through. Escaping through the room may not be an option, but it was the best place she could think of to hide the syringe.

It had to be somewhere outside the lab. Since the door to the lab was always locked—whether she was in it or not —Kat needed to hide it in a spot outside this room. If she were to have a chance to escape, it wouldn't be while she was in here.

It was too dangerous to keep it on her person, and there was nowhere for her to conceal it in the room where she slept. That left only one other place she had access to.

Doing her best to control her racing heart, Kat pounded on the door. When Walker opened it, he looked down at her with that same, guarded expression he always seemed to wear.

"Yes?"

"I need to use the bathroom."

With a small nod, he said, "You know the drill. Hold your hands out."

Terrified of getting caught, she did her best to act normal. With her hands held straight out, she stood perfectly still while Walker began to check her for anything, she may have on her.

Starting with her shoulders, he slowly ran his hands over her short sleeves before moving them beneath her arms and down her ribs. Normally, he kept going, but for some reason Walker stopped.

With his hands rested against her ribs and under her breasts, he frowned. "Your heart is racing." He slid a glance to her forehead. "And you're sweating. Do you feel ill?"

"Yes," she answered honestly. "Wouldn't you if you were constantly being felt up by the man who murdered your father?"

His face went flat, and he slowly dropped his hands. "I'm supposed to search you every time you leave. You know that."

"What do you think I'm going to do, try to kill you with a petri dish?" When the man gave her a look, she sighed loudly and asked, "Are you going to take me to the bathroom or not?"

Walker studied her a second longer before stepping to the side. "After you."

Kat walked past him, holding her breath and praying he didn't change his mind and continue the search.

When they reached the tiny room at the end of the hall, he said, "Make it quick."

"Always do," she quipped before shutting the door in his face.

Taking a minute to calm her dizzying nerves, Kat immediately went to work. Turning the faucet on to cover the sound, she quickly removed the lid from the back of the toilet.

Dipping her hand into the clear, cool water, she placed the syringe behind the toilet's small pump, hiding it as best she could before setting the ceramic lid back in its place.

After flushing the toilet to go along with her ruse, she rushed to wash her hands and face, grabbing a paper towel from the roll on the sink to pat her skin dry. Drawing in a few, deep breaths, she prayed no one would find it and opened the door.

Only Walker wasn't the one waiting for her when she walked out. It was Bukhari. And he looked pissed.

"Where is the serum?" he demanded angrily.

*Oh, god. He knows.* "W-what do you mean? I told you, it would take—"

"Two weeks," he finished for her.

"Yes. That's correct."

"You're lying."

"What? No—"

Bukhari grabbed the front of her scrub top and pulled her to the side. Kat cried out when he slammed her back against the wall. Her still-tender head made contact, but thankfully the cut Walker had stitched up was on the side, so it hadn't taken a direct hit.

With his meaty fist pressed against her chest, he held her in place. "I spoke to one of my country's top scientists. He told me if you knew the formula and had all the supplies, it would take days, not weeks to duplicate."

*Shit. Shit. Shit.*

She had to think. "Y-your scientist isn't familiar with my work. It's not like I'm whipping up a batch of cupcakes. I told you before, this project is complicated."

The man released her, and for a second, she thought it was because he believed her. She was wrong.

His hand moved lightning fast, the blow sending her straight to the ground. Kat didn't even have time to recover from that first hit to her face before his booted toe made contact with her ribs.

Crying out in pain, Kat curled into a ball, doing her best to protect her internal organs as he drew his leg back and kicked her again. And again.

"Bukhari!" Walker's voice echoed down the hallway. "What the hell are you doing?"

"She lied," the monster accused.

Walker came up beside him. "About what?"

"She said it would take two weeks to make the serum when it should be done by now."

Kat flinched, making herself even smaller when she saw Bukhari's foot begin to move again. Walker stopped him.

"Wait." Walker pulled him back. "Even if what you're saying is true, she'll be no use to you dead."

"I will not tolerate being made a fool of. Especially by an American bitch like her."

"I get that, but you need to calm down a minute and think. You beat her senseless, she won't be able to make the product until after she recovers. That'll only add to that damn timeline you're so worried about."

Lying silently on the cold, concrete floor, Kat prayed Bukhari would listen. When he crouched down beside her, she tried to move away from, but her body hurt too bad to make any progress.

Grabbing the hair on the back of her head, he pulled her face up to meet his. Fire burned in her already-tender scalp, and she was certain he was yanking the hair from its roots.

With his nose next to hers, he warned, "You have one more day to get me my serum. After that, I'm sending Walker to finish off your precious Bravo Team."

Though she fought them, tears fell from Kat's eyes.

"One by one." Bukhari finished the threat. "Starting with that boyfriend of yours."

# CHAPTER 16

"Good to see you again, Turner." The man known to him as Ghost shook Matt's hand. "Wish it was under different circumstances."

"Hey, Ghost." Matt gripped the man's hand tightly. "Trust me, so do I."

The six-one Delta operator nodded his understanding.

"You remember Dawson, our team leader?" Matt motioned to Gabe.

"Of course." The two men shook hands.

"And this is Kole Jameson. He stayed back last time, to protect his wife."

"Heard a lot about you," Kole offered Ghost his hand.

"It's all bullshit," Ghost teased.

With a chuckle, Kole shook his head. "Seriously, man. Appreciate what you did for my sister-in-law."

"How is Gracelynn?" Ghost asked, sounding sincere.

"Great. Actually, she and Nate are on their honeymoon."

With a smirk, Ghost said, "Ah, so that's why the smartass isn't here."

Matt laughed, remembering Nate's hesitation to work with Ghost and his men. Knowing these guys were going to help him get Katherine back made him even more grateful their two teams had crossed paths.

"Heard King ran into some trouble." Ghost looked at Matt. "He good?"

"He will be. Took a hit to the shoulder. Busted his collar bone, but he'll be back with the team in no time."

"Glad to hear it."

"Since these three assholes have no manners, I guess I'll have to introduce myself. Derek West." Derek held out his hand.

"Shit. Sorry, D." Matt gave the other man a chagrined smile before turning back to Ghost. "Derek's actually on Jake's team. Former SEAL and Alpha's tech guy. He's helping us out until Nate gets back."

"No, I remember. You're the one who found the pics on Gracie's phone. The ones who helped us take down that prick Yavuz." Ghost gave Derek an approving nod. "From what Ryker's said, you've done quite a bit to help figure this clusterfuck out."

Derek shrugged. "Some. Wish I could've figured it out sooner."

"You guys are here, now. That's all that matters. Come on." Looking at Derek and Kole, Ghost tilted his head toward one side of the room, where his men were standing. "I'll introduce you to the others and then we can get started.

Wearing camo gear similar to Matt's, the brown-haired captain began introducing Derek and Kole to his men. First up was Fletch. An inch taller than Ghost, the Delta operative's muscular, brightly tattooed arms were what had stuck in Matt's memory of the man.

Next were Beatle, Hollywood, and Truck. The one and only time he'd met these three was when they'd flown the team and Gracie back to the States from Turkey. Though they hadn't worked the actual op with them, Matt had no qualms about doing so now.

At barely under six foot, Beatle was the shortest of the group, the man with the slightly auburn hair had a southern drawl that could possibly out-do Derek's. With his tall, dark, and handsome feature, Hollywood reminded Matt a bit of Alpha Team's Trevor.

And then there was Truck.

The last time Matt saw him, the guy was flying the chopper. He'd known the dude was big, but seeing him standing upright was like...holy fuck! The guy was seriously over six and a half feet.

Between his enormous frame, a scar on his face, and a nose that had been broken more than once, the dude could probably just look at Bukhari and send the man running.

*If only it were that easy.*

Last up was the man who went by the nickname "Coach". Minus Truck, the six-five, naturally tanned giant also towered over every other man in the room. Matt remembered him as being fairly serious, though his strong, square jaw may have attributed to that thought.

"Heard your girl's special, like me," Coach shook Matt's hand.

"That's right. You have an eidetic memory, too." Matt dropped his hand. "Forgot about that."

"Can't imagine what that's like." Then, the man smirked.

"Funny." Matt flipped him off with a grin before turning serious. Addressing Ghost, he asked, "Can we get to work, now?"

He had a girl to save, and everything in Matt's gut said they were running out of time.

Gathering around the safehouse's large table, Ghost waited until everyone was in a spot to see the large, printed map before starting.

"Here's what we know. Bukhari's warehouse is here." He pointed to a marked spot on the map. "This is Mehrabad International here. This lot houses the airports overflow buildings. General supplies, that sort of thing. The space between that and Bukhari's warehouse is vacant. To the east of that building is the hospital for District Ten."

"Which part of the warehouse is Katherine being held?" Matt blurted.

"Hang on, Turner." Ghost held out a hand. "I know you're anxious to go in, but we need our plan to be solid first, and you and your men need all the intel we've gathered to make that happen."

Matt nodded. "Sorry. You were saying?"

He knew he was jumping ahead, but fuck if he could help it.

"One of our contacts in the hospital spotted a man matching Adrian Walker's description."

"When?"

"Three days ago. He entered the hospital empty-handed but left with a stack of scrubs. When our contact asked around, he found out Walker had sweet-talked a nurse into giving them to him. Said his daughter was home, sick with a fever, and needed something cool to wear. Apparently, she bought it and gave him several pair."

"They were for Kat," Matt mumbled to himself.

"That's what we're thinking." Fletch nodded.

Unable to keep from it, Matt looked at the Delta team and asked, "Okay, so do you have a plan of entrance yet, or do we need to figure that out?"

"Well, Turner," Derek drawled. "If you'd let the man talk, he might tell you."

*Shit.* He was doing it again. "Sorry, guys. I'm just..."

"Scared for your woman," Truck's deep voice rumbled. "Trust us. We get it."

Something in Truck's eyes told Matt the big guy was speaking from personal experience. He already knew Ghost, Fletch, and Coach had stories similar to the one Matt and Katherine were currently living. He hadn't realized Truck did, too.

As he scanned the group, Matt was shocked to find the same, knowing look staring back at him from both Beatle and Hollywood.

Damn. "Must be something about the women the Delta or R.I.S.C. men choose, huh?" Matt half-joked with the group.

"Sure is," Beatle drawled. "They're all smart as hell and tough as nails."

"I'm guessing yours is no different?" Hollywood asked Matt.

"No," he answered truthfully. "Kat's...amazing."

Beatle gave Matt a slight smirk and said, "Then let's quit standing around here shootin' the shit and figure out how we're gonna get her back."

It was the best thing Matt had heard all day.

Four long, torturous hours later, Matt and the others were finally geared up and ready to go. Using the Iranian night sky to their advantage, they'd managed to travel through the city undetected to where they were now.

With the airport overflow buildings as cover, they used their night vision goggles to watch for movement coming from the warehouse.

A combination of concrete blocks and drywall, the large structure looked strong and sturdy, but it had definite weak spots that would make for easy targets. They just had to make sure Kat wasn't within the radius of danger, should they need to go that route.

While Matt and the others had been on the plane to Iran, Delta had found a contact who'd led them to a man who'd worked on the lab's construction.

From what he could see through the thermal scope on his rifle, there were ten individual heat signals coming from inside the building.

One in the area the other team's contact said was the lab and nine more scattered throughout the building.

"The one in the lab has to be Kat," Matt whispered to Gabe, who was positioned next to him.

His team leader nodded. "Agreed."

Matt couldn't take his eyes off that heat signal. It wasn't stationary, like the others. Ones Matt assumed were asleep.

Instead Kat's blurred image would be still for a beat before slowly moving to another area of the room. After that, she'd go back to where she had started. This happened three more times in a ten-minute period.

"Fuckers are making her work in the middle of the goddamn night," he bit out angrily.

"Bukhari is desperate," Derek reasoned. "He knows it's only a matter of time before we figure out he's behind this. He wants that serum made so he can mass-market it to his entire army."

Matt got it. Didn't mean he fucking liked it. "Let's pray she's doing something to stall the bastard."

God, it was killing him to be this close but have to wait. If they went in, guns blazing, there was a very good chance Bukhari would execute her on the spot. No fucking way was Matt taking that chance.

They stayed in position, watching and waiting until they were certain their timing was perfect. That time came when two more heat signals moved into the lab.

Bukhari and Walker. Matt knew it in his gut.

"All right, boys," Ghost spoke up. "Let's do this."

Like a well-oiled machine, the two teams moved effortlessly across the open lot. Boots pressed into rock and grass, but the men had all been trained to silence their footfalls as best they could.

They were half-way to the building when the area where the lab had been constructed exploded into a fiery ball of flames.

"No!" Matt started to run forward, but Gabe's strong grip on his shoulder held him back.

"Matt, wait!"

He looked back at the man as if he'd lost his damn mind. "Are you fucking kidding me?"

"We do this together," Gabe growled.

Truck's large form appeared in front of him as the man added, "All of us."

*Shit. Fuck. Motherfucker.*

"Fine." He glanced back at the burning building. "What's the plan?"

"We go in the same way we discussed," Ghost took charge. "Only instead of your team taking the back, see if you can get through the fire and go through the lab. I don't know what the hell is going on, but they won't be expecting an attack from inside the flames. Just watch your backs."

"Roger that," Matt, Gabe, Kole, and Derek all answered in unison.

"Now go," Fletch told Matt. "Go get your girl. We'll take care of Bukhari."

With a final look, Ghost gave Matt and the others a tip of his head and said, "We'll see you on the flip side."

Not willing to wait another second, Matt took off for the building, knowing Derek and his Bravo brothers would have his back. Always.

With his heart in his throat and fear crawling its way down his spine, Matt pushed everything aside and focused on the most important objective of his life...

Finding Katherine and bringing her home.

*Hang on, baby! I'm coming for you!*

# CHAPTER 17

*Three minutes earlier...*

KAT MEASURED THE CHEMICAL ADDITIVE. USING THE dropper, she carefully added it to what was already in the glass beaker, praying she didn't pull a Todd and blow herself up in the process.

The compound she'd created wasn't the same as the one he'd used. Unfortunately, Todd hadn't been kind enough to include those in the grocery list from hell he'd put together for Bukhari. So she'd improvised.

After the jerk had finished beating on her in the hallway, Kat had picked herself up—having refused Walker's offer to assist—and painfully hobbled her way back here to the lab.

Oddly, it was the only space in the entire building she actually felt safe. Sort of. It probably had to do with how familiar it all was. Crazed murderer aside, Bukhari had done an excellent job of recreating her home away from home.

The throbbing in her head and ribs were a sharp reminder she was most definitely not at home. Familiar or not, Kat was more than ready to get the hell out of here. One way or another.

When Bukhari had been hitting and kicking her, she'd felt hopeless. Ready to give up any thoughts of escaping. She'd silently cursed fate for putting her here. Then she'd cursed the bitch even more for causing Todd's wife to get sick.

If she hadn't, he may never have been a pawn in this horrifying game. Her co-workers would most likely still be alive, and maybe...just maybe, she wouldn't be here.

That thought led to memories of the explosion, and those led her to where she was now. Or, rather...what she was doing.

Memories from that day had sparked an idea. One with terrifying consequences. But she refused to give those any thought, because at this point, they were moot.

Kat believed Bukhari when he moved the deadline for the serum to tomorrow. She also believed he'd make good on his promise to go after the members of Bravo Team if she didn't follow through. Knew, without a doubt, the cold-blooded man would kill Matt as a result of her inaction.

She was left with no other choice.

Pushing past the pain, Kat had come back in here and had gone straight to work. Not making the serum as she'd been ordered. Like hell she'd give a man like him something that could help him and his crooked army.

Instead she'd remembered one of the first formulas

they'd tested. One that had failed miserably. It wasn't harmful to the human body, but it wasn't helpful, either. A person may as well inject saline into their system for all the effect it had.

So that's what Kat had spent the night creating. She'd filled dozens of vials with the worthless drug praying Bukhari was stupid enough to believe it was the real thing. If only she could inject his dumbass with the worthless shit.

It was a scene she'd played over and over in her mind as the night had gone on. Had imagined making the man think he was momentarily invincible, right before she jabbed him in the throat with something long...and very sharp.

While she'd always believed every person's life was of value, this experience had taught her a hard life lesson. Some people truly did deserve to die.

Kat continued to work on the final touches to what she hoped would be her way out. Her plan was to wait for the right moment, and then boom! Bukhari would go up in flames. She just hoped like hell she didn't go with him.

She walked over to the counter at the far end of the room to retrieve the final ingredient. Grabbing it, Kat was half-way between the back wall and where it was when the door to the lab swung open.

*Speak of the devil.*

"Time's up." Bukhari stormed toward her.

"What?" Kat shook her head, doing her best not to run for the compound. She had to add the final chemical in order for it to work, but if he suspected she was up to something, he'd most likely beat her again. Or worse.

"Y-you said I had until tomorrow." She continued walking casually to where she needed to be.

"Close enough." He eyed the vials on the back counter. "Is this it?" His dark eyes lit up. "Is it complete?"

"Mostly." Kat nodded. "I'd still like to run a few tests. Make sure it works like it's supposed to."

"Agreed," Bukhari nodded. He picked up one of the vials before removing a syringe from his pocket. This one complete with a needle. He flicked off the plastic tip and began filling the small tube with the fake serum.

Kat's heart raced wildly in her chest. Her mind raced with so many questions. How would he test it? *Who* would he test it on?

If he purposely injured himself, he'd realize almost instantly it wasn't the real thing. He'd kill her for sure.

Bukhari walked over to her with the syringe.

"Y-you shouldn't test it on yourself. There could be side-effects we aren't aware of. Everyone's system is different, and your body's DNA makeup could reject—"

Bukhari's laugh interrupted her rambling thoughts. "Oh, I'm not going to test it on myself." He nodded to someone behind her and Kat whipped her head around to see Walker had entered the lab.

With an apologetic shrug, he wrapped an arm around her chest, pulling her back flush with his front. Kat screamed and tried to get free, but once again, the man's strength overpowered hers.

Moving her forward, closer to the man in charge, he spun her around, pushing her body against the hard, metal table in the center of the room. Pressing himself against her, Walker forced her to arch her back until her upper body was lying flat on the top of the table.

Holding her arms above her head to keep her immobile, Kat was unable to do anything but lie there and scream.

Using his body to keep her in place, Walker continued to hold her down at her wrists while Bukhari examined the veins on the inside of her left arm. Pressure from Walker's weight sent a sharp, burning pain through her already-injured ribs,

"There." He pressed against one of the larger ones. "I think this one will do nicely."

"You're crazy!" She ground out, still trying futilely to break free.

Kat winced as Bukhari pressed the tip of the sharp needle into her skin. A cool, burning sensation began spreading up her arm, and she watched with horror as he slowly plunged the remaining liquid into her vein.

"I don't know what has you so concerned. This is harmless to the human body. Yes?"

He pulled the needle free and let her go, silently instructing Walker to do the same.

The second Walker lifted himself off her, Kat sucked in deep breath. The action caused the pain in her side to ignite once more, but at least she was no longer being held down.

Angry, for so many reasons, Kat pushed against Walker's chest as she made her way past the two men.

"Yes. The serum itself is harmless." She walked backward, putting as much space between herself and the two men as possible. "But—"

"Then what are you afraid of?" Bukhari cut her off, pulling a pistol from the holster at his hip.

*Oh, I don't know. A bullet traveling at over six hundred miles an hour as it rips through my flesh seems to come to mind.*

Kat's legs went weak, and she felt as though she were going to throw up.

"This is crazy, Bukhari." Walker put himself between her and the potential bullet. "You hurt her, and the serum doesn't work, you're back to square one."

"How else will I know it works, if we don't test it?"

"Then go get one of your fucking lackeys. Not the doc I've worked my ass off to bring to you."

"The rest of your money was already transferred, so why do you care what happens to her?"

It was a valid question, and one Kat wouldn't mind knowing the answer to, but right now she had bigger things to worry about.

While the two men continued to argue, Kat inched herself away, closer to the explosive concoction she'd made. She'd barely made it when she heard Bukhari give Walker a final warning.

"Either get out of the way, or I'll shoot you first. And I won't bother giving you the damn serum."

Kat watched Walker closely, praying he'd have a sudden change of heart and take Bukhari down before he could hurt her or anyone else.

Instead, the man shook his head and said, "You're making a mistake." He then turned and started walking for the door.

"Wait!" Kat hollered for him as he passed by. She knew it was crazy to think this man, the same man who'd murdered her father in cold blood would actually help her, but she'd seen something behind his eyes.

A spec of compassion and humanity when he'd

stitched her up. He'd come to her aid when Bukhari had been kicking her in the hallway, and he'd tried to prevent the bastard from shooting her.

There had to be some bit of decency in there, somewhere. There *had* to be.

But as he made his way to the door, he simply turned and said, "I'm sorry, Katherine. I truly am." And then he left her. Alone...with a killer.

"P-please," Kat begged Bukhari. "Don't do this."

"Why not? You said the serum works, correct?"

"Y-yes, but it won't heal me."

The older man smiled the coldest sneer she'd ever seen. "I don't need it to heal you. I only need to how well it works on your pain. See if it slows the bleeding, as Anderson claimed. What more efficient way to cause pain and bleeding, than a bullet?"

Kat knew the second he decided to pull the trigger. It was the same second she moved to grab the glass beaker.

There was a loud bang before the bullet struck. At the exact same moment, Kat screamed as she threw the beaker as hard as she could, aiming directly where Bukhari was standing.

She flew back from the force of the bullet, landing on the floor as the entire room filled with a rush of incinerating heat. Her ears filled with a deafening ringing, making it impossible for her to hear anything but.

Overwhelming pain filled her entire left side. Its long, sharp nails digging their way through her abdomen, taking with them her ability to breathe.

Tempted to close her eyes and let the pain sweep her away, Kat's memory wouldn't allow it. A flash of the syringe she'd hidden in the toilet flew through her mind, and she knew if she had any hopes of surviving, she had to get to it.

Unable to hold back her groan, Kat pushed to her side, nearly losing consciousness from the trauma she'd just endured. She tried to keep her breaths even, but smoke filled her lungs every time she inhaled.

Coughing—which only exacerbated the pain—Kat miraculously made her way to her feet. Stumbling back, she fought against the spinning room to try and see where Bukhari had landed.

Through flames and dark smoke, she finally found him lying in a heap on the floor near the back. She could tell he was bleeding, though she wasn't sure of the source. And he wasn't moving.

*At least I hurt the bastard.*

Expecting his men to come rushing in at any second, Kat ignored the flames licking at her skin as she stumbled over the half-open door. The force of the blast had almost blown it off its hinges, and somewhere in the back of her muddled mind, Kat understood her falling backward from being shot may very well have saved her life.

*Irony's an even bigger bitch than Fate.*

Shaking her head to clear the useless thoughts, and the incessant ringing, Kat kept a hand pressed tightly against her wound while using the other to support herself while walking along the hallway wall.

Warm blood oozed from between her fingers, and though she had no way of knowing exactly what damage the bullet had done, Kat knew if she didn't slow the bleeding, she'd be dead before she ever got the chance to escape.

*The serum. I have to make it to the serum.*

Several muffled voices broke through the ringing. They sounded as if they were coming from behind her, but Kat refused to stop and check.

She thought she heard Bukhari's strained voice barking orders but didn't risk slowing down to see if he was coming after her.

"There!" Kat hear the muted voice from behind her. "She's down there!"

"I'll take care of her," Bukhari shouted. "You gather what you can and get out. I'll meet you at the estate."

Someone said something she couldn't make out, followed by Bukhari's very clear, "I said the bitch is mine!"

With a quick look back, Kat was opening the bathroom door when she saw Bukhari fall as he tried climbing over the rubble at the lab's entrance. Their eyes met, and he pointed the gun at her again.

Kat screamed as a bullet hit the bathroom's doorframe as she slammed it shut. Locking it—which was a ridiculous waste of time given that the door was made of wood and the man had bullets—she stumbled over to the toilet.

Hands slick with blood, Kat grunted from pain as she lifted the heavy lid off and let it fall to the floor. The white ceramic broke instantly, splintering into two, jagged pieces.

She spotted the syringe and reached for it, her wet and bloody fingers fumbling to get the plastic end unscrewed. After dropping it twice, Kat lifted her soaked and sticky scrub top, exposing where she'd been shot.

With no needle, she couldn't inject herself with the serum the way it was meant to be treated. Instead, she chose the next best thing.

Praying this worked, she bit her lip, took a deep

breath, and pushed the end of the plastic tube directly into the wound in hopes of introducing it into her bloodstream more quickly. Kat was unable to hold back guttural sound as she growled against the pain.

The stinging she'd felt earlier when Bukhari had injected her was nothing compared to what she felt now. An enraged wildfire spread through the wound, taking over her entire internal core to the point she was sure she was dying.

But then, the impossible happened.

Within seconds, the burning began to subside. Her heart rate slowed back to normal, and Kat no longer felt the pain as she had before.

*Am I dying?*

She thought maybe she was. Until suddenly, miraculously, she began to feel stronger. Steadier.

Almost frantically, she lifted her shirt to inspect the wound, shocked to see her bleeding had damn near stopped.

*Holy shit. It works!* Tears of joy mixed with the ones caused from the pain.

Kat had already known from the tests they'd run before that it had positive effects when administered through the venous system, but she wasn't sure what would happen when she'd saturated the wound directly. To actually *feel* the drug working inside her body was almost indescribable.

Knowing her renewed sense of strength wouldn't last forever, she bent down and picked up one of the two ceramic halves. Then, squeezing herself into the corner between the small vanity and door, she held the chunk of lid high in the air and waited.

Bukhari kicked the door in, and Kat had to flinch back against the wall to keep from getting struck. His momentary lapse from not seeing her like he'd expected gave her all the time she needed.

With as much strength as she could gather, Kat roared as she brought the toilet lid half down on to the man's extended arm. The gun flew from his hand, clattering on the floor as he cried out in pain. Taking advantage of the moment, Kat swung the lid upward, the edge catching the bastard's chin.

Bukhari's head flew backward, and the rest of his body followed. Landing with a thud, the unconscious man lay half in and half out of the bathroom's doorway.

Loud pops like gunshots rang out from somewhere in the building. The ringing was still present—something her scientist-trained brain made a mental note of—so it was still challenging to make out specific sounds.

Even so, everything that had happened to her these last few days, Kat was certain of one thing.

*I know what a gunshot sounds like.*

Dropping the lid somewhere behind her, Kat scrambled to pick up the gun. Her hand shook as she got into what she thought was the correct stance.

Bukhari's men had come back for him, after all. They'd see what she'd done to their boss, and that she was still alive. And they'd kill her.

*I'll shoot as many as I can before that happens.*

In her mind, she began praying as she waited to give the final fight of her life.

# CHAPTER 18

Matt felt as though his heart would explode the second he and his team headed for the blown-out wall. Ghost and the others had divided up, half circling around front, the others heading to the back.

The flames were hot and high, but Matt pressed on. Nothing was going to keep him from finding his woman.

With his gun steady, he held up his hand in a fist, signaling the others to stop. Giving Gabe a tip of his head, he motioned to where at least four men were rummaging through the debris.

Even from here, he could tell they were armed, but with their heads down and their hands full, their guns were hanging loosely at their sides.

*Idiots.* They were so busy trying to save what they could from the lab, they'd made themselves sitting fucking ducks.

Something else occurred to him. If they were trying to save what they could from the lab, did that mean Kat was gone? Had she been taken somewhere else, or…

No! He could *not* fucking go there now.

Using hand signals they could sign in their sleep, Gabe divvied up the tangoes among the team. As they made their way across the remaining distance to the damaged building, each man knew which target was theirs to take out.

Like a well-choreographed dance, the four men each took aim. Pulling the trigger on his HK-MP5, Matt shot simultaneously with his team.

The unsuspecting tangoes fell instantly. Still, Matt and the others didn't let their guard down. They'd counted ten warm bodies minutes before, which meant there were still six left somewhere in the building.

And one of those was Katherine.

Keeping his head focused and in the game, Matt quickly swept the burning lab in search of her. But he saw no sign of her or Bukhari.

With no immediate threat in sight, the team made their way across the room. They were careful to avoid the flames, while at the same time, watching their footing.

Matt had no more made his way over the broken door and into the hallway when two of Bukhari's men came running around the corner to his right.

With rapid succession shots, he took the first man out. Several bullets penetrated the asshole's chest as they hit center mass. Behind him, Gabe's gun let loose with the same, tight shots, killing the tango before the man could even reach his trigger.

"Thanks, brother." Matt gave his team leader a nod.

With a friendly tap to Matt's helmet, Gabe said, "Come on. Let's go find your girl."

At last count, that was six tangoes down, three to go,

and one amazing woman to save. But when Matt's team headed down the hallway to his left, he saw the bastard responsible for it all.

Rajif Bukhari was standing in a doorway. The son of a bitch was yards away, not paying attention to them in the least. His focus was on something else entirely.

Matt saw red as a primal, murderous rage from everything this man had caused seeped through his pores.

The deaths of Thomas Marsh and Detective Holloway. Nearly killing Zade. And—for Matt, at least—the worst of it all...

Bukhari had tried to have Kat killed before ordering her kidnapping. Who knows what the bastard had done to her since?

As much as he wanted to toss down his rifle and kill the bastard with his bare hands, his training wouldn't allow it. Instead, he went for the next best thing.

*Burn in hell, asshole.*

Matt put the fucker in his sights and slid his finger to the trigger. He'd barely started to squeeze when he saw something that made his head spin.

Bukhari bent forward, howling out in pain before flying backward, as if someone had clocked him. They must have done a hell of a job, too, because the son of a bitch was out cold.

"What the hell?"

From behind him, Derek's words mimicked Matt's thoughts exactly.

"Your girl?" Kole asked.

God, he hoped so. If Kat had done that to Bukhari, it had to mean she was okay. Right?

Keeping an eye on the unconscious man, Matt picked

up the pace. Covering the distance to the open doorway, Bukhari's still form was now blocking, he held his breath and sent up a quick prayer before peeking into the small room.

The whirl of a bullet flew past his head before slamming into the wall behind him.

"Shit!" Matt jerked his head back. It took his brain a couple seconds to catch up to what he'd seen.

Putting his hand out to signal his team to stand down, he kept his head back and hollered into the room.

"Katherine! Baby, it's me. It's Matt. I need you to put the gun down."

There was a beat of silence before he heard her quivering voice. "M-Matt?"

"Yeah, sweetheart. It's me. Can you put the gun down?"

Matt knew in his heart she would never intentionally hurt him or any of the other guys, but fear and adrenaline played all sorts of nasty tricks on the mind. After what she'd been through, he needed to do this by the book.

Otherwise, she may do something she didn't mean. If that happened, she'd be forced to live with it for the rest of her life.

"O-okay." The telltale clang of a gun hitting concrete sounded from inside the room. "I-I dropped it. I dropped the gun."

With a cautionary glance, Matt stepped over Bukhari and rushed into the room.

"Holy fuck." He hauled her into his arms. "Oh, thank God. I thought I'd lost you."

"You're here." She began to sob against his chest. "You're really here. I didn't think I'd ever see you again."

"I'm here, baby." He squeezed her against him before pulling back slightly.

"Oh, god." Her eyes widened as she realized what she'd done. "I almost shot you!"

"It's okay, sweetheart." He grinned. "You didn't know it was me." He gave her a quick once-over. "You okay? Are you hurt?"

"I-I..."

"Hey, Turner," Gabe interrupted, pulling their attention away before she could answer. "Sorry, man, but we need to get going. That explosion and all the gunfire is going to have the locals hot on our ass in minutes."

Right on cue, they heard the thump, thump, thump of the twin choppers Ghost had obtained for their extraction. That they'd been given the green light by Delta to land meant only one thing...

The rest of the building was clear and secure.

Taking precious seconds to cup Kat's cheek, Matt looked into the most beautiful eyes he'd ever seen and asked, "You ready to go home?"

Fresh tears fell from those same eyes, streaking through the dark soot clouding her perfect skin. "Y-yes."

Linking his fingers with hers, Matt used his free hand picked up Bukhari's pistol and shoved it into his waistband as he led Kat out of the bathroom.

Waiting until they'd stepped over the man's unmoving body, Kole asked, "What do we do with him?"

The look on the man's face told him Bukhari wasn't unconscious. He was dead.

*Ah, fuck.*

Apparently, Kat picked up on it, too. "Oh, my god." She covered her mouth before letting her hand drop again. "I *killed* him? I-I didn't mean to." Shocked, she looked at the others and back to Matt. "I swear. I hit him with a piece from the back of the toilet. Just to keep him from—"

"Hey, hey, hey," Matt whispered, cupping her face with both hands this time. "Look at me. You were defending yourself. He would have killed you if you hadn't hit him. His death is not on you. Okay?"

Her chin quivered, but she didn't break down. "O-okay."

"Let's leave his ass here," Gabe answered Kole's question. "His people can do whatever they want with him."

"If I have to guess, I'd say they'll probably dance around the asshole's body," Derek quipped before turning and heading down the hall. "I sure as hell would."

Matt looked down at the man who'd caused so much terror. Not only for them, but also for his own people.

Countries around the world had been trying to take Bukhari down for decades. The United States, included. In the end, he was taken out by a tiny scientist with a heart of gold.

Matt couldn't help but be filled with overwhelming pride knowing that scientist was his, and his alone.

He gave the asshole one final glance. *Not so tough now are you, fucknut?*

Resisting the urge to kick the dead man, he held Kat tightly against him as they walked away.

Using his handheld radio, Gabe gave Delta a quick update. "Headed to the extraction point with Package A. Seven tangoes down on our end, including Package B."

"Copy that, Bravo One," Ghost responded immediately. "One tango for us. Two went running your way. Sounds like you got 'em."

Gabe smirked. "You could say that. What about the last one?"

There was a slight pause before Ghost said, "Package C was not obtained."

"Motherfucker," Matt bit out. Package C was the label given to Adrian Walker.

The bastard had gotten away. Again. Matt thought of Zade, hating the idea of telling him. He'd promised to take Walker down this time. It was the one part of the mission he'd failed.

"The man can't run forever." Derek slapped his shoulder. "His time will come, brother. His time will come."

Matt knew he was right, but fuck.

"At least we saved your girl," Kole mused.

"Actually," Gabe corrected. "She saved herself."

Matt looked at the woman next to him, his chest swelling with pride again. "Hell yeah, she did."

Ghost and Fletch met them at the building's front entrance, giving added coverage, just in case.

Knowing there'd be time for introductions later, Matt simply made sure Kat knew they were the good guys as they followed them across the grass where the choppers were waiting.

About ten yards away from theirs, Kat began to move a little more slowly. All of a sudden, her steps faltered, and she would've gone down had he not had his hands on her already.

"Hey." Matt held her upright. "Easy, sweetheart. You okay?"

"No." Kat shook her head, her face grimacing with pain.

"Book it, man," Derek yelled from inside the chopper.

"We gotta get these birds in the air before someone around here figures out what we did and decides to take us out."

With his eyes still on Kat's, Matt started to pick her up. "Come on, baby. I'll carry you the rest of the way." Her fingernails dug into his shoulders, causing him to pause. When he looked back up at her, his chest tightened.

Pain clouded her eyes as Kat shook her head again. "C-can't."

Everything had happened so fast, he hadn't had a chance to assess her physical state. His thoughts worked overtime to figure out what was going on.

He'd seen the blood on her hands earlier but had assumed she'd gotten cut in the explosion. She'd been acting fine, otherwise, so Matt had guessed any cuts she had gotten were superficial. Now he wasn't so sure.

He yanked his small flashlight from the pocket at his thigh and hurried to grab her hands. Turning them over and back again, Matt saw plenty of drying blood but no visible cuts.

"I don't see any injuries, sweetheart. Where are you hurt?"

Kat swallowed, her face grimacing as she lifted the bottom of her black scrub top. Matt lowered the light to see, choking out his denial when he saw the wound there.

*No.* His world began to spin. "You're hit?" he nearly choked on the words.

Her head bobbed in a weak nod. "S-sorry." Kat barely managed the whispered word before her knees gave out completely.

Matt caught her before she hit the ground.

Looking up at him, her eyes fluttered shut as she said, "L-love…y-you."

"No!" He shook his head with the fierce denial. "I won't lose you. I *won't!*"

Lifting her limp body into his arms, Matt held on tightly as he raced to the chopper. They were literally right next door to a hospital, but given who they were and what they'd done, he knew going there would be a suicide mission.

Insurmountable fear turned his blood to ice, but he fought against it and kept going.

"What happened?" Derek's concerned expression matched the others as Matt reached their chopper. He handed Kat off to the other man long enough to climb inside.

"She's been shot!"

There was a loud and collective, *"What?"* from the others.

"But she seemed fine." Kole sounded as confused as Matt felt. The man grabbed his fist and pulled him up. "How the hell did she manage to fight off Bukhari?"

"I don't fucking know!" Matt shouted as he fell to his knees by her side. Bile churned in his gut, panic threatening to take him over. "Adrenaline maybe? Doesn't matter." He swung his gaze around wildly. "Where's the goddamn med bag?"

He'd no more said the words, and it was there. With frantic movements, he unzipped the bag, rummaging through it to find what he needed as the chopper lifted from the ground.

Several shouts came from below, men firing their weapons at the giant, metal birds. Thankfully the men behind the choppers' controls knew what they were doing.

Ghost and his team offered cover, raining gunfire down on the hostiles while the helicopter Matt was in took off. He was grateful as fuck for the men of Delta, and through his fear for Kat, felt a rush of relief when he saw Ghost and his team were in the clear.

Doing his best to control his shaking hands, Matt quickly started an I.V. Next, he administered a shot of powerful antibiotics to ward of any infection.

After checking to make sure her pulse was still present, Matt did his best to clean and dress the area the bullet had entered. There was no exit wound, which meant the bullet was still inside Kat.

Praying harder than he could ever remember, Matt kept pressure on the wound the entire way to the private airstrip where the R.I.S.C. jet was waiting. With no electronic monitors to rely on, he had to go old-school, like he had hundreds of times in the field.

Only those times were different. Those were his fellow soldiers. His brothers who'd known exactly what they were signing up for.

This time, it was Kat. And she was his…everything.

Once they were on the jet, Matt managed to keep Kat stable, but he didn't dream of relaxing. Not even when they landed at the U.S. military base in Baghdad.

A team of doctors met them on the landing strip. After giving them his medical report, they'd promptly whisked Kat away without even giving him the chance to kiss her goodbye first. That was a good thing, though. Because this wasn't goodbye.

It *couldn't* be the end. Not after he'd finally found her again.

"They've got her now, Matt." Gabe squeezed his shoulder. "She's in good hands."

Matt looked over at his team leader. "They'd better be the best. She deserves nothing less."

Hours later, they were all sitting and standing outside the building designated as the base's makeshift hospital. Matt had wanted to take her to Landstuhl, the U.S. Naval hospital in Germany. But even in the private jet, the trip would've taken too long.

Kat was strong, yes, but a person's body could only withstand a certain amount of trauma before it began to shut down. By the time they'd landed here, her heart rate had already begun to slowly drop.

Matt knew bringing her here was the right decision. He only hoped that decision resulted in her life being saved.

His phone dinged with an incoming text. Leaning against the metal building, Matt glanced down to see it was from Ghost.

*Any word on your girl?*

He responded...

*Not yet.*

Ghost wrote back...

*Keep the faith, brother. She's tough. She'll pull through.*

One corner of Matt's lips almost curled. Damn, he liked those guys.

*I'll keep you posted.*

He quickly typed out another text right after that one, adding...

*Thanks again. For everything.*

A few seconds later, Ghost wrote back...

*Anytime, brother.*

Matt allowed himself to grin slightly when he read that last text. The Delta guys may be on a different team, but they were brothers, all the same.

"You're smiling."

He looked up to see Gabe walking his way. "Ghost texted, asking about Kat."

Gabe leaned against the building with him. "Those guys are solid," his team leader acknowledged.

"Solid as they come," Matt agreed. "Not a situation out there I wouldn't want them watching my six."

"Agreed."

A few moments of silence passed before Gabe said, "You did all you could. You get that, right?"

Matt knew what the man was getting at, but he disagreed. "She never should've been put in that position to begin with."

"But she was. And that's not on you, either." He stood straight again and faced him. "You did what you had to in order to get her back. Then you kept her alive long enough to get her here. Kat's a fighter, man. We all saw proof of that. She'll pull through."

Matt blinked quickly to fight off the burning tears forming behind his tired lids. "She has to, Gabe. I've fucked up so much with her, and all she's ever done is try to protect me." He swiped angrily at a tear that had escaped, despite his efforts. "I need the chance to make it right. We need more time."

"And you'll get it. You've gotta keep the faith."

"Trust me, I am," Matt assured his friend. "She never gave up, so I won't either."

He'd no more said the words when a woman's voice caught their attention.

"She's out of surgery."

The doctor's words had Matt's eyes flying upward to meet hers. Pushing himself off the wall, he rushed over to where the woman was standing. The other men followed.

"And?" Matt asked anxiously. "Is she going to be okay?"

The doctor smiled. "I believe she will."

Matt wanted to kiss her. "C-can I see her?"

"In a minute. My team's cleaning her up. "The bullet tore through a portion of her small intestine. We extracted the bullet and removed the damaged tissue. After that, we were able reconnect the intestine and sew her back up. With proper care and rest, I see no reason Katherine won't make a full recovery."

He could barely breathe for the relief flowing through him. "Thank you." He held out his hand. "Thank you so much."

The woman shook his hand. "I'm happy we were able to help."

For the first time since she'd collapsed in his arms, Matt felt as though he could breathe.

"What'd I tell ya?" Gabe slapped his back.

Derek followed suit. "That's great news, man."

"The best," Kole piped in.

Letting out a shaky breath, Matt nodded. "You're right." He sniffed. "It's the best."

Pinching the bridge of his nose, he squeezed his eyes shut for only a second before wiping a hand down his face. Then he smiled and went to see his girl.

# EPILOGUE

Kat took a sip of her champagne, the cool bubbles tingling in her throat as she swallowed them down.

It had been nearly a month since that horrific day in Iran. Per Agent Ryker's request, after she'd been treated at the hospital in Baghdad, Kat was transferred back to Dallas.

Once they were back in the States, she was admitted to Homeland's private hospital until she was well enough to go home. And Matt had stayed by her side through it all.

He'd about lost his shit when he found out Adrian Walker had given her stitches. But it had almost bothered him more when she told him about the moments Walker had been kind and gentle. And how, at times he'd, made Kat believe he hadn't truly wanted to see her hurt.

Of course, then the bastard left her in that lab with Bukhari, allowing her to be shot and nearly killed. So, there was that.

Pushing all that away, Kat brought her thoughts back to the present and why they were here.

Today, Bravo team had come back together at Jake's ranch for a belated celebration of Nate and Gracie's nuptials. The couple had returned from their Vegas honeymoon the same day Kat was admitted to Homeland's hospital.

At first, Nate had been beyond pissed that no one had told him what was going on sooner. Especially since Adrian Walker had been involved.

However, once Jake explained it was his decision to keep it quiet, Nate relented. Though he still gave Matt crap about it from time to time, Kat could tell, deep down, the man understood.

The two newlyweds decided to hold off having a party in their honor until Kat was well enough to attend. She still couldn't believe how instant everyone had accepted her as part of the Bravo family. Part of the R.I.S.C. family, really.

Looking around at those in attendance, Kat felt such a sense of love and family. It was so strong, it was almost overwhelming. But in a good way.

All of Alpha Team had come to celebrate today. Bravo, too…minus Zade.

Her heart felt heavy when she thought of her new friend. He'd nearly died protecting her. As had so many others.

When Zade requested some time off from the team, he'd sworn to Matt and the other Bravo men he was fine. Said he needed some time to recharge before coming back to work, now that his shoulder was almost fully healed. Kat suspected that was far from the truth.

The man was hurting, and Kat could tell the pain wasn't all physical. Something had changed inside the fun-loving guy. Something she had a feeling he'd left in order to find.

"I still can't believe you shoved a syringe into your bullet wound." Olivia, Jake's very pregnant wife, spoke up. "I've seen grown men come through the ER crying and passing out from getting a few stitches. And that's after they've been given lidocaine."

Refocusing, Kat chuckled at the woman's comment. "To be fair, I didn't exactly shove it in."

The woman looked horrified. "Still. And then to fight off the Iranian Army's general...with a toilet lid, no less?"

The memory threatened to become prevalent, but Kat forced it into the background. It was still hard to believe she'd killed a man, but surprisingly, that thought wasn't what kept her up at night.

"Well I wouldn't have been able to if it hadn't been for the serum," she explained.

"The drugs may have taken away your pain, but the fighting? Girl, that was all you." Olivia raised her glass of milk in a toast. "Trust me. What you did took a lot of guts, sister."

"Here, here!" Gracie, Nate's new bride, agreed while lifting her glass of champagne.

"I second that," Sarah, Kole's wife and Gracie's sister agreed. "To Katherine the Great!"

Choking on the sip of champagne she'd just taken, Kat pressed her lips together to keep from spitting it out. After a few, hard coughs, she held her drink up with the others. "Well, thank you. Although, 'Katherine the Great' might be taking it a bit too far."

"Oh, I don't know about that, Doc," a deep voice rumbled from behind her. "I think you're pretty great."

Kat looked up from where she was sitting to see Matt standing over her shoulder. She smiled wide. "Hey, you."

He leaned down, his lips brushing against hers as he spoke. "Hey, yourself." His warm lips pressed against hers in a sweet, sweet kiss.

"And, that's our cue." Gracie hopped up out of her lawn chair. "Come on, girls. I could use a refill."

"Another one?" Sarah teased her sister. "That's like, what? Your third?"

"It's my wedding celebration...barbeque...thingy. I should be able to drink however much I want."

"Yep. Sure sounds like you need another one, Sis." Sarah rolled her eyes and snorted as she and her sister walked past Kat.

"Sure, Gracie." Olivia grunted as she struggled to stand. "Rub it in to the girl who hasn't had a single drop of alcohol in months."

Kat couldn't help but smile at Olivia's round, pregnant belly as she waddled by.

"You want one of those?" Matt asked as he crouched down beside her chair.

"Another glass of champagne? No, I'm good. But thank you."

"Not talking about the champagne, Kat."

It took her a minute to realize what he'd been referring to. She felt her eyes grow wide. "A baby?"

"Why not?" He shrugged a shoulder, his handsome face smiling up at hers. "I want to give you everything we've missed out on. Including children."

"Matt," she whispered his name. It was all she could manage to say.

"I'm not saying we have to start trying right away." He took the champagne glass from her hand and set it on the table. Taking her hands in his, he held them as he spoke. "We're both fairly young. Plus, with the new lab the military is building for you to run, I know you're going to be busy with your work. But eventually, I want that with you, Kat. I want the life we always talked about having. Together."

Kat was still in awe of the offer she'd received after Jason Ryker informed the powers that be, her serum had worked better than she'd hoped. In a week, they'd be breaking ground, right here in Dallas. Building a lab she would be in charge of.

One that would be solely dedicated to testing and creating new advances in vaccines and medications. All geared specifically for the American troops—both active, reserve, and veterans. It was a professional dream come true.

There was another dream she still hoped for. Desperately. And from what her strong, loving man had just said, it was within her reach, too.

Kat thought of the ring still tucked safely away in the lockbox at her bank. She'd never been able to part with it...now she understood why.

She'd tell him about it soon. Maybe even later tonight. Before that could happen, she needed to be confess something else.

"I want that, too, Matt." She licked her lips.

"But?"

She hesitated to answer, but knew she had to be honest with him. Always.

"I'm scared."

Matt frowned, his hands holding hers a bit tighter. "Of what?"

"Not being who you need me to be."

His dark eyes softened. "Katherine…"

"I almost shot you, Matt. You know what it's been like for me since we've come home."

She still woke up several times a week with nightmares. Memories from that night, only twisted. In her dreams, the bullet she'd shot always hit Matt, killing him instantly.

"I know, baby. You see yourself killing me, but you didn't. I'm right here."

"I know you are, but with my memory…" She looked down at their joined hands. "I can't seem to get it out of my head."

"Is that all, or is there more?"

Kat stared back at the man who knew her better than anyone. "I can't stop thinking about how my dad died because of me."

The thought was always present, in the back of her mind. The only thing that helped ease that particular pain was the letter she'd received a few days ago from her dad's attorney.

In it, her father had tried to explain his reasoning behind his actions all those years ago. Most importantly, he'd written a sincere and heart-felt apology.

Kat wished she'd been able to hear him say those words while he was still alive, but at least she knew he wasn't as cold-hearted as he'd led her to believe.

"Your father's death is not on you, Katherine." Matt looked up at her pointedly.

"Yes, it is."

"Wrong." He shook his handsome head. "Your father was killed because Rajif Bukhari wanted to use what your team created against the U.S. That, and because Sloane Anderson was an ignorant, entitled prick who thought the world and everyone in it owed him something he hadn't earned."

Unconvinced, Kat shook her head. "But I—"

"Anderson wanted the perfect life," Matt cut her off. "So much so, he couldn't accept his son for who he really was. The ignorant bastard thought it tarnished that perfect image he'd worked so hard to create. Sloane's push to make his son into something he wasn't was the catalyst that started this whole mess. After Brian's death, the guy became obsessed. With money and power. With revenge. When Walker approached him about selling the super-soldier formula, Sloane saw it as his chance to not only cash in big, but to get revenge on you for his son's death."

"Brian's suicide wasn't my fault."

"Sweetheart, I know that. Everyone knows that. Everyone except Brian's dad. Guy like that..." Matt shook his head. "Sloane was never going to accept responsibility for what happened. If he did, he'd have to admit he was flawed. Instead, he put the blame on you. For Brian's death. For everything. So the second Walker offered him the deal on the formula, he couldn't wait to say yes."

"You're right." She tapped the side of her head. "Up here, I know you're right. It's here that needs more convincing." Kat put a hand over her heart.

Matt covered it with his and squeezed. "You'll get there, baby. It'll take some time, but I promise you, you will get there."

She stared back at him a moment before whispering, "I believe you."

"Good." Matt smiled. "Because I'm going to be here, by your side until you do."

In a nervous move, Kat licked her lips. "And after?"

Reaching up, he used his free one to gently brush a few stray strands from her forehead. Tucking them behind her ear, he cupped one side of her face. "And after"—he began with a whisper, his thumb caressing her soft cheek —"after, I'll still be here. For as long as you want me to be."

"Forever," Kat rushed to say the blessed word. "I want you with me forever."

Matt smiled wide. "Forever sounds like a damn good start to me."

## ABOUT THE AUTHOR

Author of the exciting R.I.S.C. Series, Anna Blakely brings you stories of love, action, and edge of your seat suspense. As an avid reader herself, Anna writes what she loves...strong, Alpha heroes and the intelligent, independent heroines they love.

Anna's dream is to create stories her readers will enjoy, and characters they'll fall in love with as much as she has. She believes in true love and Happily Ever After, which is what she will bring to you.

Anna lives in rural Missouri with her husband and children, as well as several rescued animals. When she's not writing, Anna enjoys reading, watching action and horror movies (the scarier the better), and spending time with her amazing family.

### <u>Want to connect with Anna?</u>
*Stalk her here...*

BookBub: https//www.bookbub.com/authors/anna-blakely
• <u>Amazon:</u> amazon.com/author/annablakely

- Author Page: facebook.com/annablakely.author.7
- Instagram: https://instagram.com/annablakely
- Twitter: @ablakelyauthor
- Goodreads: https://www.goodreads.com/author/show/18650841.Anna_Blakely

facebook.com/annablakely.author.7

twitter.com/ablakelyauthor

instagram.com/annablakely

amazon.com/author/annablakely

*There are many more books in this fan fiction world than listed here, for an up-to-date list go to www.AcesPress.com*

*You can also visit our Amazon page at:*
*http://www.amazon.com/author/operationalpha*

### Special Forces: Operation Alpha World

Christie Adams: Charity's Heart
Denise Agnew: Dangerous to Hold
Shauna Allen: Awakening Aubrey
Brynne Asher: Blackburn
Linzi Baxter: Unlocking Dreams
Jennifer Becker: Hiding Catherine
Alice Bello: Shadowing Milly
Heather Blair: Rescue Me
Anna Blakely: Rescuing Gracelynn
Amy Briggs: Saving Sarah
Julia Bright: Saving Lorelei
Victoria Bright: Surviving Savage
Cara Carnes: Protecting Mari
Kendra Mei Chailyn: Beast
Melissa Kay Clarke: Rescuing Annabeth
Samantha A. Cole: Handling Haven
Sue Coletta: Hacked
Melissa Combs: Gallant
Anne Conley: Redemption for Misty
KaLyn Cooper: Rescuing Melina
Liz Crowe: Marking Mariah
Sarah Curtis: Securing the Odds
Jordan Dane: Redemption for Avery
Tarina Deaton: Found in the Lost

KL Donn: Unraveling Love
Riley Edwards: Protecting Olivia
PJ Fiala: Defending Sophie
Nicole Flockton: Protecting Maria
Michele Gwynn: Rescuing Emma
Casey Hagen: Shielding Nebraska
EM Hayes: Gambling for Ashleigh
Desiree Holt: Protecting Maddie
Kathy Ivan: Saving Sarah
Jesse Jacobson: Protecting Honor
Silver James: Rescue Moon
Becca Jameson: Saving Sofia
Kate Kinsley: Protecting Ava
Heather Long: Securing Arizona
Gennita Low: No Protection
Kirsten Lynn: Joining Forces for Jesse
Margaret Madigan: Bang for the Buck
Kimberly McGath: The Predecessor
Rachel McNeely: The SEAL's Surprise Baby
KD Michaels: Saving Laura
Wren Michaels: The Fox & The Hound
Kat Mizera: Protecting Bobbi
Mary B Moore: Force Protection
LeTeisha Newton: Protecting Butterfly
Angela Nicole: Protecting the Donna
MJ Nightingale: Protecting Beauty
Sarah O'Rourke: Saving Liberty
Victoria Paige: Reclaiming Izabel
Anne L. Parks: Mason
Debra Parmley: Protecting Pippa
Lainey Reese: Protecting New York
TL Reeve and Michele Ryan: Extracting Mateo

Elena M. Reyes: Keeping Ava
Angela Rush: Charlotte
Rose Smith: Saving Satin
Jenika Snow: Protecting Lily
Lynn St. James: SEAL's Spitfire
Dee Stewart: Conner
Harley Stone: Rescuing Mercy
Jen Talty: Burning Desire
Megan Vernon: Protecting Us

*Police and Fire: Operation Alpha World*

Freya Barker: Burning for Autumn
KaLyn Cooper: Justice for Gwen
Aspen Drake: Sheltering Emma
Deanndra Hall: Shelter for Sharla
Barb Han: Kace
CM Steele: Guarding Hope
Reina Torres: Justice for Sloane
Stacey Wilk: Stage Fright

*As you know, this book included at least one character from Susan Stoker's books. To check out more, see below.*

## SEAL of Protection: Legacy Series

*Securing Caite*
*Securing Brenae (novella)*
*Securing Sidney*
*Securing Piper*
*Securing Zoey*
*Securing Avery (May 2020)*
*Securing Kalee (Sept 2020)*

## Delta Team Two Series

*Shielding Gillian (Apr 2020)*
*Shielding Kinley (Aug 2020)*
*Shielding Aspen (Oct 2020)*
*Shielding Riley (Jan 2021)*
*Shielding Devyn (TBA)*
*Shielding Ember (TBA)*
*Shielding Sierra (TBA)*

## Delta Force Heroes Series

*Rescuing Rayne (FREE!)*
*Rescuing Aimee (novella)*
*Rescuing Emily*
*Rescuing Harley*
*Marrying Emily (novella)*
*Rescuing Kassie*
*Rescuing Bryn*
*Rescuing Casey*
*Rescuing Sadie (novella)*

*Rescuing Wendy*
*Rescuing Mary*
*Rescuing Macie (Novella)*

## Badge of Honor: Texas Heroes Series

*Justice for Mackenzie (FREE!)*
*Justice for Mickie*
*Justice for Corrie*
*Justice for Laine (novella)*
*Shelter for Elizabeth*
*Justice for Boone*
*Shelter for Adeline*
*Shelter for Sophie*
*Justice for Erin*
*Justice for Milena*
*Shelter for Blythe*
*Justice for Hope*
*Shelter for Quinn*
*Shelter for Koren*
*Shelter for Penelope*

## SEAL of Protection Series

*Protecting Caroline (FREE!)*
*Protecting Alabama*
*Protecting Fiona*
*Marrying Caroline (novella)*
*Protecting Summer*
*Protecting Cheyenne*
*Protecting Jessyka*
*Protecting Julie (novella)*
*Protecting Melody*
*Protecting the Future*

*Protecting Kiera (novella)*
*Protecting Alabama's Kids (novella)*
*Protecting Dakota*

*New York Times, USA Today* and *Wall Street Journal* Bestselling Author Susan Stoker has a heart as big as the state of Tennessee where she lives, but this all American girl has also spent the last fourteen years living in Missouri, California, Colorado, Indiana, and Texas. She's married to a retired Army man who now gets to follow *her* around the country.

www.stokeraces.com
www.AcesPress.com
susan@stokeraces.com

Made in the USA
Coppell, TX
22 June 2022

79115116R00175